Jillian of Banff XO

Barbara Baker

Print ISBNs
Amazon print 9780228630838
Ingram Spark 9780228630845
Barnes & Noble 9780228630852
BWL Print 9780228630869

Editor Renee Duke
Cover artist Pandora Designs

Dedication

Dad
(John Wackerle)

It's because of you that I grew up in the best place ever. Thank you.

* * *

Acknowledgements

Thank you to my family who are always a great source of ideas quickly followed by opinions and critiques. If you see your suggestion in my story, don't take all the credit. And if you recognize a character, be sure to keep their secrets.

A big thank you to long-time friend Dan Brunton who sent me a CBC Short Story Contest link in 2009. How exciting to have Shelagh Rogers place my story in the top three. How disappointing to follow it up with a folder of rejections and the start of this roller coaster writing life.

Determined to improve my storytelling, I attended Writescape Workshops facilitated by the lovely Ruth Walker and Gwynn Scheltema. At the first session I sat next to Jack Livesley. It was the start of an invaluable mentorship that continued until his passing in 2018. His lessons on not being verbose and read it out loud sit on my shoulder when I write and often wake me up at night with a fright.

A huge thanks to Lyndi Allison and Evelyn Pollock for sticking with Jillian through all three books. You gals are the best. Your suggestions, comments and love helped the story grow to what it is today.

Thank you, Cristy Watson, for the manuscript edits and your friendship. You took great care of my characters as you shined and buffed each chapter.

Yvonne Machuk - thank you for agreeing to be a character in the story. It was fun directing your scenes. And I'm so grateful you're a grammar nerd. Your keen eye spotted errors, and your insightful recommendations helped me complete the final review.

I greatly appreciate the time and energy everyone spent making the novel what it is today. The blame for any remaining typos rests on my shoulders.

Thank you to all the great folk at BWL Publishing for making my dreams come true.

Not to be left last by any means, thank you Johnny Reid for always playing in the background and knowing just what music my muse needs.

Table of Contents

Chapter 1

As the chairlift bounces over the towers on the way to the top of the Cascade run, I press back in the seat, so I don't have to see how high up we are. Greg leans forward, calls out to a boarder below and his enthusiastic wave shakes the chair. I clench my fists inside my gloves.

After the last tower, we lift our snowboards off the footrest and Greg raises the bar. I feel pretty confident this afternoon and my wipeouts are nowhere near as sensational as yesterday. In fact, I have not fallen once since lunchtime. Well, technically that's not true. My butt didn't dent the snow. But I did put my hand down a couple times when gravity was winning. Huge progress though.

"Yo, Greg," a ski patroller calls out waving an arm in the air as we slide down the off ramp. "Got a minute?"

Greg grabs my hand and pulls me across the slope to join a group of people with the patroller. When he lets go, I thank whoever is in charge upstairs for keeping me upright and saving us both the embarrassment of me falling.

The patroller reaches her arms out with ski poles hanging off her wrists and Greg goes in for a quick hug. My tinted goggles hide the surprise in my eyes as the others who were with her take off in different directions down the run. Maybe they've worked together on ski tours or climbing trips.

"Almost Merry Christmas Eve," she says to Greg. "Have you got any plans?"

"You bet. Jillian's aunt," Greg points at me, "is putting on a big brunch for a bunch of mates."

"That's great." She waves at me and turns back to him. "So, we have a bit of an incident. What are the chances you can help out?"

"Sure. What's up?"

"A missing kid." She waves her phone at us. There's a picture of a smiley-faced kid in a bright orange ski suit but with the helmet and dark goggles on, it's hard to tell what he, or she, looks like. She swipes the screen and a girl with huge blue eyes and short-cropped black-hair stares at us.

"She's a good skier. Thirteen years old. She was supposed to meet her family in the lodge for lunch, but she never showed up. They're new to town and her folks are panicky with the hill almost closing."

Greg nods.

"Can you go to the top and check the runs?" She points to the North American Chair, the highest lift on Mt. Norquay.

I stare up the steep run. Even from here, I can see the shadows of the huge moguls and there are only a few people making their way down.

"She's not supposed to go up there but," the patroller shrugs, "you know kids."

"I'm on it."

"I can go check the tube park and the lodge," I volunteer, in hopes her expectation isn't that I go with Greg. It would take us a week to get down that run if I was with him.

"The tube park would be good. Thanks. There are lots of people looking at the base already. Can you also check around the old lodge and the upper parking lot? She could be hiding there if she thinks she's in trouble. Her name is Olivia. Meet back at the Ski Patrol hut," she checks her watch, "in forty-five minutes. The lifts will be closed by then."

"Got it." Greg straps in his boot. "Catch you in a bit." He taps my chin before he takes off. Straight down.

"Thanks for helping," the patroller says.

"No problem."

I wait for her to leave, do up my binding and work my way over to the tube park. At the bottom, I put my snowboard in the rack and head to where people finish the ride. Lots of people shout and screech as they hurtle down their lanes, spinning on the hard packed snow while they sit inside giant inner tubes. I lift my goggles and watch for the bright snowsuit. Nothing. I go to the lineup of people waiting to go up the lift. No orange snowsuit.

The walk through the lodge is tougher because most people have their coats off, so the short black hair is my only clue. Again, nothing. I feel lame hanging out in the bathroom until all the stalls have cleared, but still no Olivia.

There's a lot of laughing at the far end of the parking lot where the trees start, so I wander over. The closer I get, the skunkier the smell is. There are six people, some even older than Greg, maybe university age, sharing tokes.

"Hey, come on. Join us," a guy calls out and gestures me over. "It's been a rad day."

Incredibly bright orange ski suit, helmet off, black-haired Olivia is in the midst of them. What the hell?

"Nah, I'm good thanks." I smile, so they don't think I'm a snob. "I have to catch my ride home." I point towards the cars and walk away, shoulders up and with purpose. A total karate training exit. Show confidence even when I don't feel it.

Shit. I don't want to be judgy. That's not my thing. Well, I try not to let it be my thing but Olivia's way younger than the rest of them and I'm sure not brave enough to walk up to her and say, "Hey Olivia, your folks are looking for you."

I grab my snowboard and take the run back down to the patrol hut.

"She's behind the old day lodge at the far end of the parking lot," I tell the patroller we met. "With a bunch of people."

"Seriously?" The ski patroller rolls her eyes. "Are they smoking up?"

I shrug. I don't want to be a narc.

After I walk back and forth from the ski racks and lodge to the Cascade Chairlift a few times, I spot a snowboarder carving down the steep Lone Pine run. I can tell it's Greg. He's easy to pick out on the hill because he is so freakin' smooth and makes it look like it's nothing to spin a 360 off a huge mogul and land it perfectly, only to do it again. I hope to be that good one day.

"Hey." I poke him in the back when he stops at the base. "Show off."

"Me?" He lifts his goggles and does a goofy-eyed grin.

"Yeah, you." I laugh.

"Olivia," a lady screeches.

We both turn to see her rush towards the Ski Patrol hut and grab her daughter in a tight hug.

"It looks like they found her," Greg says.

I don't say anything about my part in it. I mean, I'm glad I told them where she was, but I don't want Greg to think I spoiled her fun.

He swings his arm over my shoulder, and we head for his car. "I'm glad it's a happy ending versus, well, versus a not happy ending."

"Yeah, happy endings are good." I stop and pull out my phone. "Boarding day selfie." I stretch out my arm to get us both in the picture, but Greg grabs my phone, hugs me tight and our helmets tap against each other as he clicks the shot.

Great picture. I tuck my phone back in my pocket and we head for the parking lot. After our boards are in the trunk, Greg pulls his helmet off. His curly, messy hair is stuck to his head.

I tug a few of his damp locks. "Nice to see you had to work hard on the last run."

Greg steps forward and cups my chin with one hand. He stares at me and my stomach flutters...in a really good way. I don't say anything.

He tips his head. "Can I kiss you?"

"Can you kiss me? Hmm." I put on a serious expression. My brain says 'yes, dammit, kiss me' but my mouth says, "Let me think about that." *Stupid mouth.*

"Okay." He steps back, crosses his arms and gives me the sweetest smile. "Let me know when you decide."

I grab his elbows and laugh. He puts his arms around me, and I panic because I can't remember what my mouth tastes like or if I should have had a mint. I take a quick breath right before his lips touch mine. They're soft. So soft. And warm. The world stops. It really does. His tongue presses against my teeth for an instant and then retreats. He pulls back and I can feel him look at me. I open my eyes and he's right there coming in for another kiss. And what a kiss.

"The perfect end to a perfect day." He holds the car door open for me and I slide into the passenger seat.

I put on my seat belt and try to calm down the huge smile I know I'm wearing.

As Greg navigates the tight switchbacks heading back to Banff, the local radio station plays "Six White Bloomers." He grabs the dial and turns it up.

"This is the best Christmas song from back home." He mimics the story telling and I join in with the lyrics, tapping the beat out on the dashboard.

When it's over he turns the radio down and glances over at me. "Do you ever miss Toronto and your friends?"

Wow. That came out of nowhere. *And I can't even remember the last time I texted anyone from home.*

"I used to. A lot." I look at his profile and shrug. "But things got busy here and they have their lives there and...I don't know. I guess I kind of don't have much in common with them anymore."

He nods. "Yeah, that happens."

When exactly did I stop wanting to get back to Toronto? I can't remember. And when did I start thinking of Banff as home?

"Grandma Got Run Over by a Reindeer" starts, and Greg turns up the radio again. We both belt out the song, a bit off key and I add a few made up words when I can't remember the real ones. I gaze out the windshield with a perma-grin on my face.

Since Christmas break, Greg and I have been hanging out a lot. The vibe is different, even cozier than our months of fun times chumming around as just good friends. I hoped there'd be a kiss at some point, but I also did not want to do anything to ruin our friendship if it wasn't ever going to be more than that. It couldn't be any more perfect than it is now.

"Hey," I turn to him. "Any chance you can give Steph and me a hand hauling up a table from the basement before you go to work?"

"No problem. For sure I can help."

Parked in the back behind Aunt Steph's house, Greg passes me my helmet and coat and puts my snowboard in the garage.

"Steph," I shout from the back porch into the kitchen as Bucky rushes by to go out for a pee. "Greg's going to give us a hand with the table."

"Perfect," she says as she walks into the room. "Hi, Greg. Ready for Christmas?"

"As ready as I'll ever be," he says.

After we lug the table up, I grab Greg's hand. "Come see the tree."

He lets out a complimentary whistle when he steps into the living room.

"I did it all except for the tinsel." I lean in and whisper, so Steph doesn't hear. "She's got this thing about hanging tinsel. She does it one piece at a time. And when we take the tree down, it comes off the same way."

He chuckles.

"I know, right? Bit of a control freak, hey?"

Greg points to the archway where a sprig of mistletoe hangs and backs me up until we're under it. He raises his eyebrows, checks over my shoulder, gives me the most adorable smile and leans in. Another kiss. Another soft, warm, unrushed kiss.

"See you tomorrow," he says, as Bucky rushes back inside.

I watch Greg go. My cheeks need to cool off before I face Steph and I want to stand here and soak it in. Soak in all the parts of my perfect life. Who would ever have thought it could be this good. Especially in Banff, three thousand miles away from home.

* * *

"Time to get up," Steph shouts. "I need your help.

As I come down the stairs, I see the mistletoe and smile. Those kisses with Greg were different than any kiss I have ever had. I am definitely no expert on kissing but most of the ones I have had felt, I don't know, flippant, almost obligatory. Like the date's over and you know it has to happen and it does and it's all awkward and feels inconsequential. Greg's didn't. It felt like it meant something. To me, anyways. Did it mean anything to him? I hope so.

I wrap my arms around my housecoat and squeeze myself for a few more seconds, reliving them before I call out to Steph, "Merry Christmas Eve."

"You're in charge of bacon, scrambled eggs, pancakes and toast," Steph says from the shortbread-smelling kitchen. "They'll be here at eleven."

"There's lots of time." I grab a bowl and box of cereal as she rushes from the stove, waving cookie sheets in the air.

What would my holiday have been like if I had gone to Denver to visit my dad and met my new-to-me stepsisters and stepmom? Maybe I will find out next year. For now, I only have to deal with Steph's silly craziness and spending time with Greg.

"What have we forgotten?" Steph's eyes dart around the kitchen. "Will we have enough food?"

"Relax. Don't go all mom on me. This is not a big deal."

"Not a big deal? I have never entertained without your Oma telling me what to do." She shakes a flipper at me. "I don't cook for crowds, and I want this to be the best damn Christmas Eve brunch they've ever been to."

"There's the festive spirit." I give her a hip check on my way to the table. "They're friends. They have nowhere else to go and they're not judgy. Besides, you could feed them this and they wouldn't care." I lift the box of cereal in the air and shake it.

"That's not the point. Now work with me. If Oma's looking down on us, I want her to be proud."

"Her ashes are in a box, on the shelf, next to Opa's." I point towards the living room. "She's probably got better stuff going on with him than spying on us. Quit stressing."

Even though I try to lighten Steph's mood, my heart hurts that Oma and Opa won't be here. Our first holiday without them. Oma would whip a meal together and Opa would entertain everyone with his stories. I sigh. It seems forever ago since they were here, and yesterday, all in the same instant.

"Don't think I didn't see that kiss under the mistletoe," Steph says.

I stare in my bowl. Shit. Really? She saw it? My face gets hot, but I say nothing.

"I'm going to be like snot on a stick every second Greg is here." She snorts. "Trust me, there will be no hanky-panky in this house."

I swallow and make my voice casual. "No one says *snot-on-a-stick* or *hanky-panky*."

"This is not an English lesson. You know what I mean. I may not be fabulous at this mother gig, but I know what kind of trouble that kiss can get you into."

I don't want to bring up the whole "you were a pregnant teen and ditched me on your sister" drama because it's Christmas, and intentionally upsetting Steph will ruin the mood and any opportunity for me to be with Greg.

"When did *you* have your first kiss?" I paste a genuinely curious expression on my face and turn to her. "Like, you know, one that was real."

"Don't change the subject." She shakes the flipper at me again. "This is about you, Jillian. Not me. You're only fifteen."

"Come on. How old were you?"

"I want to tell you a story." Steph leans against the counter for a few seconds. "When I went to my ten-year high school reunion, they gave out a ton of awards – one for the person who moved the furthest away, one for the person with the coolest job. You name it, there was an award for it." She sighs. "You know what they gave me?"

I shrug.

"They gave me a watermelon."

"Because...you like watermelon?"

"No." Her nostrils whistle. "Because I was the first one to get pregnant."

"Oh, burn." I shake my head. "But I thought Oma and Opa kept it a secret."

"It was, but you know how secrets work. Especially in a small town."

"What did your friends say?"

"I didn't have many friends." Steph laughs. "Your Opa and I spent any spare time out in the bush, hiking, riding, skiing. When he bought me a horse, if he wasn't around to do something, I was at the corrals."

"I'm sorry."

"You don't have to be sorry. I'd hang out with him over anyone else. He was the best." She tips her head at me and gives me *the look*. "The point is, I am only telling you this because I want *you* to have every opportunity to do amazing things with your life *and* with those kinds of kisses, *you have to be careful*. Very careful."

"Got it."

All of a sudden, Steph's eyes zip from the counter to the table, to me. "Coffee? Are you doing the coffee? Or am I?"

"I will do coffee." I grab the pot.

Wow. This is awful early in the morning for such a big share. And what mean people. Total jerks. Why would Steph stay in Banff if that's what people thought about her? But then, she does love a challenge. Any kind of challenge.

The doorbell rings.

Bucky lets out his happy-to-see-you bark and Steph freezes. Her eyes open wide, like a grizzly bear is walking into the kitchen.

"They're early," she hisses.

"Chill." I give her an uber-big smile and go to the door as Bucky pushes his way past me. "Greg. Hi." I pull my housecoat shut to hide my flannel PJ's while Greg wrestles with Bucky.

What's he doing here so early? I haven't done my hair or even washed my face yet.

Greg smiles. My face gets warm and my heart stops. It. Just. Stops. Until his smile droops, and his eyebrows get all scrunchy. Oh no. We spent so much time together. We kissed. Was it too much? My boyfriend status has always been sketchy. How does Mom say it? 'Waiting for the other shoe to drop.' What if it's dropping now?

"Merry Christmas Eve," Steph calls out to Greg.

"To you too." He waves at her.

Both Greg's eyes are red. He didn't go drinking, did he? He's not old enough to legally drink in Alberta. Not that he doesn't drink. I've just never seen him get hammered.

"Greg." I hug my sides. "What's wrong?" *I know what he's going to say, and I don't want to hear it. Not now. Not on Christmas. Not ever.*

He closes his eyes.

Yup. I'm right. Incoming bad news. I bet he wants to just be friends again. How can I just be friends again? This is not fair. *Why do guys ditch me when I least expect it? This is even sooner than normal. What the hell?*

His face looks like he's in pain as he stares at me.

"Is everything okay?" I hug myself harder.

"No. No, everything is not okay."

"What's wrong?"

Greg grabs me in a bear hug. His body shakes against mine. He pushes me back, hands on my shoulders, and lifts his head to meet me eye to eye.

"What?" I mouth.

"Suzanne has been shot."

It takes my brain milli-seconds to digest the information. This is not about *me*. His sister has been shot.

I grab Greg's hands and squeeze them. "What...what happened? Is she okay?"

He blinks fast.

"My folks are trying to get me a flight home right away. Mom says it's bad. They don't know if she'll..."

"Don't talk like that. Suzanne's the toughest girl I know." I grip his forearms. "What happened?"

"She was at a uni party with a bunch of friends. Someone brought a gun. Two died. Three are..."

I go in for a hug again, so he doesn't have to be tough, and so that I don't embarrass him by watching his face.

"Three are...holding on."

"Suzanne's fit. She's strong. Healthy," I mumble stuff into his parka to chase the sadness away. "You'll see. She *will* be okay."

We stay there for a bit and then he gives himself a shake. And the hug is over. My heart connects the dots. Shit. Seriously? I get the best kisses ever, and he has to leave. Shit. Shit. Shit. Not about me. *This is not about me.*

He slides a hand into the pocket of his parka and pulls out a red, foil wrapped little box. "Merry Christmas. I'm sorry I'm going to miss everything, but I've got to get going."

"Hey, wait. I'll get yours. You can open it on the plane." I rush to the living room, grab his gift from under the tree and run back. "It's nothing really, just something, I don't know...I hope you like it."

We exchange gifts and I stare at the bow on the red box, hating myself for being upset he will be in Australia when we had all these plans to snowboard and skate and hang out. I bite my bottom lip, force a smile, and look up at him.

"She will be okay, Greg. She will. You'll see."

He says nothing. And then he puts one arm around my back, leans in and kisses me. My heart pounds so hard I'm sure Steph can hear it. I know she's watching. But I don't care. Greg presses his cheek against mine.

Damn it. *Idiot person bringing a gun to a party. Crazy, stupid world.*

"I have to go." Greg steps back. "I'll email as soon as I can until I switch my phone plan. Who knows, I might even get on Facebook." He lets out a sarcastic groan. "I'll let you know what's going on as soon as I get a chance."

"For sure. Take care of Suzanne...and yourself, and your folks."

One more solid hug and he leaves. Before he closes the back gate, and is gone, I mouth, "I like you. A lot."

Chapter 2

"Poor Greg." Steph's fingers squeeze my shoulders. "That's awful. I feel sorry for all of them."

"Me too."

So I don't have to talk, I mix the pancake batter a bit too aggressively and it slops onto the counter. I stare at the mess. Steph turns the radio up a notch and cheerful Christmas music fills the room. I wrestle with being sad, and mad, and disappointed. It takes a few rounds of mad and disappointed before I give myself hell. This is not about my missing out being with Greg and having fun. Grow up. Deep breath. And a silent prayer because it can't hurt to ask for help. *Please let Suzanne be okay*.

Steph makes exasperated sighing noises as she arranges platters of cookies and squares. I have no idea why she's so stressed about this brunch. It's not like Tom is coming. He and his sister, Mika, my almost best friend, are stuck in Lethbridge with their aloof mom. Mika called it their *duty visit*, and since Tom isn't coming, Steph has no one she needs to impress. The fact that she's freaking out is borderline funny because she's always in control...of everything.

I put Mickey Mouse pancakes on one plate for Kyle, the only kid coming to the brunch, because his mom is batshit crazy most days, and then put ordinary ones on a bigger platter beside a stack of buttered toast. Turkey bacon spins in the microwave. Check, check, check. Having to do stuff helps me not worry about Suzanne and whatever Greg is walking into.

The coffee maker light is *not* on. With deliberate, slow movements so I don't spook Steph into a frenzy thinking I forgot, I make a pot, turn it on and run upstairs to get ready.

Bucky barks when there's a knock at the back door. It makes me jump. Could it be Greg? Maybe he didn't have to go after all. I shake my head at my stupidness.

Steph calls, "They're here."

I hurry down the stairs, and when I get into the kitchen, I point a finger at her. "Relax. We are ready."

Kyle, his great-gramma, Mrs. Bronigan (an old friend of Oma and Opa's), and Eddy, Steph's dreadlocked best guy friend, all shout, 'Merry Christmas Eve.' Bucky barks at all the excitement and the noise level in the kitchen gets so loud. Then everyone fills their plates from our buffet style brunch set up along the counter and heads to the table.

"Have you been good?" Eddy points a pancake-loaded fork at Kyle. "Santa is still watching."

"Santa isn't real." Kyle gives Eddy an exaggerated child's eye roll. "That's kid stuff."

"And..." Eddy shakes his fork. "You're a kid."

"Am not."

"Are too."

"Okay guys." Steph laughs. "If Kyle is too old to believe in Santa that leaves more presents for Jillian and me."

"Mom says Christmas is a chemical scam," Kyle says.

"Pardon?" Steph leans forward on her elbows.

"It's...," Kyle scrunches up his face and stares up like the answer is written on the ceiling, "a commercial scam. That's what it is. She says people get sucked into buying shit..."

"Kyle Bronigan," his great-gramma smacks the table. "You watch your mouth young man. So close to the Lord's Day. What will he think of your swearing?"

"Mom says your Lord doesn't care about me. Just like Santa. They're not real GG." Kyle's serious voice and stern seven-year-old expression raise a few comical eyebrows.

"Well then, I guess I'll give your presents to someone else," Mrs. Bronigan says.

"That's not fair. They're not from Santa. They're from you," Kyle whines. "They're *my* presents."

Everyone laughs and then constant chatter follows with people's plans for the holidays and New Year's Eve. I'm glad it's noisy. No one notices I'm quiet as I get over my pity party. Greg and I were going to bring in our first New Year together. *It's not about me, I tell myself again.*

"Well." Steph stands. "How about some dessert? Let's clean this round up." She points at me and starts stacking plates.

We clear away dishes and the doorbell rings again. I freeze.

"Merry Christmas Eve," Barrett calls out. "Sorry I'm late. I had to," he walks up to me and drops his arm over my shoulder, "drop Greg off at the airport."

"Oh. So, you know?" I look at the goofy Santa hat and pompom which bobs across Barrett's forehead. "How's he doing?"

Barrett turns to me and says in a low voice, "How do you think he's doing?"

"I know, but is he like, okay? Is he doing, okay?"

"He's doing his best." Barrett gives me a side hug.

"You need food." Steph grabs a clean plate, piles on leftovers, and hands it to Barrett. "Sit and eat."

"Yes, Ma'am." He salutes her and heads to the table as the room erupts into noise again.

While everyone catches up with Barrett, Mrs. Bronigan grabs Steph's arm, taps my leg with her cane and ushers us towards the living room. I glance over the top of Mrs. Bronigan's head at Steph, who raises her hands in the air at me like she doesn't know what's going on either.

"Can you gals keep Kyle here for a while?" Mrs. Bronigan whispers.

"What?" Steph says. "Keep Kyle? Why?"

"His mom, well, she's, she's..." Mrs. Bronigan looks at the floor and huffs before she looks up at us. "She's on another bender. In the wind somewhere. I would take Kyle to the senior's lodge with me, but the visitor room is already booked. Besides, he's too young to stay there by himself. Some hoodlum stayed at his house with him last night. I can't take him back there. It's not safe."

"But it's Christmas tomorrow," I say. "What about his presents?"

"Ahh," she taps her cane on the floor. "You heard him. The boy doesn't believe in Santa. Or the Lord. Not my doing. Trust me, I tried. His mother's brainwashed him."

Steph and I stare at her.

"So, can you?" She lets go of Steph's arm and clasps her hand to her chest. "Can you take him? It will only be a few nights, maybe a week or two. That's all. I'll take him to the lodge for the afternoon and supper and bring him back around seven each night."

"Okay," Steph pauses. "Sure, I guess." She looks like she's convincing herself, Mrs. Bronigan, and me. "He can stay here."

Wow. Steph and I have a hard time keeping each other in line and we've never had to look after Kyle without Opa's supervision. Poor kid. Here's hoping we don't lose him.

"Thank you. You girls make your folks proud." Mrs. Bronigan says. "Both of you. You really do." And she hobbles back to the kitchen.

"What the hell?" I hiss. "It's Christmas. We have a pair of pajamas and that remote control car for him. He needs more on Christmas morning."

"We'll figure it out." Steph pats my shoulder and we both go back into the kitchen like nothing happened.

Card games, sweets, coffee and overlapping conversations go on for hours. It's exhausting, but it does distract me from spending all the time worrying about Suzanne and Greg.

"I'm done." Eddy gets up. "I need a nap to digest this food before I go to work." He pulls a package out of his coat pocket and passes it to Kyle. "You know, just in case you decide to believe in Christmas."

"Wow, thanks Mr. Eddy." Kyle's eyes are huge. "But I didn't get you anything."

"Christmas is for kids." Eddy ruffles Kyle's hair, hugs Steph and me, and leaves.

The others follow and I whisper to Barrett to hold on. When everyone is out the door, I turn to him. "I need to buy presents for Kyle for Christmas morning."

Barrett's eyebrows scrunch up. "Why?"

"His mom is awol. He's staying here for..." I shrug. "I don't know for how long."

"Lego. Kids love Lego. You can't lose."

* * *

"Santa came," Kyle shrieks as he busts into my bedroom.

I pull my pillow over my head to hide from the light. "You don't believe in Santa, remember?"

"But he came. There are so many presents under the tree, and he ate all his cookies and drank the milk you put out. He was here. Get up." He slams my door and runs to Steph's room.

I peek out from under my pillow. It's still dark outside. Steph will love Kyle's excitement this early. I grab the picture on my dresser of Greg and me snowboarding.

"Is Suzanne okay?" I whisper, then check around the room to see if anyone heard. Stupid, I know, like who would hide in my room. Once I confirm I *am* alone, I kiss the picture.

"Hurry up," Kyle yells as he pounds down the stairs.

"Hold your horses, Mister," Steph shouts.

I follow her downstairs where Kyle jumps on the spot like an excited baby kangaroo.

"We have traditions in this house." Steph puts her hand on his head to hold him still. “Just because Mr. and Mrs. Meier aren’t here to supervise doesn’t mean they get thrown to the wind.”

Kyle twists his head out of Steph’s grip and looks at me. “What’s she talking about?”

“We have to get fruitcake, coffee, and shortbread ready before we open presents.” I walk by them and into the kitchen.

“I don’t drink coffee. I’m just a kid,” Kyle wails.

Steph winks at me.

I mouth, “You’re mean.”

“Okay, Kyle. Here’s your job.” Steph steers him towards the living room. “You sort the presents by name. Put them in piles but no peeking or shaking. We’ll get breakfast.”

“You’re going to drive him crazy.” I pour water into the coffee pot.

Steph shakes a finger at me. “Patience is a virtue.”

“Oh, stop. He’s a kid. An excited kid who didn’t believe in Santa Claus yesterday. Think about it. What if we’re giving him his best Christmas?”

“Don’t get all sappy. It won’t kill him to wait.”

After we have everything ready, I follow Steph into the living room with our tray of treats.

“This is my pile, that’s Miss Steph’s and there’s Jillian’s.” Kyle points at them as he hops around his.

Steph walks over to the mantel and puts a fancy teacup and a tiny plate of fruit cake between Oma and Opa's boxes of ashes. I bite my lip. Oma loved everything, every little thing, about Christmas. And Opa encouraged her—especially all the baking and cooking.

How's Mom doing today? Is she alone? At least Steph and I have Kyle to keep us busy. What if Mom has no one? She's used to being here for Christmas. Not in Germany. Alone. Come to think of it, I haven't heard much from her. Incoming sigh. Maybe she met a guy. Maybe she's not alone. And that's why I haven't heard from her. There's so much I don't know about her life right now and the cheap phone plan she bought me doesn't allow overseas calls.

"Are we ready?" Kyle's excitement trumps my reflective moment. "Can we open them?"

"For someone who goes on about the materialistic aspect of Christmas, you seem pretty jacked," Steph says.

Kyle tips his head at her then looks at me. "What did she say?"

"She's trying to be sarcastic and funny."

Steph puts her hands on her hips. "I *am* funny."

I shake my head as Kyle puts his hands together like he's praying. "Please, can we open them?"

"Here's the rule," Steph says. "You need to read the tag before you rip it open, so you know who gave it to you because you'll be writing thank you cards for the gift."

"Most of mine are from Santa," Kyle shouts. "I don't have to thank him. It's his job."

Steph shakes her head at me. I shrug. *What else was I supposed to put on the tag?*

Kyle sits on the floor, turns packages around and around, shakes them, squeezes, and then rips them apart. His smile and squeals are the best.

I start to open my presents, saving Greg's for last. Smelly bath soaps from Mrs. Bronigan, a cool patterned neck tube for boarding from Eddy, and clothes from Steph. Fashionable clothes, and not too bold. I am impressed.

"I have all the receipts in case you don't like them, or they don't fit," Steph says.

"No, they're great." I nod at her. "Nice work."

"You think just because I'm a park warden and have to wear a green uniform I don't have any fashion savvy?"

"Well," I wink, "you wear your uniform a lot."

Steph throws a wad of Christmas wrap at me.

"Open mine." I pass her a green foil-wrapped box.

She holds it out in front of her.

"Will it scare me?" She winces. "Or blow up?"

"No."

Ever so slowly, she peels the tape off and unfolds the paper. Then she flips it over, her eyes dart from the picture to me to the picture, and she blinks super fast.

"Stop it. No tears, remember?" I make a frowny face. "We promised."

"It's lovely, Jillian." She holds up the framed picture of Oma, Opa, Mom and Steph sitting on the back step of the house with Bucky sprawled out in front of them. No one is looking at the camera and they all look so chill. "Thank you. It's lovely."

I took the picture a year before the shitshow happened last summer when I found out Steph was my bio mom. And Dad, Dale (I still don't know what to call him) wasn't even in the picture. In fact, he didn't know I existed yet. You'd never know any of that drama was about to unfold from their quiet expressions in the picture. Frankly, the whole thing still takes getting used to...for all of us.

My mom, Anita, is Steph's older sister. And Anita raised me. When I found out *who was who in the zoo* and reacted, not well I will admit, Mom had no choice but to explain everything. There was so much talking. Her talking. Me listening. She kept going back to *we thought it was the right thing to do.*

It was a memorable few days figuring it all out, and even now I sometimes shake my head. So many secrets and lies. I still call Anita *Mom* and Aunt Steph, well, most times I call her Steph, unless I'm pissed at her, and then I use Aunt Steph. Sometimes she's like a cool, much older sister, and then she has moments where she can be a bossy old cow, almost like she's trying to fill the mom role but isn't sure how to go about it.

I pick up Greg's gift and run my finger over the shiny paper. I would never have met Greg if Mom hadn't sent me here. I smile. I didn't see that coming...something good coming out of having to live in Banff.

Sometimes I think Mom took the job overseas so Steph and I can do the mother-daughter bonding thing, but I think we've bonded as much as we're ever going to. Besides, having one mom is plenty, even when we don't live in the same house anymore. Mom seems to sneak into my head when I least expect it *or* when I do stupid stuff and then I remember her old sayings she referred to as teaching lessons.

The house phone interrupts my thoughts.

"I got it." I set Greg's gift down and run to the phone. Maybe it's him. I take a breath before I pick up. "Hello."

"Jillian," Mom's voice echoes at me. "Merry Christmas."

"Merry Christmas, Mom." I force a smile in my voice so she can't tell I'm disappointed it's her and not Greg. "I was thinking about you. How are you?"

"Oh, I'm busy. It's not a normal Christmas here but that's okay. The time goes fast."

Mom asks a ton of questions. *What are we doing? Who's cooking? How are we handling the first Christmas without Oma and Opa?*

"Hey, I meant to tell you," she interrupts before I can respond to the last question, "if you're interested, there's a trunk in the attic with lots of old stuff from your grandparents."

"Uh-huh." I glance at Kyle shaking the giant box of Harry Potter Lego. "What about it?"

"I thought you and Steph could go through it and sort it out. I don't know if Steph remembers it's up there."

"Okay, sure."

She rambles on about the dinner she's heading to and then a late meeting, and it all reminds me of how far away she is.

"Can I talk to Steph?" Mom says after she winds down from her recap of what she has been up to.

"Sure. Just a minute. Merry Christmas, Mom. Love you." I point to Steph. "Mom wants to talk to you."

I pick up Greg's present again and pretend I'm not eavesdropping on their conversation. Mom is Mom. Life right now is about her and her work. And I have to admit I am kind of okay figuring mine out here with Steph.

When did that become my thought process – *I'm okay with figuring it out here with Steph*?

Greg's gift is light and neatly wrapped. I shake it. Something slides around inside.

"What is it? What did you get?" With his new remote-control car in hand, Kyle hovers over me.

"I don't know."

"Well, open it and find out."

I lift out a delicate, silver bracelet with two charms on it. A snowboarder and a hiker with a walking stick.

"Boring." Kyle goes back to driving his car through the wrapping paper scattered on the floor.

I put the bracelet on my wrist. It weighs almost nothing, and the reflection of the Christmas lights twinkle on the shiny silver. It's so personal. I feel guilty about giving him the carabiners with his initials engraved on them and the high-tech backpacking bottle with cool graphics. I know he can use them when he's climbing. They're practical. Besides, it's the thought that counts, right? Nope. I still feel like I cheaped out on the personal aspect for Greg.

Chapter 3

My morning routine now starts with checking emails for anything from Greg. Again, nothing. I know he's got more important stuff going on but it's hard not to be a part of it, even from a distance. Just to hear if Suzanne is okay.

I read Mom's short email which gives a rundown on how busy she is and that she hopes I am helping Steph out. It sounds as if I am one of her clients and she is going through the process of staying in touch. It is kind of funny how she never asks anything personal, like she's afraid I might tell her life is not fabulous and then she would have to deal with it. I send her my weather report type response. I forever have Oma to thank for teaching me how to say nothing with something.

Before I shut my laptop, an email from Dale pops up. Dale? Dad? I still don't know what to call him. Dad makes him sound too familiar. I only met him once and we've sent a few emails back and forth since then, so I tend to go with calling him Dale.

My finger hovers over the keyboard. Shoot. I feel guilty. I sent their presents in the mail with a letter apologizing for not coming to spend Christmas with them. I hope they got it. My guilt simmers when I realize they never called, and this is the first I have heard from them in two weeks.

I open the email and a picture of them together on a ski hill pops up. Dale and his wife on the outside. Jules and Jessica, my younger stepsisters, in the middle. Arms draped over each other. Big smiles. My guilt fades completely. They look happy. Maybe my not going to meet them was best for all of us.

Jillian,

I hope you had a good Christmas with Steph. We decided to take off to Vail for a ski holiday. The snow was superb. I think you would have liked it.

Thank you for the Canadian souvenir gifts. That was thoughtful of you. We all look forward to coming to Banff in the summer and spending some time getting to know you. I hope you will be able to fit us into your schedule.

If you ever need anything, you have my number. Please never hesitate to call. The very best of wishes for the New Year.

Dale

I reread it a few times. The *I hope you can fit us into your schedule*—is that a slam at me for cancelling at the last minute and not going to see them? Or am I reading more into it than I should? I find it tricky with texts and emails. When I can't see the person's face, like in a real conversation, I tend to dissect the written words. Sometimes too much. And it can distort the meaning. Besides, it's not like I know him well enough to figure out what he means, even if he was here. Maybe he really does just hope I will have time to hang out with them in the summer.

I send a reply.

Dale,

Thanks for the note. The picture looks like you all had a great time. Yes, Steph and I had a good Christmas. It was nice to be with her as we spent our first one without Oma and Opa. Thank you for the money and the Christmas card.

Happy New Year to all of you, too. Have a great winter. Let me know when you plan to come to Banff. See you next summer.

Jillian

I reread mine in case *he* dissects my words. I doubt he would though. He's a busy man. And I have not said a lot of anything. Similar to a weather report. I shut down my laptop and try not to be disappointed that Greg never sent anything.

"You have your mopey face on." Steph shakes a finger at me.

"Me?" I point to myself, then to her. "What about you?"

"I am not moping."

"Oh really?" I cross my arms over my chest. "So, you're going to say you haven't been pissy ever since Tom called to say they're staying longer in Lethbridge?"

"I am not pissy."

"Really? You barked at Kyle last night because he forgot to put his bowl in the dishwasher."

"I did not."

"You did."

"Really?" she whispers.

"Yes."

"Oh shit. Is he okay? Do you think he hates me? What should I do?"

"Steph." I walk over and put my hands on her shoulders. "Kyle didn't notice. He's got thicker skin than both of us. Besides, Tom will be back in a few days. You can get all kissy face then."

"We don't do kissy face."

I groan.

"We don't." She shakes her head and all I can do is smirk. How naïve does she think I am?

"After Mrs. Bronigan picks up Kyle, why don't we go to Norquay? I can snowboard. You can ski," I suggest. "We can get rid of some of this missing-guy-energy we've got going on. Kyle won't be back until suppertime."

Steph agrees, so we rush around to get Kyle and ourselves ready and it gets a bit chaotic with who needs to take what to get out the door. Even Bucky doesn't know whether to lie down or sit up and pay attention to all the rushing about. But we manage, and in no time Steph and I are on the road to Norquay.

When we get off the lift for our first run, I do up my binding and pendulum down the steep part of the Cascade while Steph schusses to the bottom. Show off. Just as I push off again to link another turn, a spray of snow hits me from behind. My arms windmill as I attempt to counterbalance an incoming butt slam, but it doesn't work. A boarder stops on the downhill side in front of me.

He pulls up his goggles and says, "Hey. Sorry about that, mate."

I have no idea who he is and am totally embarrassed I'm on my ass. "No biggie," I say as I push myself up. Maybe if he talks a bit more, I can figure out who he is. Or if this is a ski hill pick-up line. Cute, but I'm not interested.

"How's shredding?" he says.

"It's my first run today." I wouldn't call my snowboarding status at the *shredding* level, but it's cool he thinks it might be.

"How's Greg? Have you heard from him?"

Ah, Greg's friend. *How sweet is it that he knows I know Greg?*

"No, not yet. He's kind of busy."

"Yes, I bet he is." He frowns. "Poor bloke. Hope it goes well for all of them."

I love his Aussie accent. Or maybe it's just because it reminds me of Greg. There are so many people in Banff and on the ski hill from Australia and New Zealand. Steph says they come to work and board for a season and then never go home.

"So, how's the snow?"

"Great." He looks around as if he doesn't want spies to hear. "It's actually quite shitty, but you know, any day on the hill is better than being somewhere else. Later Jillian." He waves. "Hope your guy gets back soon."

He takes off and makes wide swooping carves like a pro. One day, that will be me. With lots of practice.

My guy? He called Greg my guy. I smile so hard my goggles lift off my cheeks.

Run after run, I follow Steph down the hill. We head over to the Spirit Chair and my confidence grows right up until I get too cocky and barely save myself from slamming into the hill. Focus. Full attention to turns required. I pick up speed again, catch an edge, complete an unintentional cartwheel and land on my side. Damn. Definitely not shredder material yet.

"Thanks Steph." I slide my board into the back of her truck. "That was fun."

As she drives home, I mention, "Greg was going to teach me to drive. I signed up to take the learner's test in January."

"Aren't you the one who drove my truck down a fire road last summer? Illegally." Steph laughs.

"I don't think that counts."

"I'll take you driving when you get your learner's licence."

"Thanks." I sigh with minimal enthusiasm. I know she means well but driving with her and driving with Greg are not the same.

"I get it." Steph socks me in the shoulder. "I do. But he'll be back before you know it."

I get a sense she does *get it*. Is this a bonding moment? It makes me smile that Steph and I might actually be on the same page about guy stuff.

"Hey, if I teach you," she says, "and when Greg comes back, he takes you out to show you how to drive, you can act like a pro."

That would be pretty cool.

When we get home, I put on my big girl panties and decide to be the first to send an email. The time difference is a killer but maybe he's online and can answer right away.

Greg,

Hi. How's Suzanne? And how are you doing? I don't know what else to ask but please know I've been thinking about you guys a lot.

Steph and I went boarding today. I even made it over to the Spirit Chair and came down a steep pitch with only one wipeout. A huge improvement on my part. Insert happy face emoji. I ran into a friend of yours. He sprayed me so badly I fell over. Really. I just fell over right in front of him. So embarrassing. He said to say hi. Maybe asking him his name would have helped. Sorry. I didn't.

Thanks for the bracelet. It's so pretty and I wear it all the time. It's almost a good news bad news gift—it makes me think of you way too much. Sappy, hey?

Christmas flew by. Kyle is staying with us for a while but we're not sure for how long. It's kind of complicated with his mom being awol. He keeps Steph and me busy.

I hope things are going okay.

I debate how to sign off. I don't want to be a clingy, needy girlfriend.

Jillian of Banff

I stare at my inbox for a few minutes. Nothing.

Because I feel guilty Bucky was locked in the house while we were on Norquay, I take him for a long walk along the Bow River by the canoe dock.

"What the hell," I whisper when I see this huge husky in the shadows between the wolf willow branches and frozen river. The very same husky who showed up last summer at the Cascade numerous times and then again at the helicopter crash site in the fall. The husky no one else, people and Bucky included, ever acknowledge seeing. "What are you doing here?" I whisper.

Bucky sniffs the tree trunk, then pees on it. He has no interest in the husky. And seriously, how can he pee so often?

The husky doesn't come closer, but he watches me.

"Okay. I get it. This is your space. We'll leave." I tug on Bucky's leash, and we turn around and head past the Bow View Lodge towards the streetlights and home.

Once inside the back door, Bucky heads for his bed.

"Hey Jillian," Steph calls out. "A cougar's been spotted down by the river. I'm going to check it out. Mrs. Bronigan is taking Kyle out for burgers and will bring him back around seven."

"Sure," I say. *By the river? A cougar?* "Be safe."

I stare at her back as she heads out the door. Was the husky watching out for me because of the cougar? Did he know it was close by? Or was he just creeping me out for kicks and giggles?

I make a sandwich and head to my room to check my email. And there it is in my Inbox—a letter from Greg. My index finger is slow to hit open as I hold my breath.

Hey girlfriend,

Oh my God. He called me *girlfriend.* Just like that. Not like he had to or anything. Now I feel bad not saying anything cute to him.

I miss you. Ever always here for you even if it's just a note. Sorry it's taken so long to write. It's been rough. When I'm not at the hospital, I'm driving someone to or from the hospital, getting food or running errands. When I'm done, I sleep hard and fast.

An international plan for my cell phone is too pricey, so I nabbed Dad's computer for a few minutes. He's got an old one he's booting up for me to use, so that will help, and I can write more often.

Suzanne is unconscious. A good thing for now, the doc says. She coded yesterday, but they brought her back. Mom almost had a heart attack. It was bloody awful but they're still hopeful she can pull out of this. Like you said, she's tough. She'll need to be. There's a long recovery ahead of her if she can get through this stage.

Mom is whipped but I can't get her to skip a day and stay home to rest. Pop goes to work for a few hours and then comes after lunch. I've tried to convince them we need a schedule, so we don't all burn out, but they're not there yet.

Thanks for the sweet gifts. Once things settle down, I'll put them to good use on a trek.

I think about you and miss you loads. Catch you later.

XO Greg

Ah, heart melt. Thank you, Greg. I exhale because I didn't realize I was holding my breath.

How awful for all of them. I wish there was something I could do. Other than stay in touch, there's not much. I can pray, you know, just in case someone really listens to that stuff.

I stare at the ceiling and whisper, 'whoever's up there, if you've got time, can you please take care of Suzanne and help her through this?' My heart hurts for them.

Greg,

Thanks for the update. I'm so sorry this happened, and I hope Suzanne comes out of it soon. It must be awful to see her like that and to watch your parents trying to manage it all and be tough and invincible. What a nightmare. Please know I'm thinking about you all and sending healing thoughts.

There's nothing else new here, but I thought I'd let you know I got your email. I hope you have an okay day of it.

Take care. Miss you too.

Jillian of Banff XO

I finger his bracelet on my wrist and press on each charm.

* * *

When New Year's Eve finally comes, I am so done with doing stuff to stay busy. I feel grumpy. Greg hasn't sent any more emails. I've eaten so much junk food and now I have a massive zit attack on my forehead and chin. Tonight, I will binge-watch my favourite movies, eat healthy snacks and write a list of *Things to Do* for next year. That should give me some positive mojo and get me into a healthier norm before Greg comes back.

The doorbell rings as I switch channels.

"Jillian, come here," Steph calls.

Seriously? I'm comfortable and cozy.

"Jillian!"

I kick the blanket off and stomp into the kitchen.

"What..." I stop when I see Barrett. "Hey, hi. What's going on?"

"Happppy New Year," he slurs.

"I think your friend might be under the influence." Steph walks up to me and looks me in the eyes, inches from my face. "I don't clean up barf. Make sure there's no barf," she says in a gruff whisper. "And don't wake up Kyle."

"Got it."

She pats my back and heads upstairs.

"Barrett." I shake my head at him. "What's going on?"

"Nothing."

"Are you okay?"

"Nope."

"You're drunk." I head to the cupboard to find a plastic bowl in case he does barf because I also do not clean up barf.

"Yup."

"Why?"

"There was beer. I drank it. Then I drank some more."

"But you don't drink."

He lifts his hand and points a finger at me. "Correction. I don't drink well."

I glance at the ceiling and whisper, *'Mika, you owe me, big time. I'm a huge fan of your boyfriend but not when he's drunk.'*

Barrett's usually so on his game and practical and chill. *What the hell got into him?* I put on a pot of coffee and grab snacky food to sober him up, hopeful he doesn't upchuck. Begrudgingly, I peel a Christmas orange for myself.

"Are you going to get sick?" I pass Barrett a cup of black coffee.

"Nope."

I put the bowl in his other hand. "Just in case."

"Okey dokey." He wobbles a bit.

"Did you drive here?"

"Nope."

"Are you going to stick with monosyllabic responses?"

"Yup."

I grab a tea towel and lead the way to the living room, remove the fancy pillows and point to the end of the couch. Barrett falls onto it and closes his eyes. I put the towel on the carpet and the barf bowl on top of it.

"What do you want to watch?" I point the remote at the TV and switch off my chick flick.

"Don't care."

"Okay, we'll watch the ball fall in New York. People there are having way more fun than you and me."

"I miss Mika," Barrett whines.

This is so *not Barrett*.

"Do you think she found a better boyfriend?"

I roll my eyes at the TV. Drunk talk. It's the worst. Guys never talk mushy stuff but give them alcohol and they turn into melodramatic idiots. Barrett will feel so stupid tomorrow...if he remembers any of this.

"She's with her mom and Tom." I flick through the channels. "I doubt she has time to boyfriend shop."

"You sure?"

"Yes." I pass him the chips. "Only eat them if they stay down."

Chip crunching and coffee slurping noises. I glance over and Barrett sits up a bit straighter as New York's New Year's Eve festivities scroll across the screen. There are so many partiers, music and a lot of kissing. *Lucky people.* I hum along with the song they're playing.

When the midnight ball finally falls, Barrett stands up.

"Happy New Year."

"Hey, easy," I shush him and reach out to stop him from stumbling.

He leans in, eyes closed, lips puckered.

"No way. No offense but no way. You chill." I grab his shoulders and steer him back onto the couch. He grabs my hand. "Barrett. Stop it."

"I miss Mika."

"I know. You mentioned that. She will be home in a few days."

"She hasn't answered any of my texts."

"Barrett, she never texts." I close my eyes and exaggerate a sigh. "She hardly even turns her phone on. The only reason she has it with her is to keep Tom off her back. It's his big brother role. He thinks a cell phone is the next best thing to pepper spray."

He plunks back onto his corner of the couch, and I perch on the edge of the opposite end, switching channels until I get to *Big Brother*.

"Yeah," Barrett says with more guy enthusiasm than I expect.

We debate the characters and their chances of pulling off a win. I sigh. My first New Year's Eve in Banff. Not how I visualized it. I lean back and try to force my eyes to stay open until Barrett leaves.

The side of my face rubs against something that doesn't feel like my pillow. I wipe drool off my cheek and open one eye. A car chase flashes across the TV screen at the same time that I feel an arm across my shoulders.

Who's arm? Greg? I almost bolt upright until I remember he's in Australia. I look at the sleeve. Barrett. It's Barrett's arm.

What the hell?

I slide off the couch onto the floor and wait. No response from Barrett other than whistle noises from his breathing. I crawl across the room towards the kitchen light.

One last look, Barrett is still sound asleep. Small blessings.

"Well, hello there," Steph says in a quiet voice.

I stare at the floor. Fuck. I groan and stand up.

"What's going on?" Her finger taps the table.

"Nothing."

Steph tips her head and gives me the I-am-not-buying-it look.

I hurry to the table, lean down and whisper, "Seriously, nothing. Nothing at all. We must have fallen asleep watching *Big Brother*. I was waiting for Barrett to sober up and go home." The words tumble out as my brain tries to replay how I ended up asleep on the couch with his arm around me.

Steph stares at me.

"Honest."

"Did you get into my beer?"

"No." I pull my head back. "I don't drink."

"Neither does Barrett, usually."

"Seriously, Steph, I didn't drink anything, and nothing happened." I give my shoulders a tiny shrug to make sure my bra is where it's supposed to be. Nothing happened, I tell myself. We. Fell. Asleep. That's all. *Right?*

"Do his parents know he's here?"

"Yes."

"Well, if he's spending the night, you're coming upstairs now."

We sneak up the stairs so none of them squeak. Steph peeks in on Kyle and we each go to our own room. When I wake up on New Year's Day, I tiptoe downstairs. There is no one on the couch.

"What?" my mouth says without a sound. Where's Barrett? I know we left him here.

Chapter 4

"Tom," Steph says in a way louder voice than normal.

I nudge Kyle and turn the TV louder to give them privacy. She hasn't seen Tom for almost two weeks. If it were Greg who came back, I'd want a bit of alone time too. Longest Christmas holiday ever. I can't believe I'm thinking this but I'm glad school starts tomorrow.

"I'm hungry," Kyle says.

I glance towards the kitchen. "How about I challenge you to Mario Kart first?"

Kyle jumps up and grabs the controllers. As always, since my skill level at the game is lower than beginner, I bubble my way through too many levels, but it keeps Kyle amused and he laughs a lot at having to always rescue me.

"Hey, Jillian, Kyle." Tom walks into the living room.

I control my reaction to seeing him because his super hotness, for an old guy, catches me off guard. He looks younger somehow. And happy. Really happy. Not that he's not usually happy but it's a different type of happy eyes and smile look he's got going on. Or maybe it's just because he's wearing jeans and a t-shirt and not his ugly green Park Warden uniform.

"How was Lethbridge? And Mika, how's Mika?" As soon as the words leave my mouth, I get a twinge of guilt. I haven't heard from Barrett for three days. *What do I say to Mika? Heck, what do I say to Barrett when I see him?*

"It was good," Tom says. "Much better than I thought it would be."

He glances back at Steph, and she gives him an uber exaggerated smile. What's going on? Did Steph tell him about Barrett and me?

"Mika got a new job," Tom says. "She'll be working at the Information Office in Banff and she's applying to go to the University of Lethbridge for September."

"What? She's giving up working at the stables? She loves that place." I stand up. So many thoughts bounce in my head but Mika leaving trumps them. "Why? Lethbridge is forever away. I'll never see her."

"You know what?" Tom drops his head, shakes it then lifts it up and says, "I shouldn't have said anything. It's her news to tell and she's excited. Pretend you heard nothing from me. Promise?"

I look at Tom, then Steph, and back to Tom.

"Promise?" Tom points at me. "Please. She'll bust my balls."

I laugh at the visual, knowing full well Mika is capable of doing that.

"Okay." I run my finger and thumb across my lips to zip them, but damn, Mika never said a word about any of this. I thought we were friends. "Is she home?"

"Yeah, Barrett's working, so she's ironing her uniform to start tomorrow."

"Ironing?" My eyes open wide. "Hey Steph, can you stay with Kyle so I can go see her?"

"I can stay by myself." Kyle's bottom lip sticks out. "I'm not a baby."

"I know you're not but if you *are* ever here alone," Steph says, "you call 911. Okay?"

"Why would I be alone?"

"Just in case, ever." Steph puts her hands on her hips. "Got it?"

"Yes, Miss Steph."

Tom takes three big steps over to him, picks him up like he's a pillow and puts him over his shoulder. "You're coming with us, buddy. We'll teach you everything you need to know about ice fishing."

"Really? Yahoo. I'm going fishing."

I pause outside Tom and Mika's apartment and take a breath. My plan is to not say anything about the whole Barrett incident unless she mentions it. And if she does, then I'll play it down so it's not a big deal. Because it's not a big deal.

"Hey, stranger." Mika pulls me into the living room and gives me a hug.

She gives me a hug. Crazy. She's not a hugger unless it's a mandatory hug-required situation. This isn't.

"Hi." I hug back, hopeful she doesn't sense my surprise at her greeting. "How was Christmas?"

"It was a blast."

I did not see that coming. Maybe her mom's not as awful as she makes her out to be. Or maybe she did find a new boyfriend. If so, poor Barrett. He'll be crushed. At least she's not acting awkward, so maybe he hasn't said anything.

She pushes me back from the hug. "Barrett told me."

I panic and know my eyes are huge.

"How's Suzanne?" she says. "Have you heard anything?"

"No change yet." Inward sigh of relief. Not because there's no change in Suzanne but because that's what Mika is talking about. "She's still in a coma."

"That sucks. I'm so sorry. I bet Greg is going crazy."

"Yeah."

We walk to her bedroom and the first thing I see is a well-pressed National Park ugly green uniform hanging from a coat hanger on the closet doorframe.

"What's this?" I point and fake curiosity.

"It's my foot in the door to becoming a warden. Tom got me a job at the Information Office. I'm going to get my high school diploma by correspondence classes while I work there and then I have two years of university." She takes down the hanger and waves it in front of her. "I start tomorrow and hopefully when I've got my degree, they'll remember me, and I can get a warden gig."

My lips do a perfect oh-I'm-so-surprised expression. Even Tom would be impressed.

"Information Office? University?" I tip my head. "What's going on?"

She does a recap of their time in Waterton National Park and how spectacular the place is. She says it got her thinking about her future, being able to work outdoors and still be with horses *while* she helps protect the environment.

"Stop." I put my hands up. "Who are you and what have you done with my almost best friend Mika?"

"Almost best friend?" She punches me in the shoulder. "I go away for ten days, and you replace me?"

"You do know you're irreplaceable?" I laugh at her serious expression. "No really, where's this coming from? You didn't even want to see your mom and now you're career planning. What happened?"

Mika takes off on another enthusiastic dialogue (with lots of hand actions) about all the advantages and benefits of working for the government in such an awesome place. I sit on her bed, watch her big grin and animated movements, and it makes me happy. She's had a rough go at life. I'm not sure how Barrett will react about her leaving in the fall, but this is Mika super-jacked, and I've never seen it before. It looks good on her.

"Tom and I saw a pair of bald eagles circling. Tom figures they might have been guarding a kill. It was so quiet, and we just stood there watching them. It was amazing."

I smile because I'm not sure how awed I'd be about eagles flying because, like, isn't that what they do? But I say nothing because it's obvious it had an impact on her.

"And this bobcat with last year's kitten, they were out hunting..." and she's off again all excited and talking fast. It's cute. Throughout it though, there's no mention of her mom, but she's in such a great mood I don't want to spoil her by asking how the visit went, in case it was crappy.

As I listen, I remember the incident at the river with the husky and Bucky and then Aunt Steph having to go check for the cougar. I let Mika unwind a bit before I say, "Hey, you know, with all those animal encounters you had, do you ever believe they're maybe, I don't know, ones meant for just *you* to see? Like a spirit animal or something?"

"What?" She squints her eyes. "You think, because I'm native, I'm one with the animals? Some kind of wildlife whisperer?"

"No, no. That's not what I meant. I just wanted to know..." Shit, this is not going how I want it to go. I try to ease into it better. "Something bizarre happened and I can't figure it out. Maybe there's nothing to figure out." I ramble on because I don't mean to offend her, I'm just curious. "I thought maybe you'd..."

She bends over, her hair flies in the air and then she's upright again, laughing, as if I just told the best joke. I have no idea what's going on. And no idea how to react. Is she on something?

"Relax." She shakes my shoulders. "I'm jerking you around."

I don't move because if this is her kidding around it's a tad bit frightening.

"You don't have to be native to see animal spirits," she says. "My grandparents, I think they're ravens. Remember when we were in the Cascade, after the whole poacher incident, there were those two ravens flying over us?"

I do a quick replay in my head of us tying up the poacher and remember Mika pointing at the birds flying away.

"Yeah, I do. And then there were two more at the corrals when you agreed to meet with Tom."

"Yup, I saw them a lot when I lived in the bush. And then I saw them once in a while when I took trail rides out from the stables." She does a big inhale and holds it for a second. "I'd get this feeling someone was watching me and when I stopped to check it out, I'd see them together on a branch, or post, watching me."

"Cool."

"I don't see them much anymore though." Mika grins. "Maybe they're not worried about me anymore. Or maybe someone else needs them more than me. Or maybe it was all just my imagination. You know, too much time alone. Who knows." She smiles. "Why do you ask?"

"There's this big husky. I saw him with you when we first met."

She shakes her head. "I didn't have a dog."

"Yeah, well, I know that now. But then, I thought he was like your guard dog. And he terrified me. But Bucky never reacted. Ever. And no one else mentioned him."

She doesn't say anything.

"I saw him again, this week, down by the river." I rush through my tale because it feels surreal talking about it out loud and I don't want her to laugh at me. "Bucky didn't react. And then Steph got a call about a cougar sighting."

"Whoa." Mika puts both hands up like she's stopping a bus. "You do know the difference between a dog and a cougar, right?"

"Very funny." I snort. "Someone spotted a cougar along the river trail where I was walking. And when I was there, the husky sat in front of me kind of daring me to go past him. Which I didn't because he creeps me out."

"It could've been a warning. Or maybe you were in the wrong place at the right time.

Coincidence maybe." Mika shrugs. "Hey, did you hear Tom's great news?"

Whoa, so much for my husky question, I guess. "That he's taking Kyle ice fishing?"

"No." She brings her fingers to her mouth.

"What?"

"Shit." Mika scrunches her eyes and mouth up. "I'll let him tell you."

"You can't do that. That's not fair. What's going on?" I stand. "Hey, is he going to propose? Is that why Steph was acting odd this morning?"

Mika laughs. "No."

"Then what? What's going on?"

"Hey, how's snowboarding going? Have you been able to get out much?"

"Don't change the subject. Tell me what's going on."

"I can't really. I'm sorry. I shouldn't have said anything." She lifts her hands in the air. "Don't worry though, I'm sure you'll find out soon."

* * *

I check my email before I get ready for the first day back to school. Nothing from Greg. Is that good news or bad news? I finger his bracelet and decide to send him a note.

Greg,

Back to school today. I'm looking forward to the distraction. It was the longest Christmas holiday ever. I hope things are improving for Suzanne. I just thought I'd send you another quick note to let you know that I think about you all a lot.

Miss you. Take care.

Jillian of Banff XO

I debate adding more XO's but decide against it.

"Can you take Kyle to karate class tonight?" Steph hands me a plate of toast. "I'm meeting Tom after work."

"Hey, you can come and take the class with me." Kyle spits bits of cereal out as he waves his spoon in the air. "Miss Steph says you used to do it. You can practise with me."

My whole karate gig seems a lifetime ago. It's been over seven months since I took a class in Toronto. I was training to get my red belt this spring. That will never happen here.

"I didn't bring my Gi," I say.

"That's okay. Not everyone has a uniform." Kyle gives me an encouraging smile. "Just wear sweats. We can kick some ass."

"Hey, language." I shake a finger at him and fight back a smirk at his kid cockiness. I put on my listen-to-me adult voice and say, "That's not what karate is about. It's about making you into the best person you can be physically and mentally."

"Yeah, yeah, that's what Sensei Geri says too. But kicking some," he grins, "butt is fun. So will you come with me?"

"Sure. Finish up and get ready for school. I'll walk with you." I turn my back to him and say in a low voice to Steph. "What's going on with you and Tom?"

"Nothing." Steph avoids eye contact.

"I think your nothing is something. Mika knows what it is, but she wouldn't tell me."

"And she shouldn't." Steph gives me her serious don't-piss-me-off eyes. "It's none of her business."

"And that just makes it sound a lot more than nothing. What's going on?"

"Adult stuff." Steph sighs. "Don't worry about it. I'll fill you in when we figure it out."

"I'm sixteen this summer." I lift my hand and put my thumb and index finger an inch apart. "I'm this close to adult status."

She shakes her head and walks out of the kitchen.

"You can't avoid telling me forever," I call after her.

What's going on? And why am I the last to know? I glance at Kyle who's got his cereal bowl to his lips, slurping like Bucky and totally oblivious to everything. Technically, I guess I'm not the last to know.

Kyle chatters all the way to school about his sensei and this girl in his class who sounds like a mini girl version of Karate Kid.

I tap the top of his toque. "I'm thinking, Mister, you have a crush on this gal."

"Do not." He looks up and tries to give me a mean look but there's a smile trying to escape. "She's just really good. She's Sensei's kid."

"Ahh, so you're crushing on the teacher's kid?"

"Am not."

It amazes me how he's such a great little person considering his mom bails on him so often, and his dad, well, he's an ass when he does turn up. Kyle acts like his life is the best. Maybe staying with us, maybe this is the best he's had in a while. The thought makes me feel good about helping Steph out with him.

"See you later," I say, as we reach his elementary school.

He runs through the gate.

Steph hasn't mentioned when Kyle's going home, and Mrs. Bronigan isn't around as often as she used to be. It's as if he's now a part of us, which is not a big deal other than Steph and I have to co-ordinate stuff more to have someone home with him. It's not an issue right now since my life is pretty darn dull. But it is bizarre he's living with us.

I hurry to get to school so I can avoid Barrett at our lockers.

The hallway is full of chatter and greetings. I wave at familiar faces and get a few waves back. Bonus.

I grab my books and head straight to class. Teachers dump speeches on us about acing exams because our futures depend on it and then they hand out practice tests.

Since there is not much going on with Greg gone, I might as well be productive in my spare time (because I have a ton of it) and try to make the honour roll. Won't Mom love that? Look at me joining Mika with planning for the future.

"Hey." Tony, a short guy with super curly hair from chemistry class leans against Barrett's locker. "Why don't you join us for lunch. It's freezing out and," he opens his eyes super wide, "there's a *big* chess game today."

"A chess game?" I try to hide the nerd alert going on in my head and scan the hallway for Barrett.

"It's kind of lame but fun. Come on."

"I didn't bring a lunch."

He digs in his pocket and pulls out change. "The junk food machine is operational today."

I look at the loonies in his palm. Why not? It's better than walking home to eat alone or running into Barrett. I pick up two loonies.

"I'll pay you back." I close my locker, walk with him to get snacks and head up the stairs to the lunchroom.

Along one wall, kids sit on tables and, through the large, wired glass windows, watch volleyball intramurals in the gym below. Tony leads the way to the end of the room where two guys hunch over, no surprise, a chess board.

“Guys.” He taps the table, and they lift their heads. “This is Jillian.” He points to me.

They smile and look right back at the chessboard. Burn. My feelings should be crushed but it’s kind of funny. Chess. A girl. And chess wins. I guess I am just that dull.

“Derrick, Gary.” Tony points to the top of their heads and then pulls chairs over for us. He turns his chair, so the back faces the table, and straddles the seat. “Who’s winning?”

This really *is* all about a chess game. My smile is way too cheesy and I’m glad none of them see it. I sit next to Tony. I’m the only one making a noise with my chip crunching, so I try to soften them in my mouth first to reduce the crunch factor.

Derrick must be the oldest. He’s got a moustache. I bet he’s in grade twelve. I haven’t seen him around but that means nothing. I tend to walk through the halls focused on not doing something stupid that will make people notice me. Poker-straight-haired Gary with studious, black glasses must be in grade eleven. He doesn’t look as old as Derrick, and I haven’t seen him in any of my classes.

Opa taught me the basics of chess when I was a kid, but it wasn’t my thing. Mainly because he never let me win. Derrick has more pieces on the board which means nothing. Checkmate can happen when you least expect it.

I listen to their monosyllabic dialogue and the occasional fist to the table *thud*. Nerds. Yup. But I'm not alone.

A group of giggly girls come in and head for the gym viewing window. They're junior-highish age. Grade seveners maybe, but it's hard to tell. They look made up and wear magazine fashionable clothes. One of them is Olivia, the missing girl from Norquay. She glances our way, totally scans past me, and focuses on the guys. I watch her watch them and then one of her friends grabs her arm and they're back to watching the volleyball game. For the new girl in town, she's made a lot of friends already. Not exactly how I started out here but good for her.

"No!" Derrick throws his hands to his head. "Good match, bro."

Together they put the pieces back in a little wooden box and fold up the board.

Like I just walked into the room, they drill me with questions. What do you think of Banff? Do you ski? Snowboard? Got a job? Miss home? My face gets warm from all the attention.

"Whoa." Tony puts his hands up. "Keep it in your pants. She's got a boyfriend."

The fact Tony knows about Greg surprises me. It's not like Greg went to school here or that he'd be a chess club groupie on any level. I have to say though, Tony's statement is quite the icebreaker. While the guys laugh it off, my face heats up again.

"I don't usually lose," Derrick says to me. His voice is deep, and he looks woodsy in his red and black flannel shirt.

"Whatever," Gary snorts. He checks his watch and, as if it's a signal, everyone gathers their stuff. "Nice to meet you," he says, and they walk away.

"Tomorrow?" Tony points at me. "Same time, same place."

"Ah, sure, I guess."

Barrett waves at me in the hall. I smile and attempt a casual wave, but it feels stiff. He's a guy. I doubt he notices. Besides, maybe I'm the one being weird about this. Maybe he doesn't remember anything. Maybe there is nothing to remember.

My backpack weighs a ton. This *being academic* might also be a physical workout. I do a mental check of the classes I had and the homework assignments, so I don't forget anything.

As I slip my lock on, Barrett shoulder checks me and says, "Hi."

I snap the lock shut, turn, and give him a cheesy smile. "Later. I have to pick up Kyle." And away I go down the hall, walking fast so if he's watching, he gets that I'm in a hurry. I feel like a jerk but am glad to have Kyle as an excuse.

"Okay then," I hear him call out. "Catch you later."

* * *

"Sensei Geri." Kyle does a traditional karate bow in front of his instructor and then stands at attention. "This is Jillian. She's a blue belt in something but she doesn't have her Gi with her and she has to bring me here," he talks so fast, "so is it okay if she trains with us? I can teach her the stuff."

The stern-looking lady in a black Gi looks me up and down before she says, "Yes."

"Thanks Sensei." Kyle grabs my hand and pulls me into the last row. "You stand behind me and do everything I do."

I glance over all the heads of the little people and am thankful there aren't any kids from high school here. Kyle is so jacked I will not let him know how silly I feel.

During the warm-up exercises, Sensei steps in front of me and assumes a wide stance with her hands behind her back. When I finish my final burpee she says, "Show me a front stance."

I drop into it.

"Weight distribution?"

"70 – 30, Sensei."

"Horse stance."

I switch stances. "50 – 50, Sensei."

"Back stance."

"30 – 70, Sensei."

"Fighting stance."

Again, I switch my position, bend my knees, and put as little weight as possible on my front foot.

"Distribution."

Shoot. My brain scrambles to remember but can't find the numbers. "A little bit on the front and most on the back."

The class giggles. Great. Nothing like keeping the little people amused. My face gets warm. It's good to know not only guy situations make me blush.

Sensei Geri gives me the slightest fragment of a smile before she moves on to drill another student.

By the end of the class, my shirt sticks to my back. Man, am I out of shape. These kids aren't even sweating. Note to self—get in shape and study. My time will be so full I'll hardly miss Greg. Not!

"That's Kimberly." Kyle does a cool looking-not-looking glance towards a girl with two ponytails. "Don't stare," he whispers and pulls me towards the door.

The cold air feels good on my face, but my sweaty body is not as appreciative.

"You did pretty good." He shrinks his neck into his parka as we walk home. "We can practise after school every day, and you can come to all my classes, and you'll get really good in no time."

I smile at his encouragement. It's cute to have a seven-year-old as my optimistic cheerleader.

Chapter 5

I wave the permit in the air at Steph. "I got my Learner's Licence."

"Way to go." She claps. "How many did you get wrong?"

"Really? That's your first question? You're so like Mom, you know that, right?"

"We're sisters. It's possible we share a few traits."

"I only got one wrong. It was about what you do if a car is passing you on a highway and another car is coming. Would you slow down, speed up or remain at your same speed?"

"Remain at your same speed."

"I don't think so. If you slow down, he can get in safely."

"But the other car won't know you're slowing down. You're supposed to maintain your speed, so he doesn't have to second guess what you're doing."

"Whatever. So," I say, as I fill up a glass of water with my back to Steph. "Are you ready to talk about what's going on with you and Tom?"

Silence.

I turn and watch her avoid eye contact as she sweeps invisible crumbs off the kitchen table.

"Is everything okay?" I step beside her. "Are you alright?"

Her mouth opens to say something, but she stops.

"Steph, you're freaking me out. What's going on? Are you guys okay?"

I sit down across from her which forces her to look at me. Her fingers tap the table as if it's a piano. Nice distraction but she doesn't play the piano.

She finally says, "It's complicated."

"Come on. I'm not a kid. How complicated can it be? You're together or you're not together."

"Tom is applying for a transfer."

That does not sound life threatening, but I don't say anything.

"A transfer to Waterton. Four hours from Banff."

"Oh." Okay. Still not life threatening but I get the complicated now. "And?"

"And..." She pinches her lips together. "He wants me to go with him."

"Like...marry him, and go with him, or move in with him, or what?"

"Not marry." She rolls her eyes. "There are two jobs open. He wants me to apply for the other one."

Uh-oh. What? No. Not now. I can't move again. What happens when Greg comes back and I'm gone? I press on Greg's bracelet and try to calm the panicked look my face wants to assume. *I can't leave Banff. I don't want to change schools again. What the hell? Right. A bit of quick self-talk. This isn't about me. Yet, it is.*

The cuckoo clock tick tocks. I want to say so many things like, *seriously, now? What am I supposed to do? Greg will be back. I can't be in Waterton. And what about Kyle?*

"Don't worry. It's not going to happen." Steph shakes her head too many times as if she's convincing herself. "I'm not moving."

I exhale way louder than I should.

She goes to the fridge and stares at the contents.

"Are you going to apply for the job?"

"Where are the apples?"

I point to the fruit bowl on the counter mere feet away from her. She shuts the fridge door harder than necessary, grabs an apple and sits down again.

"Steph, are you applying for the job? This is serious. This affects all of us. Kyle, me." I point to Bucky sleeping in the corner oblivious to the conversation. "Even him."

She takes a huge bite and chews like it's an aerobic workout.

"So, are you going to let me know? Are you applying for the job?"

Steph swallows and stares at the apple. I want to grab it from her, so she focuses on our conversation.

"It's not happening...it might happen. If it does happen it'll take months to process.

The government doesn't do any transfers fast."

"So, we *might* have to move?" I hold my breath.

"Not likely."

"But not likely means there's a possibility we might?"

Steph pinches the stem of the apple and spins it.

"Jillian, please don't worry about it. Okay?" She finally looks at me. "I have a lot to think about. When I get my head around it, when I figure out if I even want to leave this," she waves her hand holding the apple around the room, "we'll talk. But for now, go with *no*, I'm not applying. Tom and I can figure out how to make it work for everyone."

Her *no* is not convincing. I do not need this. Not now. Not ever. Maybe if I do an amazing job in school, maybe she'll make it a definite 'no' so I can finish off the year here. I just have to study hard, nail my exams, help with Kyle and convince her this is where all of us need to be. Not a small feat but I can do it. I know Steph is waffling right now. I just need to help her to unwaffle and choose to stay here.

* * *

In my dream, I hear someone call my name. A voice I recognize but can't place. It's been such a restless night fading in and out, worrying about what Steph will decide and what I can do to convince her not to move, or what I can do if she does move. I feel drained, so I lie still and try to figure out who's calling me.

"Jillian, phone!"

The lights in my room go on. I shade my eyes to see Steph standing in the dark hallway waving the phone at me.

"Remind him about the time difference." She drops the phone on my stomach, walks out and slams my door.

"Hello," I whisper. Why I whisper, I don't know. *Still in dream state?*

"Hello, Jillian of Banff."

"Greg? Greg." I sit up and pull the covers to my shoulders as if he can see me. "How are you? How's Suzanne?"

"It's so good to hear your voice. This is the highlight of my day."

I tiptoe over, turn off the big light, scoot back to turn on my reading light and then snuggle back under my blankets. "What's going on? Is Suzanne okay?"

"She's apparently coming out of the coma. I'm not sure what that means because she seems the same as she was yesterday, but the doc is optimistic she'll be awake in a few days."

"That's fabulous." I feel myself relax. "How are your parents? How are you?"

"I'm knackered. I think I could sleep for a solid week and then maybe I'd feel human again. Suzanne's got a long way to go. A ton of rehab. An old cobber from school is helping me run mom back and forth so that's been a huge help."

"What a good friend. You're lucky to have him helping you out."

"He's a she." Greg laughs. "Chris has been a mate since we were in nappies."

A visual of Greg and a little girl in diapers sitting on a step, zips through my head. I give myself shit for going down that path while he goes on about splitting his time between being at the hospital and working his way through grade twelve courses online so he can get his diploma.

"Maybe if I nail my exams, Mika and I can graduate together. We can have a small party when I get back to Banff."

"For sure." I pull myself out of pity mode when he mentions coming back to Banff. "We'll definitely do that."

"I probably won't be back until March. I might even miss all the boarding."

I bite my bottom lip, so I don't sound whiny. "March?"

"There's just so much stuff to do and Mom doesn't like Suzanne to be alone. She's burning herself out and with Pop back at work I need to stick around. It's okay. It'll be March in no time."

"Gotcha." *I guess. What else am I supposed to say? Seriously? March? That's two months away.*

"How's the snow?"

We chatter on about nothing really, but I get over my pout because it's so good to hear his voice and it feels like he's right next door. I want to ask Greg about the person who did the shooting, whether or not they caught them or if they're running around loose still. That would be terrifying for everyone. But I don't want to ruin the mood he's in. I guess he'll tell me when he is ready to talk about it.

"Reckon I better say goodbye. It will cost me a bundle when Mom gets the bill."

"Thanks for calling," I sigh. "It's so good to hear from you."

"Next time I'll borrow the laptop and we can do a video chat."

"That would be cool."

"Thanks, Jillian. I feel heaps better hanging out with you. Miss you."

"Me too. Bye." I pause and wait to see if he says anything else but there's the *click* and he's gone. I squeeze the phone.

* * *

Study, school, karate class with Kyle, watching chess games at lunchtime, and always checking my email becomes my new norm. When it's not freezing outside, I walk over to the Cascade Mall with the guys at noon to change up the chess venue. People stare and that's fun to watch. None of them hit on me which hurts my ego a smidgeon. Not that I'd act on it, but still, it's a bit of a burn. They're super sweet to me though and it's nice to pass them in the hallway and get high fives and waves.

For the last few weeks, Mika's been wrapped up in her new job and studying to write her diploma exams and Barrett's working after school, so locker chats are quick. He seems distracted. I'm not sure if that's a good thing (it's not about New Year's) or maybe it's a bad thing (he's distracted because of New Year's). What's Mom's saying—'Leave well enough alone? Don't dig too deep or you will uncover stuff you should have left alone?'

I hate that I am avoiding Barrett. But I don't know what to do. Do I ask him what happened? Do I tell him what I suspect happened? *No, that would be so ballsy and presumptuous.* But what if it is right? What if something did happen? Shit.

For now anyways, it is what it is. I just hope we get to a point where we can move on and be like we used to be. I miss him, and his cheerfulness and goofy antics.

* * *

"Help me with these boxes," Steph shouts from outside my bedroom door.

Seriously? It's Saturday. My *do-nothing* day. Not like all my days outside of school are *do-nothing* days but Saturdays are the sacred ones. I mutter as I crawl out from under my warm covers and peek down the hall. A stack of boxes blocks the stairs.

"What are you doing?" I grumble. "And why so early?"

"These are Oma and Opa's boxes that your mom mentioned when she called at Christmas." Steph puts her hands on her hips. "It's crappy outside. I'm off. Kyle will be with Mrs. Bronigan most of the day. I thought we could hang out and sort through them."

"You did, did you?" I roll my eyes at her pathetic attempt of keenness to encourage me to be eager enough to sort through boxes of old stuff.

I help lug them down the stairs and put them in the living room. Oma labelled them by years, so we line them up in order. After Kyle is gone, I settle down in front of the oldest box and open it. A pressed stack of checked cloth hankies sits on top of a floral embroidered runner which covers a stack of old picture albums. A peculiar combination of stuff. I know the hankies are clean, but I finger them as if they're not and set them aside. I grab an album and sit on the couch.

There are lots of small black and white pictures with decorative edging and people I don't recognize. I look closer and try to spot Oma or Opa when they were kids. No luck.

After three albums of unknowns, the next album has bigger pictures, straight edges and some are even in colour.

"Hey, is this Oma?" I bring the album to Steph. "With some friends. Looks like maybe high school. Look at those skirts. Wow."

"Yup. They were dolled up to go dancing. Your Oma loved to dance and sing, and I don't mean karaoke. She would get right on stage with the band."

"I didn't know that."

Now that I recognize more people it's fun to flip through the pages. They were young once. Hard to believe.

I freeze when I see a picture of a big husky and a little girl in Oma's kitchen. The little girl is me. And the husky is just like the one I keep seeing. What the hell? I peel the plastic off the picture and bring it up close.

"Hey Steph." I walk over to her. "Whose dog is this?"

"Oh, that miserable beast. They called him Dog. Your Opa found him on some hike, and the owners never came to claim him."

"Dog? That's not a very creative name."

"They didn't want to get attached because they were sure the owners would come and when they never did, Dog stuck."

"Why did you call him miserable?"

"I tried to get that mutt to like me. I walked him. I gave him treats on the sly, but he never took to me or Opa. Stupid mutt. If he'd known how much I wanted him to like me he could have at least been a bit friendlier."

I flip through the pictures looking for others of Dog.

"For whatever reason, Dog liked you. No one ever said he was real smart." Steph laughs. "He was just mean."

"Hey, that's not nice."

"Lighten up. I'm kidding. *I* even grew to like you." Steph snorts. "There should be lots of pictures of him. I figured he would eat you in your sleep."

"And you never stopped him?"

"You're here, aren't you?"

"Funny."

Steph laughs. "You and Oma were his favorites. When you came to visit, he never let you out of his sight. He even let you ride him around like a horse."

I flip through more pages and find lots of pictures of him, some with me in them. *What are the chances this is him, the husky I keep seeing?*

"What happened to him?"

"Gosh," Steph pauses. "I'm not sure. I was at college when he disappeared. He never came back. I'm not sure how hard your Opa would have looked for him though."

"How old was he?"

"No idea. Look at this." She holds up a frilly white baby's dress. "Your christening gown."

"I'm christened? Really? Who was religious?"

Steph folds the dress and tucks it back into the dry cleaner bag. "Oma didn't want to take a chance on your future. She figured getting you christened couldn't hurt."

"I don't remember her ever going to church."

"They went to the United Church for a long time. You know, the one on the corner across from the CIBC," Steph says. "After you were christened, someone suggested your Opa should wear a tie to church and that was it. Your Oma figured if they were more concerned about what he wore than the fact she'd dragged his butt there, they could find better things to do on a Sunday." Steph laughs. "Most people knew better than to mess with your Oma. They never went back to church."

"Yup, I can totally see her reacting like that." I look up at Steph. "Were you at my christening?"

She shakes her head. "My being your biological mom was not, ah, common knowledge. Your mom took you."

"I guess that would have been awkward." I flip through more pictures looking for Dog. *Could he still be alive? Why wouldn't he come home if he was?* Maybe it's one of those other worldly existential things...if such a thing actually exists.

* * *

"What're you doing tonight?" Tony says as we head up to the lunchroom.

"Nothing."

"Want to come out with us, me and the guys? Have a few brewskies. Friday night fun."

"I'm not old enough."

"You think I am?" Tony looks around and then back to me with a comical grin. "We'll pick you up around eight. I know where you live."

"I didn't say yes."

"But you didn't say no."

"You know where I live?" I stop and turn my head to face him. "Are you stalking me?" As soon as the words come out, I wish I could take them back.

"Yeah," he says.

Okay, high alert. What the hell? Now he gets more than chess-weirdo status.

"Joking." He socks me in the shoulder. "My stepbrother used to date your aunt."

"What? Steph dated a high school guy?"

"No," Tony says. "That *would be* disturbing on so many levels. He's fifteen years older than me. Long story. Blended family. My stepdad is older than Santa Claus. Peace. Love. Blah, blah, blah." He shrugs.

"Got it. Nice to know Steph has had a life."

* * *

"Jillian," Steph shouts up the stairs. "You have company."

I turn into the kitchen and see Tony and Derrick standing in the back porch. Steph, with a hand on her hip, looks at me. *How badly did she interrogate them?*

"Hi," I say. "You've met Steph."

"Yup," they answer in unison.

"We've met before." Steph points to Tony.

"Oh." I tip my head at her and almost smirk, but her expression stops me.

"Be home by eleven," she says and walks towards the living room.

I feel awkward. Is it wrong to go out with them? It's not like I'm going to do anything. Just hang out. Greg won't mind. I know he wouldn't want me moping around waiting for him to come back.

Tony unzips his parka a bit, pulls out a flask and waves it in the air. "We'll have us a small party."

"Not here," I hiss, and push it back into his coat with a quick glance to make sure Steph didn't see.

"Of course, not here." He zips up his jacket. "Come on."

Go? Don't go? What can it hurt? I grab my coat and Derrick winks at me. I pull a scarf off the hook and duck my head, so he doesn't see me blush. *And why am I blushing?* Stupid me. It's not a flirt wink. Just a sneaking-out-of-the-house-to-drink wink. They both know about Greg.

"Where are you going, Jillian?" Kyle walks across the kitchen towards me. "You're going to come back, right? To take me to the tournament tomorrow, right?"

"For sure." Shit. I forgot I promised I would take him. It starts at eight AM.

"No, you won't." Kyle squints his eyes and puts on a mean face. "You'll be all wrecked and tired and you'll think of some dumb excuse about why you can't take me, and I will have to miss the whole tournament."

"I would never do that."

"Yes, you would. Everyone does." He stomps out of the room.

What the heck? That's so *not* Kyle. *Did he see the bottle of booze? Is that why he's all pissy?* He thinks I'll let him down like his mom does? Shit.

"Hey." I lift both hands at Tony and Derrick. "I'm sorry. I forgot. I've got a thing in the morning. Another time, maybe?"

"A thing?" Tony says.

"Yeah. I promised Kyle I'd take him to his karate tournament. It starts early. Sorry. You guys have fun."

I'm not sure if I'm glad Kyle reminded me about the tournament or disappointed I'm being all responsible about it. Being responsible blows kahunas. I spend the evening doing homework, studying and trying to be an overachiever, while checking my inbox a bazillion times. Nothing from Greg.

* * *

Lots of young kids in karate uniforms line up to face the sensei as they give the opening speech about sportsmanship, fair play and no contact. I find a chair along the wall of the gymnasium and settle in. These tournaments go on forever. I smile at Kyle when he sees where I'm sitting.

Six separate rings are marked off. Four blackbelt instructors with stern or grumpy (hard to tell) faces sit in chairs at the head of each ring. When I first started karate, their expressions terrified me. As I worked my way up to blue belt, I realized it was all part of their intimidation factor.

Kyle squirms on the floor next to Sensei Geri and his group while he waits for his turn to do his yellow belt Chung Gi kata.

"Hey." Derrick sits down in the chair next to me.

I try to stop the what-are-you-doing-here look that wants to run across my face. "Hi. What..."

He shrugs. "These things take hours. No offence to any karate students, after you've seen a few of their..." He waves his hand at a kid in a ring.

"Kata," I say.

"Right, kata. After you've seen a few of them, they all start to look the same." He nudges me. "Know what I mean?"

"I do." I point to Kyle's group. "It's way more stressful out there. And the time goes by a lot faster when you're competing instead of sitting here."

We watch the kids do their bow, introduce themselves, shout out their form and perform their kata. I squeeze my hands together when it's Kyle's turn.

"He did good," Derrick says.

After Kyle bows and steps out of the ring, he waves at me with a big smile.

"So, you do karate?" I glance at Derrick.

"No. I'm more into..."

"Chess."

"Chess, hockey and baseball."

"That's a wide range. But you know about this?" I sweep my hand across the gym.

"A bit." He smiles. "Besides, I thought you could use some company."

I stare straight ahead. I know he knows about Greg. So, he's being friendly just because he's a nice guy? How freakin' sweet is that? Guy friends are the best. No expectations.

We chat and point and watch. He gets some snacks, and we share them. After Kyle finishes sparring, he comes over and Derrick high fives him.

"Nice work buddy," he says.

"Thanks." Kyle grins. "I'm done. Sensei said I can go."

"I'll give you guys a ride home," Derrick says.

"That's okay. We can walk."

"My treat."

I'm not sure what his game is but I'm going to go with *he's just being nice because he's a nice guy with nothing to do on a Saturday morning*. And he's super easy to talk to. Besides, Bucky didn't bark at him when they came over last night. That's totally a good sign. So, he's being a friend. Just a friend.

At the house, Derrick doesn't get out of the car, and I don't invite him inside. I don't know why, but I don't.

"Thanks for the ride," I say. "And thanks for hanging out with me."

"You bet." He waves and I close the passenger door.

"I could eat a whole bag of cookies." Kyle rushes up the back steps.

"How about I make you chicken fingers and fries instead?"

After Kyle inhales lunch I help him out with a new Lego creation in the living room.

He pulls the instructions out of my hand. "I can do the rest myself."

Ouch. I can tell when I'm not needed, so I head back to the kitchen. Steph and Tom's whispering stops me in the hallway. When did they get home? I lean my head towards the sounds, ear tuned to the kitchen, to eavesdrop.

"She will understand. It's a huge promotion for you," Tom says. "Besides, Waterton is beautiful."

What's going on? Did Steph already apply for the job? And who will understand what?

"I don't know if I can do that to her. She's got Greg when he comes back. She's got school and she's working so hard at her grades. She studies all the time. It's not fair to make her move now."

I stretch my neck further, so I don't miss a word. What the hell? She said not to worry about anything. Now I'm worried.

"Come on. I want us to be a family," Tom whispers. "Mika can come up from Lethbridge. She and Jillian can be like sisters. We'll all be together under one roof. Who knows. Maybe we can have our own, too."

Lip smacking noises.

I scrunch my eyes shut. It's not like I don't know they're doing it but hearing it out loud is disgusting.

"You've got this all figured out," Steph says.

"Well, you know, if...when we get married, I assumed..."

Married? They're getting married?

"Hold on. One thing at a time. We have a lot more talking and planning to do first to get both of us on the same page before we tell anyone else."

My heart thumps so loud I'm surprised they can't hear it.

"Jillian," Kyle calls. "Can I have some juice?"

I freeze. Steph steps into the hallway and by the look on her face I know she knows I heard everything.

"There's juice in the fridge, Kyle," she says, then steps in front of me. "We'll talk later," she whispers.

I don't trust my voice, so I don't say anything and head upstairs. What is Tom trying to do? Ruin my life? I thought he liked me. Well, in reality, it's not Tom. Steph must have applied for the job. *She's* the one who's going to ruin my life. Not fair. I can't move again. I don't want to move again. Why do they have to screw with my life now that it's actually working? Well, it will be working a lot better when Greg gets back.

And right then I think of Mom and feel a tad guilty when I realize I haven't thought about her in quite a few days.

Not that Steph gets off the hook, but I whip up a quick email to Mom with a weather update and a few test marks she'll be proud of. Send. Then a quick one to Greg to ask how things are going with Suzanne and mention I miss snowboarding with him. And I miss him. I say nothing about the shit show Steph might be causing in my life. I hit send and an email from Greg comes in at the same time.

Jillian,

I bet the snow is awesome. Hope you found some new mates to board with. I miss you.

Pop tries to be this rock for everyone, but I can tell he's starting to cave. Small change in Suzanne—she can breathe on her own. Doc says this is a huge improvement. Time goes so slowly at the hospital. Sitting here watching Suzanne do nothing is brutal.

Pop gave me his old laptop, so I can work on my grade twelve Social and English classes when I'm here. That's one of the reasons I'm using proper typing format and sentence structure. Practice makes perfect, right? I want to get my diploma before I turn eighteen and this gives me something to do so I don't drive myself nutso while I'm at the hospital. I feel daft complaining. It's not like Suzanne can help it, but it sucks.

Thanks for listening to this diarrhea. Enough about my life. How are you? I miss you. Did I say that already? I do.

Ah, heart melt. My face gets warm.

I'm glad this program has spell check, so I can fix all those wavy red lines under my typos and don't come off looking like a dolt. Insert smiley face emoji. Did you smile?

I'm glad you got your Learner's Licence. I can't wait to teach you to drive. I'll have you parallel parking in no time.

It's foggy here tonight. Without the stars it feels claustrophobic.

How's everyone? Barrett? Mika? Your aunt/mom? I think I'm rambling so I'm going to sign off. Let's set up a good time to call next weekend. It'll be like a long-distance date.

Take care. Miss you.

XO Greg

PS – If the red squiggles under words are typos, what are the blue lines?

I read it over a few times and miss him like crazy all over again.

Greg,

The blue lines suggest you might need some type of punctuation—comma, hyphen, that kind of stuff. They're not as serious as the red squiggles.

I can't wait to chat. It'll be almost like you're in town. Not really, but it's better than just emails. How about Sunday 8 PM Alberta time, which is 2 PM Monday Aussie time? Would that work for you? If not, let me know what time does work. I can't wait.

Miss you too.

Jillian of Banff XO

Sunday nights are early nights for Kyle so after supper, as I plan what I want to say to Steph, I throw in a load of laundry. I need to be calm and logical. I need to make Steph see that staying in Banff could be a win for everyone. At least until August when I turn sixteen. Then maybe I can talk her into letting me stay here alone. Maybe with Eddy checking on me. He's like a big brother to Steph. She would trust him. I can't take care of Kyle on my own but maybe his mom will be back by then.

"Jillian," I hear Kyle shout.

"What's up?" I peek in his room. He's on the floor stuck to sheets of red and blue construction paper and the biggest bottle of white glue. There's glue everywhere. I can't help but laugh. "What are you trying to do?"

"I squeezed it, and it was stuck so I squeezed harder, and it blew up and I couldn't stop it and my picture is ruined and I need to have it done for school tomorrow."

The kid who marches through his insane life without faltering, is having a glue meltdown. I wonder what's really going on with him.

"Hey, it's okay." Tiptoeing to avoid the blobs of glue on the floor, I grab the bottle and put it on his desk. "I'll help clean it up and then we'll start again. You stay right there. I'll get paper towels."

"Miss Steph will be so mad."

I lift his chin up and smile at his sad face. "You don't think she's made a mess before? Trust me, she won't be mad." I wink at him. "Besides, we'll get it cleaned up before she even finds out."

Who knew white glue was not the easiest thing to wipe off, but we get everything tidied up and start over on his Valentine's project.

"Okay." I hold up the finished poster and take a step back. "What do you think?"

"It's pretty good," Kyle says.

"Great. You get ready for bed." I put the paper on his desk. "Let it dry flat overnight and we can roll it up in the morning to fit in your backpack."

"Thanks for helping."

"You bet." I scruff up his hair. "Bedtime."

After I switch my laundry to the dryer, I head downstairs to talk to Steph. Only the stove light is on in the kitchen. And there's a note on the table.

Jillian

Had to step out. Might be late.

Steph

I shake the paper in the air. What the hell? Is she with Tom? Are they continuing to talk about how they're going to ruin my life? Shit. And who do I look like? Kyle's mom? Steph didn't even tell me she was leaving. How did she know I didn't have plans and staying home to watch Kyle would screw them up? Right. Because I never have plans. Doesn't matter. She still should have told me.

Chapter 6

"Hey," Barrett pulls back my locker door and gives me squinty eyes. "Are you like...ignoring me?"

"No." I give an exaggerated no-way-would-I-do-that look so I can hide the sleeping-with-him-on-the-couch flashback. "Why would you think that?"

"Because you literally go the opposite direction every time you see me."

"I do not."

"Suit yourself, but you do." He opens his locker. "Or maybe it's your new friends. Maybe you've replaced me." He peeks around my door and gives me a puppy dog sad face.

"You're irreplaceable, Barrett." I fake a light punch to his chest.

"Just be careful," he says.

"What do you mean?"

"Come on." He scrunches up his eyes. "For a big city girl, you're kind of naïve."

I step back. "Burn."

"No. It's sort of cute but you need to watch yourself. Derrick's the marrying kind and he's currently on a rebound."

"What?"

"He just got ditched. He's trolling."

"What exactly are you talking about?"

"Never mind. Just don't get too friendly or you'll give him the wrong idea."

"Stop right there." I get in his face. "I am not interested in Derrick. Got it? We are friends. And. I. Am. Not. Naïve."

Barrett's lips tighten in a straight line and his eyes become googly round. "You are."

And away he goes. The jerk. What's he thinking? I'm interested in Derrick? That's crazy talk. Derrick is nice. And I am doing nothing wrong by being nice back to him. Besides, has Barrett forgotten about Greg? I sure haven't.

At noon, I rush to my locker, pull on my coat and as I get ready to head home, Tony calls out, "Lunchroom."

"I got a thing," I say. "Tomorrow maybe." I wave over my shoulder and head towards the doors.

Now I feel guilty about ditching them. They're fun to hang out with. A great distraction from missing Greg and avoiding that conversation with Barrett.

But Barrett's comments got to me. I know he's wrong. I know he's reading way too much into Derrick and me. We are just friends. That's it. End of story. Besides, I can have guy friends. It's not like Greg would expect me to hole up and be a loner just because he's not here. That's not who Greg is.

Part of me hopes Steph is home, so we can talk, and the rest of me wants *me* time to settle myself down.

It figures she's not home and now I have to deal with everything myself. I run upstairs to send Greg a quick email to let him know I'm thinking about him and hoping they're seeing improvement in Suzanne every day. I tell him exams are done and I feel good about how I did. Then I erase that line and tell him I did fabulous on my exams, because I really did. Mom was even shocked, and it takes a lot to shock her.

Again, I want to ask him about the shooter, but I don't know if it's my place. And Greg hasn't mentioned anything about the person, so I close the email with the fact our new semester starts, and I plan on nailing it too.

Right after I send the email to Greg, I get the idea to do a Google search about the incident.

Why didn't I think of it before?

I search 'Christmas shooting university Australia' and up pops a bunch of newsclips. Oh my gosh. He tried to shoot himself too. But he survived and is in a psychiatric ward recovering and awaiting assessment. I speed read through a few articles. *He thought he was playing a game. He didn't know the gun was real. He missed taking his medication for days.* I put my hands over my face. I can't read anymore. They must all know this. And he's alive and those other people died or were hurt. *I can't imagine how they feel about any of it.*

I walk downstairs in a daze.

* * *

"Hey, Jillian." Eddy brushes the snow off his coat and steps into the back porch. "Is Steph home?"

"She's in the shower. Do you want a coffee?"

"No, I can't. Thanks though. I'm off to work. Can you give this to her for me, please?" Eddy hands me a brown envelope. "It's research material she was asking about." He pulls out his phone. It always surprises me when I see him with one. The first time I met Eddy he lived in a tree fort in the woods. And now the guy's got a phone. "Tell her I'll send her another link."

"Look at you, Mr. Technology. Of course, I'll tell her."

There's a knock at the door. We both look up as Barrett steps inside the back porch. I'm thankful Eddy is here so I can avoid any awkwardness having to talk to him alone.

"Eddy." Barrett takes off his boots. "How's it hanging?"

"Do you kids really still say that?" Eddy laughs. "I have to make a mile. Catch you two later."

Barrett waves his hands in the air. "Do adults really still say, 'make a mile?'"

"I'm out of here." Eddy jostles Barrett for a few seconds. "Catch you on the flipside."

Barrett and I both groan.

"You kids have no appreciation for coolness." Eddy waves and is gone.

Crap. Now just the cuckoo clock ticks and I fake a huge smile at Barrett. Where's my next distraction? I put the envelope on the table for Steph and look around the kitchen expecting, I don't know, someone to jump out of the fridge and rescue me. It figures Kyle would sleep in when I need him, and Steph would decide to have the world's longest shower today. I listen for footsteps but nope, I hear nothing.

"I am done playing this game. Why are you being such a jerk?"

"Whoa." I put my hands up. "First, I'm naïve and now I'm a jerk. What the hell?"

"Fine. I was being nice using jerk. You're being a bitch. You ditch Mika and me and treat me like I have the plague every time you see me. Don't say you don't." He crosses his arms. "I'm not leaving until you tell me what's going on."

"Bitch is a bit harsh." I get a glass of water so he can't see my face.

"Is it your new friends? Is that why you're avoiding me? Us?"

"No. I already told you. They're just friends."

"Then what? What changed?"

I suck it up and face him. "New Year's Eve."

"What about it?"

"You were drunk."

"Uh-huh."

"I woke up on the couch. Lying on the couch. In front of you. You were hugging me."

"You're kidding, right?" Barrett tips his head. "That's why you've been a bitch for over a month?"

"I didn't know how to, you know, talk to you about it. You were hugging me. Hard. I couldn't tell Mika."

Barrett does a lap around the table, stops, and crosses his arms again. He says nothing and just gives me this I-cannot-believe-you look.

"What?" I point at him. "What would you have done?"

"I would have talked to me about it." He drops his head and shakes it.

"Stop that."

"You want to know what happened?" He lifts his head. "You were sitting by my feet, and you were crying. I tried to talk to you, but you didn't say anything. You just kept crying. I thought maybe you were doing it in your sleep." He shrugs. "I couldn't get you to stop. I figured you were missing Greg. So, I gave you a hug and you flopped down on the couch in front of me. I put my arm around you so you wouldn't roll off and faceplant onto the floor."

"No."

"Yup."

I scrunch up my face, totally ashamed I thought the worst. "Really?"

"Really."

I am such an idiot. *Why am I such an idiot?* I go from *I think Barrett and I might have had a moment* to feeling stupid.

"Barrett, I thought, I don't know. You were drunk. I thought maybe..."

"You thought I tried to get in your pants?" He gives me his goofy-eyes grin and embarrassment heats up my face.

"Shut up. Don't even talk like that." I hush him in case someone hears us.

"Hey, after you've been such a bitch, relax. I'm just messing with you. Besides, it was two in the morning. I wasn't drunk anymore. When I woke up, you were gone so I figured you got over whatever you were sad about and went to bed."

"I'm an idiot. I'm sorry."

He shoulder checks me. "I'd never cheat on Mika, and I'm not dumb enough to mess with Greg's girl."

I hang my head. "I feel stupid."

"You should."

"Thanks asshole." I fake a punch to his stomach.

* * *

"Can we talk?" I say to Steph as I dry the dishes. "Kyle can't hear us."

Silence.

"Tell me what's going on."

"I applied for the job in Waterton." She pauses. "They offered it to me."

"I heard that part. Are you taking it?"

"I don't know yet," she says in the quietest voice.

"What does that mean? Are you, or aren't you?"

"Jillian, I just found out. I need to look into a lot of things and figure out some logistics and details."

"Aren't we a detail?" I point towards the living room where Kyle is and then to myself. "Don't we count for anything? Like a vote?"

Steph puts her hands on my shoulders. "I know you think this is probably going to blow your world up, but I'm trying not to let that happen. I want to figure it all out and see how I can make it work for everyone."

"That's going to be kind of hard when Waterton is not next door." I toss the tea towel on the counter and head for my room.

"Jillian," Steph calls, but I keep walking.

What if I guilt her into not taking the job? I could whine and pout. I can tell she hasn't decided yet, so it might just take some swaying to get her on my side, so I don't have to leave Banff. At least until I'm sixteen—plenty old enough to take care of myself.

What was in the envelope Eddy dropped off? Research on how to screw up my life by moving to Waterton?

If Mika wasn't going to Lethbridge, she and I could live together. Darn Mika for getting career oriented when I need her. I pull up Google for some fact-checking about sixteen-year-old rights and responsibilities.

* * *

"Barrett," a female voice calls out from down the hall.

We both close our lockers and turn.

"Barrett." Mrs. Machuk, the French teacher, holds out a piece of paper. "There's a grade ten field trip to the Frank Slide area which is a great opportunity to learn some Alberta history. I would appreciate it if you would talk a few of your friends into signing up. There will be a meeting in the lunchroom at noon on Thursday. I expect you to be there."

Barrett looks at the paper and says, "Do they have to be in French class?"

Is Barrett's face getting red? Oh my God. He *is* blushing.

"They need to have a pulse, are not currently suspended, and are registered in this school. Those are the only requirements." Mrs. Machuk smiles and walks away.

And Barrett watches her.

I sock him in the shoulder. “You are totally checking her out.”

He grabs my arm. “Shhh.”

When she’s out of sight, he whispers, “She can hear grass grow from inside a bomb shelter.”

“But you were, weren’t you?”

“No.” He scrunches up his eyes. “Besides, what if I was?”

I punch him in his bicep.

“Stop it.” He grabs his arm. “Just because I’m with Mika doesn’t mean I can’t appreciate fine women.”

“Gross. She’s a teacher.” I roll my eyes. “Listen to you talking like you’re such a player.”

He waves the paper Mrs. Machuk handed him and says, “You should come. It will get you away from missing Greg and out of class for a few days.”

“Dodging the bullet, are you?” I snort at his avoidance of further discussion about Machuk and grab the sheet to skim through it as we head outside. It’s nice hanging out with Barrett again and not having to look for an escape route every time I see him.

“I’ll check with Steph. See if she’d be okay on her own with Kyle. Last week she forgot it was early dismissal, and he called me to pick him up.”

“Look at you, being all responsible.”

"Someone has to make sure we don't lose him. Steph has her phone turned off most of the time, so he kind of needs me."

On Thursday I head to the room where the Frank Slide field trip planning meeting is happening. I recognize a few faces and see Tony goofing around in the back with a bunch of guys. He grins and the conversation we had about him stalking me flips through my head. No, he's not stalking me. He's just going on the field trip so he can ditch classes like most of the kids in the room. I turn to the front and listen to Mrs. Machuk.

"In case you nod off during the information part of this session, there will be a handout with an itinerary of the trip."

A few kids groan.

"We'll be going to Frank, Alberta. Who's found it on the map?"

I don't want to be the keener, so I keep my hand down.

"No one?" Mrs. Machuk's lips press together tightly. "Good. Your enthusiasm warms my heart. Who signed up because they wanted to learn a bit about Alberta history?"

I can't let her suffer so I raise my hand. She points at me. Another hand raises and then another. Phew. It's nice not to be the only nerd in the room.

"Who's coming because they want to ditch classes for a few days?"

Numerous hands raise, including Barrett's. I elbow him in the ribs and mouth, "Seriously?"

"Thank you for your honesty but you'll still have to apply yourself and complete the course work."

More groaning.

"Here's the information you need. The most important piece is the parental permission slip. I need them back by next Friday. Please do not practise your artistic cursive writing skills." Mrs. Machuk gives the class a sarcastic smile that gets her message across loud and clear. "A list of items you need to bring is also included and some information about the area. Humour me and, at the least, scan through the information."

Kids jostle to get out of the room when the bell rings.

"I think this is going to be fun," I say.

"Yeah." Barrett nods. "We don't have to come to class. That will be the fun part."

"Have you ever been to Frank?" I flip through the sheets Mrs. Machuk handed out.

"Why?"

"Because it's got some cool history."

"Excuse me." Barrett stops in the middle of the hallway, faces me and puts his hands on my shoulders. "Who are you and what have you done with Jillian?"

"No, seriously. Lots of stuff happened there. It's interesting."

"Again, who are you?"

I push his hands off and make a fake angry face at him.

* * *

"Jillian, can you please come up here," Sensei Geri says.

From my spot at the back of the line, I step out to the side, march to the front of the class, bow to Sensei and assume neutral stance.

"Can you hold a kick bag?" She passes me a black padded kick shield. "We are going to practise all the kicks for next week's belt test. It will go faster, and they'll get more turns, if we have two lines going."

I try not to show the wow expression my face wants to assume. She has never asked me to help before. Sensei hands me the kick shield, positions me a few feet away from her, and instructs the class to make two lines and practice their roundhouse kicks first.

Before the first kid steps up, I stand sideways, slip my arms into the shield's straps and brace the pad against my body. The kid puts his fists up, gets into a fighting stance before he twists and throws his back leg at me. *Wow*. He has more power than I thought he'd have. I sink lower and tighten my arms up to take the impact better. Mini Karate Kids rotate from line to line, winding up their best kicks as Sensei instructs them on what they need to work on.

I see the mischief in their eyes when the force of their kick throws me off balance and I have to reposition my feet. Cocky little jerks.

On our way home, Kyle says, "I think you'll get a belt soon. You know the kata and Sensei likes you. No one but her ever holds the bags."

"You're my biggest fan." I ruffle his hair as we walk up the back steps. "I'm glad I can help out."

"How'd it go?" Steph calls out from the kitchen, "Do you need a snack before bed, Kyle?"

"Sensei Geri really likes Jillian." Kyle rambles on about the class while Steph gets him a bowl of cereal.

There's a knock on the back door and Mika rushes in before I can open it. Her eyes are scary in a panicked kind of way. Mika does not panic. *What's going on?*

"I need you," she says.

"What's up?"

"Trust me. I just need your help."

"Is everything okay?" Steph walks towards us. "Are you okay, Mika?"

Mika's face shifts from super stressed to this big fake adult-pleasing smile.

"I'm just working on this thing, and I have to get it done and need a bit of help." She grabs my arm and almost convinces me, but her eyes are still way too intense.

"Okay," Steph says slowly. "But it's a school night." She gives me a look that says way more than her words. "Don't be too late."

I look down at the sweats I'm wearing, and Mika throws my parka at me. "You're fine. We're not going anywhere fancy. Get your boots on."

"Stay out of trouble you two," Steph says in the voice she uses when she means *don't screw up*.

I zip up my coat and keep up to Mika, who is jogging to her truck.

"You're freaking me out," I say. "What's going on?"

"Barrett is racing."

"Racing what?" I slam the passenger door shut. "What are you talking about?"

"A bunch of kids are racing down the Norquay road. I think Barrett is with them."

"No way. Barrett would never do *anything* to hurt his truck."

"We had this argument at my place. He was talking about these guys racing the switchbacks and I said it was stupid and he defended them about not having anything to do in town and I told him again his friends were stupid, and he stood up and gave me the strangest look and walked out without saying anything. I yelled at him to come back." Mika spews out more words in one breath than she usually does in a day. "Why would I yell at him?"

"Slow down. I think you might be overreacting." I put a hand on her arm. "Barrett is not stupid, and he'd never do anything like that."

"He was mad. Really mad. He wouldn't tell me where he was going. I can't believe I yelled at him like he was some little kid."

"Probably not your best moment, but relax," I say. "You know Barrett better than that. He's not going to do anything to hurt his truck even if he's mad at you."

"But the fight started because I was talking about looking forward to going to school in Lethbridge and I said stuff I shouldn't have said about new experiences and broadening my horizons and he got really quiet, and I got mad that he wasn't participating in the conversation." She takes a breath after she finishes.

"Broadening your horizons? Wow. You never thought to idle back on your excitement when he got quiet?"

"No. Why would I? I *am* excited and he was putting a real downer on my mood."

"Hey, slow down." I point out the windshield. "Look at all the cars. The flashing lights."

"I knew it. I knew he'd do it. Oh my God, it's all my fault. What have I done?"

"Calm down," I say as an ambulance and fire truck, lights flashing, sirens blaring, scream past us. "We don't know if Barrett did anything."

Mika hugs the shoulder by the recreation centre as a policeman waves cars over to stop. She rolls down the window and we watch him talk to the drivers in front of us. I can hear Mika's breath come in gulps.

"He's okay." I rub her shoulder. "Did you call him?"

"No. I didn't know what to say. I didn't want him to think I was checking up on him."

"There's been an accident. The Norquay road is closed," the policeman says. "Take the exit and head back into town." He moves to the car behind us.

"I told you something awful was going to happen," Mika chokes out the words.

"You don't know it's Barrett. Let's go back to town." I pull my phone out, turn it on speaker and call him.

"Yo," Barrett answers.

"Hey, how's it going?" I say to him as I turn to Mika and smile.

Silence.

"Barrett, what's going on? Are you okay?"

"Yeah."

I hate it when people give monosyllabic responses. It makes it hard to figure out what's going on with them. What's Mom's expression—'like pulling teeth or something?'

"Are you at home?"

There's a pause before he says, "I am."

"Can we come over?"

"Who's we?"

"Me and Mika. Can we come over?"

More silence.

"She's worried about you. She thought..." I stare at Mika's profile in the dark cab and try to figure out what to say. "She said you were upset. We thought we'd stop in and make sure you're okay."

"I'm good."

Click.

I stare at the phone.

"The upside to that is," I put my phone back in my pocket and try to insert a positive spin in my voice, "we know he's okay, but someone on that road isn't." I point at the blue and red flashing lights as the emergency vehicles race up the switchbacks to the ski hill.

"I'm an idiot," Mika says.

"Borderline. Maybe." I laugh to lighten the mood.

"You're not supposed to agree."

"You called it. Not me."

Mika snorts.

"He's okay. You guys will figure this out. Give him a bit of time and then go see him. Do *not* just text or call. *Go* and see him."

She sighs, and is quiet for a few seconds before she says, "You know what? It kind of bothers me."

"What bothers you?"

"That you know Barrett better than me."

"No, I don't."

Chapter 7

The hallway at school is super loud with chatter. Kids everywhere in big groups, lots of hand gestures. Mondays are usually quiet, like everyone is hungover from the weekend. But not today.

"What's going on?" I shoulder Barrett as I open my locker, hopeful he's not mad about last night.

He talks into his locker. "Accident on Norquay."

Not exactly monosyllabic and his response is informative.

"Were they trying to night ski without lights?"

"Nope," he says, still talking into his locker. "They were racing down the switchbacks. Missed a corner and hit a tree. One was in grade seven. Stars helicopter flew her to Calgary. Olivia someone."

I freeze. Now *I'm* the one staring at the inside of my locker. Olivia? The kid who was smoking up with those older guys? That Olivia? I try to think of another Olivia in this school. Maybe it's not her. It's not like I know everyone. But she'd be in grade seven. She's not old enough to smoke, let alone drive.

Who was she with? What the hell? The news startles me. It's not like it's my fault she got hurt but I still feel shocked she was involved in it.

And off Barrett goes to class. Not a good-bye. Nothing. Derrick high fives me as he passes by. It's nice to see a familiar smile because I think it's going to be one of those days. I hope Olivia is okay. I mean, I don't even know her but that sucks. She probably just wanted to have fun. To fit in. And I hope Mika and Barrett figure it out. I hope I can get out of being in the middle of their shit storm. Barrett and I just got over the whole New Year's fiasco and now this.

When Friday finally comes, I head home with thoughts of sleeping in on Saturday. That was the longest week of school ever. I cannot believe I am thankful for the chess club at noon, and karate classes, and walking Bucky to fill in the evenings. *How sad is my life that sleeping in tomorrow is all I'm looking forward to?*

"Hey," Tony shouts, as he crosses the sidewalk carrying a snowboard. "Got a minute?"

"Wow, that's some sweet board. What's up?"

"Any chance you can hang onto this for a few days?"

I scrunch up my face and look at the shiny, sparkly snowboard obviously meant for a princess of sorts.

"I didn't know you were a boarder."

"I'm not." He laughs like I told the best joke. "It's a present for a friend. I've got to get to work, and I don't want to haul this all over town."

"Ah, sure. I guess. I'll put it in Steph's garage."

"Keep it safe, okay?" He holds it close. "It's worth a fortune."

"For sure."

"You're the best." He passes me the snowboard and pats me on the back. "Catch you later."

I tuck the board under my arm and finish my walk home. The garage is a disorganized haven for boxes and second-hand store cast offs. Steph can't park inside because it's so cluttered. Near the back, there's a tall steel cabinet which looks like a ski locker and when I open the door, it's empty. I glance around the garage. After Tony takes the board back, I can put a bunch of boxes into the cabinet and make space to park the truck. Maybe Steph will give me bonus points for being intuitive to her needs.

"What are you cooking?" I call out to Steph when I step inside. "It smells amazing."

"Roast beef dinner and all the fixings."

"What's the occasion?" I turn the oven light on. "Even Yorkshire puddings? Wow. Is the queen coming?"

"No, but Mika, Barrett and Tom are."

"Mika and Barrett?"

"Don't worry. I have intel." Steph taps the side of her head. "They were spotted kissing, so we can assume they are over whatever they were arguing about."

"You have intel?"

"Tom told me."

I wave my hand at all the dishes and food she's got on the counter. "Did I miss someone's birthday?"

"Nope."

"Then, what's going on?"

"Nothing's going on." She flaps a tea towel at me. "Get cleaned up. Tell Kyle to wash his hands."

When Steph says, 'nothing is going on' with that tone, something is definitely going on. Is she finally going to let us know what she and Tom are up to?

I stop in front of my computer. I'll be quick. I open my email, and up pops not one but two messages from Greg. Oh my gosh. Tiny happy dance in front of my desk while I open the last one.

Jillian,

Do you have time at 9 PM your time tomorrow night to do a video chat? Let me know. No worries if you're busy. I just thought I'd take a chance and see if we can catch up.

XO Greg

Another faster happy dance. And a quick response.

Greg,

Yes. I can do 9 o'clock tomorrow night. Can't wait. Steph has this big supper thing going on tonight. I'm not sure what she's up to and I didn't miss anyone's birthday, so something is up. Stay tuned. Mika and Barrett are coming too so I'll say hi to them for you. Chat tomorrow.

Jillian of Banff XO

I open Greg's first email.

Jillian,

Hi. I miss you.

He kills me with his sweetness right at the start.

Suzanne opened her eyes yesterday. We know she recognizes us. Insert a giant Aussie sigh. The doctor says she's a fighter and he believes we'll notice improvement every day now. Mom and Pop both slept for 18 hours after. They were knackered. It is my turn tomorrow to catch up on sleep. I feel like I've lost a month of my life. I doubt I'd have the strength to snowboard or climb for a day. I feel like a sloth, and I feel selfish being a whiner about it considering what Suzanne's going through.

Now that she's conscious they're planning stages for her physio, which they say will hurt like hell and drain the shit out of her, but they don't want her to lose any more muscle tone, or it will only get harder.

Sorry for the details. It helps me sort it out to write about it. All in all, a huge improvement and a big relief.

How's Banff? Congrats on acing your exams. What else have you been up to? How are Mika and Barrett doing? Are you boarding much?

Miss you again.

XO Greg

They must be over-the-moon ecstatic about Suzanne's recovery. Maybe Greg will come back sooner than the end of March.

Stop it. It's not about me. *Quit making it about me*. I need to be happy for them. Greg thinks he's selfish. I'm glad he can't hear my thoughts.

Tomorrow night I get to see him, sort of.

"Hurry up," Steph shouts. "I need a hand with the finishing touches."

"Coming." I twist my hair into a messy ponytail then go and knock on Kyle's bedroom door. "Get washed up, buddy. Steph's got supper ready."

He jumps up from his Lego creation like he's got springs in his legs. "Are we having chicken fingers and fries?"

"Nope. But when we are done eating, you will tell Steph whatever we're having is delicious. Let's get going."

I stop dead in my tracks when I step into the kitchen and see Mika and Barret coming in from the back porch all jazzed up in dress clothes. Bucky stands in front of them with his tail wagging, waiting for a free handout or at least a scratch behind the ear.

"Hi," I say. "You guys clean up good."

"Go to the living room." Steph points at them. "Jillian, you stay here. I need extra hands."

"I can help," Mika says.

"Living room." Steph points again.

"Yes, ma'am." Barrett salutes her and steers Mika out of the kitchen.

"Can you set the table?" Steph gestures to all of Oma's *company is coming* dinner dishes. Another indicator Steph's 'nothing' really is 'something.'

When we have everything all ready and fancy looking for the meal, Steph calls out, "Okay, supper is ready."

We settle in around the table and the bowl passing begins as plates get loaded and conversation fills the room.

"How's school?" Tom passes me the gravy boat.

I laugh. "It's school and I go, and I come home, and I study and then I go back again."

"Try not to make it sound so exciting," Steph says.

"And Jillian's doing good in karate," Kyle pipes in with a mouth full of mashed potatoes.

Steph waves a fork at him. "Chew with your mouth closed, please, young man."

"Yes, Miss Steph. This is better than chicken fingers and fries."

"Thanks Kyle." She smiles at him.

Through the entire meal everyone talks about random stuff. But not the stuff I want to hear about. Everyone is having fun and teasing, but throughout it I try to figure out what the heck is going on. Steph freaked doing Christmas Eve brunch and here she is being all domestic and preparing and serving a meal without freaking out once. I don't get it.

After everyone leaves, I start to tidy up.

"Hit the hay, mister," Steph says to Kyle. "It's past your bedtime."

"Can I play a game? Just one?"

"Not tonight. Your GG will be here early to pick you up."

"Fine." He trudges off like he's going to detention. His exaggeration is adorably cute.

"So," I say with my back to Steph, "what was this all about?"

"I wanted to get everyone together. I thought this would be a good start."

"A good start to what?"

Steph lets out an ominous sigh. "In figuring out what comes next."

"So, what comes next?"

She puts both hands up. "I don't want you to panic or freak out."

"Well, that's a shitty way to start. Now I want to panic *and* freak out."

"Sorry." She covers the leftovers with plastic wrap and puts them in the fridge, totally avoiding eye contact. "It's not going to happen right away."

I don't say anything.

"Maybe at the end of the school year, depending on how things are going, there's a possibility of..."

"Cut the crap." I cross my arms over my chest. "Just say it. What's going to happen?"

Steph looks at me. Her face scrunches up like she's in pain. "I'm seriously thinking about accepting the Waterton position, but we have a lot of details to work out. I want you to be involved the whole way. We just have to think out of the box to figure out a solution that will work for all of us," she says. "I don't want you to worry. We'll make it work. I promise you that."

I chew my bottom lip but say nothing.

"Talk to me." Steph squeezes my shoulders.

"We're moving?"

She shakes her head. "No, that is not a definite at this stage. Maybe I can work my shifts there and come back on days off."

"What about Tom? I doubt he'll appreciate that. And what about Kyle? I can't take care of him myself. I have school and studying."

"I'm working on it. Trust me. Mrs. Bronigan and I are discussing scenarios. I hope Kyle's family comes through for him, so it's one less ball I have to juggle. We have got lots of time to get to the details."

I want to scream but the words I want to shout are mean, and once I say them, I won't be able to take them back. If I have any chance at all of staying in Banff, I have to help Steph figure this out, so I don't have to move.

“Jillian, tell me what’s going through your head right now. What are you thinking?”

“I’m kind of full, and tired, and I’ve still got homework to do.” I close the dishwasher and turn it on. “Thanks for supper. It was good.”

“Jillian,” Steph calls out as I walk up the stairs, but I ignore her and head to my room.

I don’t know why I even try to fall asleep. My brain runs in circles thinking of ways to help out more, make Steph’s life easier, and look like a super star so she changes her mind about this whole Waterton thing.

My heart hurts. Like, literally, it feels as if a weight squeezes it, when I think about Greg coming back and me not being here and not being able to see him every day. How can Steph be so selfish? And what about Kyle? What’s going to happen to him? He can’t live in the seniors’ lodge with Mrs. Bronigan. And she’s the only stable one in his family. Will he have to move to Waterton too?

Now my head hurts.

I get up and check my email. Nothing. I don’t want to say anything to Greg about this yet. He’s got enough going on already. I smile when I remember we’re doing a video chat tomorrow night. I’ll pretend none of this shit is happening. I just want to hang out with him like life is normal, and he’s here and all is good.

The papers and permission slip from Mrs. Machuk are on top of my homework. I grab the information sheet, turn on my lamp and crawl back into bed. There's a small road map on the bottom with a dark line going from Banff to Frank, Alberta. A few towns are marked on the way and there are lots of stretches with nothing except altitude contour lines, which are on the west side of Highway 22.

I read the notes about the Crowsnest history, the coal mines, disasters and ladies of the evening. It makes the past seem like the black and white movies Mom and I used to watch. After I finish reading, I turn off the light and will sleep to take over.

Darn Steph. Why now? Why can't she have a career change when...I don't know, when I leave? But I don't even want to leave. Shit. Sorry Mom. Even though you are across the world, and I hardly hear from you, you sneak into my thoughts at the oddest times. Love you.

* * *

Bacon smells fill the stairwell and loud cartoon voices come from the living room. I must be the last one up.

"Morning," Steph says in a quiet voice and hands me a plate of bacon and eggs and toast.

I pull my head back and scrunch my eyes up at her. *Is cooking her new thing to warm me up for potential life changing events?*

"Why are you up so early? And why are you cooking again?"

"It's not poison." She pushes the plate at me. "I'll get you coffee."

What is she up to now? I sit down and eat while I wait for the other shoe to fall.

"I want to assure you everything will be okay, and I don't want you to waste your time worrying or stressing about all of this." She sits across from me and puts her hands on the table. "I mean it when I say it's not going to ruin your school year. I *promise* you that."

I nibble on bacon and watch her face.

"I really mean it, Jillian. And I know you don't believe this, but we," she points at me and then herself, "we'll figure it out together."

It's too early to argue that there's no way I'm moving to Waterton. And I need to stack my deck, so I get her on my side. The end of school is over four months away. I have time to work out the best-case scenario. I'll even get Mom on my side if I have to.

"Please, trust me," Steph says.

"Okay, sure. And thanks for breakfast." I give her a half-assed sarcastic smile. "I'm going to get nervous though every time you cook now, you know that, right?"

"I like to cook."

I shake my head.

"Okay, maybe it's my therapy. It helps me think."

"Stop thinking so much."

"Do you want to go boarding today? Kyle will be with Mrs. Bronigan," she says. "We can call Mika and Barrett—see if they want to come."

"Sure. Why not."

I smile when I remember Greg is calling tonight. I'll be able to tell him how my boarding is doing.

"Maybe we can get you over to the Mystic Chair," Steph says. "We can try a few of the longer runs."

"You think I'm ready? It's supposed to be a lot steeper."

"If it's too steep, you can pendulum down, or you can slide on your butt."

I groan. "Right, because that's a classy way to get down the slope."

Chapter 8

"Do I look okay?" I spin in the doorway to the kitchen.

Steph pulls her head back and eyes me up and down a few times. "Where are you going?"

"Nowhere. Greg and I are having a video chat, remember?"

"Oh, right. Sorry, I forgot. New age dating."

"He's a bazillion miles away. It's the only way I get to see him."

"Australia isn't a bazillion miles away."

"You know what I mean." I spin again. "Do I look okay?"

"How much of you is he going to see?"

"That's not the point. I want to look nice. It's been forever since I've seen him."

"It's only been a few months."

"Stop it. Do. I. Look. Okay?"

"Yes, you look great. Even if you didn't, he wouldn't care."

I pace across the kitchen a few times. Grab a glass of water. Decide against it in case I spill it and have to find something new to wear.

"Wow, you're wired," Steph says. "Relax. You look perfect. Just be yourself and be sure to say hi for me."

When Greg's face pops up on my screen, I catch my breath. Oh my gosh. I miss him too much and I force a smile, so I don't look sad.

"Hi, Jillian of Banff," he says in the softest, sexiest voice.

I've never thought of Greg as sexy. But right now, wow, uber-sexy.

"Hi."

We watch each other without saying anything. I hear myself sigh and hope it isn't obvious.

"I miss you," he whispers.

"Ditto."

Silence.

He shakes his messy curls and says, "Enough sappy. What's new? Tell me everything. What have you been doing? What are the snow conditions like? How are Barrett and Mika? Do not leave out any details."

I'm glad he asks so many questions because it's a good distraction from sitting here with my heart missing him. After I answer them all and tell him about the epic runs on the Mystic Chair, with limited butt slides down the steep parts, we go back and forth with how Suzanne's improving, his course work, and how his folks are finally taking turns with visiting hours and taking time for themselves to catch their breath.

At a pause in our chatter, I whisper, "I read about the shooting online."

Greg nods but says nothing.

I try to fill the void feeling awkward and stupid for bringing it up. "It's so awful."

His mouth opens and I hear his long exhale. He closes his eyes and I really regret having started this because his face falls like there are no muscles left to make a smile.

"There were days when it was so brutal with Suzanne," he starts in a quiet voice. "I wished the bugger would have died." He shakes his head. "Then I'd think I'm glad he didn't. He needs to be held accountable for what he did, and he needs a lot of help. The bloke has a ton of issues. They have to help him, so he never does something like this again."

All I can do is nod and watch Greg's eyes.

"I go down a dark hole when I think about it, and it's hard to crawl out without being mad...so freaking mad. It saps out all my energy and it *doesn't* help anyone. I have to walk it off. Literally, walk it off, so I don't spiral." He takes a big breath. "Anyways, enough about that." He taps the screen. "Have I mentioned I miss you?" And ever so slowly his cheeks lift, and a small smile reappears.

I put a few fingers up to touch his. "I miss you too. Steph says hi," I blurt out. *What a mood killer*. God, I can be such an idiot.

"Say hi back for me." He chuckles. "It's so good to see you, Jillian. This makes it easier than just emails. Maybe we can chat every weekend, to check in, see how each other's doing."

"I'd love...like that. A lot."

"Deal. You and me, girl."

I melt in his smile.

"Goodnight," he says. "Sweet dreams."

"Bye."

I see his hand reach across his keyboard.

"Ready?" he asks.

I reach for the close button. Before he disappears, his lips kiss the air and mine follow. When the screen goes black, I feel the heat in my face. Will I ever grow up? Even long distance, he makes me blush. I hug myself.

* * *

"The bus will leave at eight AM sharp, Monday morning," Mrs. Machuk says. "I would like you to get into groups of three. You are responsible to make sure you're all accounted for when I do headcounts. Pick your group before we leave, or I'll pick them for you."

There's a lot of grumbling.

Barrett points at me and then another guy across from him. I recognize him from a class but we're not on a first name basis.

Nameless guy looks at me, grins and turns to Barrett. *Way to take charge, Barrett.* I smile at him and am glad to be a part of their group.

"Each student can bring one backpack or suitcase equivalent in weight to what you can carry on your back. One sleeping bag and foamy per student. We would all appreciate it if you remember your personal hygiene products. Food for the two nights will be provided, and we'll be responsible for all the cleanup. So, let's not mess up the accommodations we'll be using." Mrs. Machuk moves to the front of her desk. "We'll be sleeping in a conference room. There will be further discussion on the bus regarding appropriate behaviour, so the information has greater potential of being retained." She looks down at the papers in her hand and shuffles through them.

Barrett leans over and whispers, "That would be the sex, drugs, and rock and roll discussion."

I mouth, "What?"

"I can hear you," Mrs. Machuk says. without looking up.

Barrett points to his ears, then to Mrs. Machuk. "Told you."

"I can still hear you." She looks up and hones her sight in on Barrett before she waves the papers in the air. "Here are extra permission slips for those who have misplaced theirs. Have them signed. The ‘signed and returned’ aspect are crucial to coming on the field trip.”

* * *

Check email. Countdown to weekend virtual date with Greg. School. Chess at noon. Karate with Kyle twice a week. Supper preparations. Homework. Check email again. Repeat. Screen time with Greg, good test marks and karate with Kyle are the highlights. Oh, and the chess club. They are a lot of fun, which passes the noon hour since Barrett is now involved in badminton intramurals.

Mika loves her new gig at the park’s information office and Barrett has a part-time job after school. We almost have to make dates to get together and I don’t always want to be the third wheel with them, so it’s nice to have the chess club guys to hang with. It makes the days go faster.

Derrick challenged me to a game last week. I guess he didn’t really challenge me. The other guys didn’t show up at noon, so I was his only option. He was super competitive, and it got a bit intense. I couldn’t handle the no talking, so I did a few dumb moves and let him win. He was jacked he won but I’m pretty sure I could have taken him.

Before leaving for school, I check my email one last time and up pops a note from Greg.

Jillian,

I have some exciting news. Suzanne is doing so well that I'm going to take a break from the hospital and go surfing with some mates. I can't wait to tell you about it on Sunday. I should have some great pics to show you too. I know you would love surfing. Maybe one day I can teach you. You picked up snowboarding so fast I know you'd be great at it. I'll catch a wave for you.

Hugs. Miss you loads.

XO Greg

Well, that made my day better on so many levels. Maybe if Suzanne is doing so well, he'll be back in Banff sooner than later. I shut my laptop and smile. What would I do without Greg on the other end of my emails?

* * *

"Hey Jillian," Steph calls.

I stick my head out my bedroom door. "What?"

Steph stands at the bottom of the stairs. "Let's go to Sunshine tomorrow. I heard they got a lot of snow this week."

"Sure. Sounds great."

"Departure time will be eight o'clock to beat the rush and get first tracks."

Fabulous. Boarding tomorrow will make the weekend go faster and Sunday will happen sooner.

My alarm goes off in my still dark bedroom. What the heck? I try to register why I would set an alarm this early on my sacred sleep-in day. Right. Going to Sunshine with Steph. I crawl out of my warm bed to get ready.

Steph swings her truck keys at me. “You drive.”

“What?”

“You have your learner’s licence and you have driven before. The road will be quiet. No time like the present.”

“Greg is going to teach me.”

“I know, but you could impress him with how good you are by getting in a bit of practice.”

Seatbelts on. I turn the key and Steph’s truck roars to life in the quiet, dark back alley. D for drive. It all comes back from my time at the Cascade cabin when I drove the truck to get help for Mika. It feels cool to be in the driver’s seat again.

“That’s it. You’ve got this,” Steph says in a calm voice.

I ease out of the back alley, signal and head towards main street. At the red light, I tap my fingers on the steering wheel. Mom’s expression pops into my head and I nod in agreement. *It is like riding a bike.*

Across the intersection and out of town we go. The truck bumps over the tracks, and then it's straight to the overpass and a slow merge onto the highway with the other early birds heading for the ski hills. It takes a bit to get used to the headlights in my eyes, but driving on pavement is way smoother than driving on a fire road.

"This is our turnoff." Steph points at the Sunshine Ski Resort sign. "There is a parking lot after the overpass where you can pull off. I'll drive the rest of the way in case the road is slippery."

I know that parking lot.

My breath comes in puffs, and I focus on my driving so panic does not set in. I never told Steph what Kyle's dad did when he kidnapped me. Well, technically, he didn't kidnap me. I got in the car willingly because I thought he was taking Kyle and me to Steph's house to see if she wanted to join us for supper. But he kicked me out at the parking lot Steph wants me to stop at, and then he drove off with Kyle, leaving me to walk back to Banff.

Deep. Slow. Breaths.

I pull into the spot, stop the truck, and with my eyes only on the route around Steph's truck and to the passenger door, we switch places. I bite my bottom lip as Steph drives up the road.

"Great work," she says. "Greg will undoubtedly be impressed."

I nod and press my back into the seat until my freakout moment passes and I can breathe normally. The road narrows and

Steph navigates the tight corners as she follows the line of taillights ahead of us.

In a few minutes we're at the parking lot and getting our gear out.

"Darn," Steph says as the gondola sways. "I was hoping it wouldn't be a windy day."

Snow pelts against the windows and I peer out at the gray morning. There are lights further up and a number of white strips against the mountains, which must be the runs. Steph tightens her boots and zips up, so I do the same.

"Here we go."

The gondola slows down. I follow Steph out and grab my snowboard from the rack. Wow, this place is way bigger than Norquay. There are four lifts which start from here. And some of them go up pretty high.

"Look at you hot dogger," Steph says, after our first run down on Strawberry.

I laugh. "You don't call a boarder a hot dogger."

"Well, that is what you call a good skier, and you did really well coming down there."

"Thanks."

Each time she takes me down a different run. It's slow going with the flat light but once the sky clears, it's fun to go faster, and I feel more confident. I can see forever, and the views are to die for. Wait until I tell Greg I was up here.

Steph doesn't offer me the keys at the end of the day, which is okay with me. My legs feel like Jello, and the parking lot is busy with people leaving. On the way down the road, I grin at the day. My snowboarding feels so much better. I can't keep up with Steph, but I'm not that far behind. With more practice, maybe I'll be a shredder before Greg gets back.

Sunday takes forever to get to video chat time. With the field trip next week, my motivation to do homework involves a lot of procrastinating. After supper, I shower and get spiffed up for Greg's call. And I wait. And wait. I finally send him an email to see if he's going to be online soon. Nothing. Did he forget? No. He wouldn't, would he? I leave my monitor on in case I hear him ring, then lie on my bed and stare at the ceiling. At some point, I wake up and my lights are off.

What the heck. Why didn't he call?

Dumb scenarios run through my head. I try to hold on to the one where he had such a good time surfing that they decided to spend an extra day. I force myself to stick with that one, so the '*other girl*' scenarios don't take over.

Chapter 9

I'm impressed that everything for the field trip fits in my pack, and my sleeping bag and foamy are strapped to the bottom.

"Geesh," I groan, when I heave it onto my back. "I'm glad I don't have to hike with all this stuff. Getting it to school will be enough."

"Have fun." Steph slaps my pack so hard I have to double step to stop from falling.

"Will you miss me?" Kyle tips his head and grins.

"Of course, I will." I scruff up his hair. "Don't lose Steph. You know how she strays if we don't keep an eye on her."

"What does stray mean?"

"You know, keep her in line." I fake boxing punches at Steph.

"Got it," Kyle says while Steph protects her ribs, so I don't make contact.

"Have a good time without us. Don't forget to brush your teeth."

"What am I, three?" I wave over my shoulder as I head out the door. "I won't have cell reception all the time so stay out of trouble. Love you guys." I keep walking, as if it was the most natural thing to say. I must be getting soft. I used the 'l' word and it's not even daylight yet.

On the way to school, I try to kick my mood about Greg not calling last night. Not even an email to explain why. Inhale. Exhale. I force myself to stick with the *surfing is so good, he stayed longer than planned* idea. A visual of him catching a wave runs through my head and I smile. Not that I know anything about surfing but I'm sure Greg's good at it.

The orange cheese wagon sits at the back of the school, while everyone jostles to get their packs off. Barrett, the other guy in our group who now has a name (Brad), and I stand together and wait for Mrs. Machuk to tell us what's next.

"You are representatives of our school. Because you're from Banff people will remember if you pull any pranks, more so than if you were from *Nowhereville*, Alberta. Remember that and behave accordingly." Mrs. Machuk scans the group. Pause for effect no doubt. "Use common sense. If you have to ask yourself if what you're doing is wrong, then it probably is. If *I* have to talk to you about anything, it will not go well for you. Do not let the school down. Do not let me down. And do not embarrass any of us with any of the above."

Most of us turn away and roll our eyes.

"Don't roll your eyes," Mrs. Machuk says.

Wow. Not only is her hearing amazing, her ability to see what we hide from her is also uber impressive.

"Let's get going," she calls out, raises her hand and points to the bus door.

"Yo," Tony shouts, as he jogs up. "Sorry I'm late. It won't happen again," he apologizes to Mrs. Machuk.

"Your permission slip, please." She holds her hand out.

"Got it." He puts down his pack and digs through a few outside pockets before he pulls out a crumpled piece of paper.

Mrs. Machuk unfolds it, turns it sideways, then back again and looks at Tony. It's as if she doesn't believe what she's reading but finally says, "Get on."

* * *

When the bus stops in Black Diamond, Mrs. Machuk says we have two hours to check out the town and grab something to eat. She repeats her *behave* spiel but before she can finish it, a girl asks where the mall is. Mrs. Machuk closes her eyes, shakes her head, and mouths something no one can hear.

She fakes a smile at mall girl and says, "The museum is open on Railway Avenue."

"Where's that?" someone else asks.

"Next to the railway." Mrs. Machuk points to where a train sits on the tracks. "The only building with the word museum on its sign. If you don't go into the museum, at least read some of the plaques on the streets. Make me proud. There will be a short quiz after we head out."

So many groans.

"Catch you back here." Brad waves at Barrett and me then heads away with a few guys.

"Don't get lost in Hicksville." Tony pats my back as he walks away. "It's not the big city, but it's not Banff."

"These old towns are so fun." I zip up my parka as Barrett and I cross the street. "They have so much character. The stores with square false fronts," I wave my hand towards the building, "I can visualize women wearing long dresses and bonnets carrying baskets of fresh bread and eggs coming out of the stores."

Barrett stops in the middle of the road and scrunches up his eyebrows.

"What?" I grab his arm and pull him onto the sidewalk. "Didn't you read Laura Ingall's book? Or Anne of Green Gables...cute old towns with quirky people?"

Barrett does a slow headshake, like I'm speaking French.

"Don't your parents watch those old shows? Mom had this boyfriend, so she put a TV in my room with this massive VCR and a pile of tapes. I'd turn up the volume, so I didn't have to listen to them."

"Gross." Barrett gags.

"Yeah, tell me about it. But the shows were fun. Mindless, cheesy entertainment."

"You do realize that now you sound like a history nerd, right?"

"I do not."

"Do too." He throws an arm around my shoulders and gives me a solid squeeze before we walk past a colourful painting of rolling ranch lands in the window of a gift shop. "But I'll still hang with you, even if you're nerdy."

"Did you even read the brochure on the Crowsnest Pass? It has everything. Ghosts, mine disasters, bootleggers. Cool stories. Harlots. You know what those are, right?"

Barrett throws his hands in the air. "This is supposed to be a break from school. You know, F U N. Quit spoiling the *fun* part."

"Come on, can't you imagine it? No phones, using an outhouse because that's your only option, no showers, a bath once...well sometimes once a month only."

"Nerd. Stinky nerd in a month." Barrett pinches his nostrils. "Let's go grab something to eat."

I pull out my phone and take a few pictures of the street before we head down to check out Marv's Soda Shop for lunch. The walls in the restaurant are decorated with black and white posters from the Elvis Presley era. They even have juke boxes in each booth. Old fashioned, milkshake glasses decorate the front counter where a purple haired waitress, dressed as Minnie Mouse, grabs menus and shows us to a table.

After we inhale the best ever chili cheese dogs and poutine, I drag Barrett to the museum and read a few plaques. A bunch of kids head back towards the bus, and we follow them.

"Headcount," Mrs. Machuk says, as she stands at the front of the bus and starts pointing her finger up and down the seats. "Check for your partners."

"Brad." Barrett stands and turns towards the back. "Gotcha bro." He plunks back in the seat. "My work here is done."

"Thanks for being so responsible," I say.

There is banging on the bus door and the driver opens it.

Tony rushes up the steps.

Mrs. Machuk's head counting finger pauses in the air and she turns to him. "Next time be early, versus almost late."

"Got it."

What's his game? This cocky side of Tony is new for the guy who hangs out with the chess club.

Satisfied we haven't left anyone behind, Mrs. Machuk taps the driver's shoulder, and the bus leaves the town behind.

"How did Black Diamond get its name?" she says. "Did anyone find out?"

"Coal."

"Yes. What other resource did they find in the area?"

"Oil," says the same voice as the one who gave the coal answer.

I glance at Barrett. "You knew that, right?"

He shrugs.

"What river runs through the town?" Mrs. Machuk glances up and down the aisle.

Silence.

"The Bow," someone shouts.

"Good guess but it's wrong. The Sheep River runs through the area. There's another hour and a half to Frank, so get comfortable. Keep your hands where I can see them at all times should I choose to check." She watches us for a bit, then turns and takes her seat behind the driver.

Out the left windows, the snow-covered farmland runs into rolling foothills, and on the right, the fields run into the distant mountains. The cloudless, bluebird sky, an Alberta trademark, makes it look like a postcard from the gift shop in town. I take a few pictures out my window. The bus movements make the photos look blurry – kind of a cool effect.

Oh my God. Barrett is right. I glance at him as his head taps on the window when the bus goes over bumps. This is the first time I have been out of Banff in forever and here I am, taking in the scenery. I really am a nerd. I'll be talking about weather soon. A visual of

Oma and her weather conversation starters comes to me and makes me smile.

The bus is quiet as fence posts zip past. Kids zone out with ear buds, a book, or they sleep. I open a page in my notebook.

Greg,

I missed not seeing you on Sunday. I hope everything is okay with Suzanne. Maybe things got busy. It happens but I will admit I had a bit of a pity party not being able to hang out with you. I can't wait to catch up next week.

Remember the field trip Barrett talked me into going on? He said time would fly and we would get out of classes. Well, I'm on it and am now in a bus heading for Frank, Alberta. We were just in this cute town, Black Diamond—land of historic coal, and oil tales, and ranching versus farming. It became a town in 1929. The false fronts on the shops on main street make it look like the set for an old western show on TV. I expected ladies in big hoop dresses to stroll out of the stores but nope, only people in jeans and parkas. There's my history lesson for the day, just for you, because Barrett isn't interested.

Is Suzanne still improving? I can't imagine being in a hospital bed 24/7. And the bedpan and already chewed pureed food, ack. But she's got this.

How are you? Online classes going okay? I hope you had a fabulous time surfing. I've never asked, but are there lots of climbing spots around you? Is that where you learned to do it?

Snowboarding has been awesome. I'm sorry you're missing it, but we've had a ton of snow, so hopefully you'll be back for a few spring boarding days.

Anyway, I'll take a pic of this letter and email it to you, so I don't have to type it out. Notice the neat cursive writing? I'm glad Mom made me take that class. Resumé worthy, no doubt. Insert smiley happy face. Chat on Sunday. Can't wait.

Miss you. Take Care.

Jillian of Banff XO

The wind whips around when we get off the bus at the Frank Interpretive Centre. I tuck my head and hurry inside. Somewhere on the drive down, the sun disappeared behind the clouds and a cold gust took over. *Look at me. Incoming weather report.*

"You'll get used to the wind," says the man holding the door.

Inside the building, Mrs. Machuk talks to an older man in a blue uniform. Provincial Park blue uniforms are not as ugly as the green National Park ones Steph and Tom wear. We all stand around with our backpacks at our feet, not quite sure what to do.

"This is," Mrs. Machuk raises her hand and points towards the blue uniform guy, "Mr. Fisher. He will be showing us around the centre."

"Hi," Mr. Fisher says. "Welcome. Let's get you to the auditorium and you can drop off your gear. Please follow me."

Down hallways and after two right turns, we get to a big room with chairs stacked along the wall.

"This will be your sleeping accommodations, and through there," he points across to another door and a partially open bifold, "is the eating area. There are supplies in the fridge for breakfast and lunch. Your supper will be catered."

A few yay responses.

"Find yourself a piece of floor space and settle in. I'll be back in fifteen minutes to give you a tour of the rest of the facility. The washrooms are through there." Mr. Fisher points to another set of doors.

Awkward shuffling follows because we don't know what to do, but when Mrs. Machuk and Mr. Fisher leave, kids jostle to get to a spot they'll call home for two nights. I head for a space by the window.

"Great pick." Barrett drops his pack next to me.

I glance around to see if Brad is following and then turn to Barrett.

"What?" He lifts his hands in the air.

"You know you don't have to babysit me."

"I'm not."

"Really?" I watch his expression.

"Really."

And just like that, he sets about unrolling his foamy and sleeping bag, like camping out next to me is the most natural thing to do. I thought Barrett would want to hang with his guy friends and do dumb guy stunts but nope, here he is next to me. It's kind of sweet.

Did Greg put him up to it? No, Greg would never do that. First off, he's got way bigger things to focus on than me on a field trip and second, Greg's not like that. I don't think. I guess I assume that, but we have been apart more than we've been together so how would I know? Gosh, I press my finger on his bracelet and roll it against my wrist, why didn't he call?

Maybe this field trip really is a good distraction.

I undo my gear and shake out my thin mat before I check my phone. Only one bar flashes. Minimal reception. I put it into airplane mode to save the battery but will still be able to use the camera.

"Okay, let's go on a bit of a tour," Mr. Fisher calls out.

Pictures of Turtle Mountain before and after the rockslide hang from the lobby's walls. Out the big windows, ginormous rocks, some the size of Steph's truck, fill the valley. I look from the field of debris, up to where they used to belong, and back down again. Unbloody believable. Like a giant smashed the mountain into rocks and then threw them everywhere.

“The archives are on the top floor.” Mr. Fisher points to the stairs. “There is more information and a collection of souvenirs at the guest services shop. If you have questions, ask anyone in a park uniform. They’ll be able to help you.”

I shake my head as I read a plaque about how a whole family, except the father who was working down in the mine, were killed while they slept. Families lost everything. Houses. Lives. There is one article where a family was in the same house but in different rooms. A kid walked away without a scratch and the rest of the family was never found. I shake my head.

And then there are stories of people who happened not to be asleep in their beds for unusual reasons—a girl working at the hotel stayed overnight for the first time instead of walking home and a man stayed in the barn with a sick animal—they survived. But their families didn’t. So many bodies never even found. Which means they’re under all that rock. Just bones now.

The miners working underground dug their way out. Not one of them was hurt. I shudder because Suzanne pops into my head and how she survived, and some others didn’t. Was it just luck? Same as the miners who survived?

She’s okay. Suzanne is going to be totally okay in time.

I take a deep breath and move on to focus on the exhibits.

“Amazing,” I whisper to no one and move on to the next display and find another story of a house left unharmed when ones on either side were demolished.

“Ninety seconds, that’s all it took,” Barrett says from behind me.

“I know. Unbelievable. And they had no idea it was going to happen.”

“Well, some knew it would happen one day.” He points to an information board which explains how a native aboriginal band avoided Turtle Mountain because they believed it was bad medicine. They called it, ‘that mountain that moves.’

Now we have so much technology and gadgets and detectors. Back then, not so much. I wonder if we’d know today when something like this is about to let loose. But I still hear about earthquakes and volcanoes and stuff that just happens without warning, so maybe it’s not so different.

“Take notes for me,” Tony says as he passes us. “Could it get any more boring? Maybe there’s a movie playing somewhere.”

“That would be in the theatre room.” Barrett gestures to the Theatre Room sign above the double doors.

“Thanks bro.” Tony heads towards it.

Barrett mumbles.

“What did you say?” I move beside him.

“I said, ‘Don’t call me bro’.”

I glance in the direction Tony disappeared and back to Barrett. “You’re not a fan?”

"You're just realizing that?"

I shrug. "He's okay."

Barrett's eyes get big, and he's got his goofball face on.

"He is," I say.

"If you say so." Barrett walks off to another display.

He's never judgy. Why doesn't he like Tony? Wait a minute. Is he watching out for me again? My knight, Mr. Barrett. Keeping me safe from the world. I stare at a picture of an old street in Frank and grin.

In the next section, as if there wasn't enough death already, the display describes other mine accidents and so many more lives lost in the Crowsnest Pass. They had to dig mass graves because there were just too many to bury individually. So many widows and orphaned kids. What a tough life. I feel a tinge of guilt for how good I have it.

"Hey Nerd," Barrett calls from somewhere down the hall.

I walk toward the sound.

"There's food."

I follow him.

"Remember the F-U-N part of getting away from school?" Barrett pokes me in the shoulder.

"Sorry. It's...I don't know, interesting. Like in our lives, there is no way we've seen anything like this. Or could we even deal with the aftermath?"

"You want to die in a rockslide?"

"No. Of course not. But even their lives, before and after, were so tough. Hard work all the time. Outhouses forever. No TV. No technology. It's like roughing it every minute of every day."

"And," Barrett puts me in a headlock and noogies my skull, "I repeat my, 'don't be a nerd' remark."

I slip out and punch him in the ribs. "I am *not* a nerd."

He waves his fingers in the air and mouths *'nerd, nerd, nerd'* as we enter the eating area.

After the pizza party, I wander back to the displays. Through an open door, I see a girl bent over a big table. She stands up and groans.

"Can I help?" I say as I walk into the room.

She jumps around.

"I'm sorry. I didn't mean to scare you."

"Maybe it'll help." She stretches and arches her back.

"Maybe what will help?"

"Maybe getting scared will reactivate my brain and I can figure out how to finish this." She brushes her hands on her pants. "Hi, I'm Afton."

"Jillian. Hi." I wave my hand over the board which resembles the inside of a tiny house minus the roof. Outside the house she's got branches for trees stuck in putty, a pile of pebbles, mini farm animals in a corral and a few people scattered around.

"What're you doing?"

"We have a group of grade four kids coming next week. I want to make a diorama to show them what a typical house and yard in Frank looked like in 1903." She walks to the other side of the table. "Today, kids are so plugged into their phones, most of them wouldn't know what to do with themselves without it."

"Yeah, I guess."

She stares at the table. "What would you do, if you were a kid, this is your house, you've finished your chores and your mom said, 'go play'?"

"I don't know. I guess I'd go get a toy to play with."

"You have two." She picks up a piece of cloth. "Pretend this is your apple head doll."

"Okay. Where's my other toy?"

"Outside." She moves a tiny straight twig and puts it by the door. "What would you do with it?"

I shake my head.

"Hopscotch. X's and O's. Hangman." She draws miniature examples of each on the dirt in the front yard. Then she scatters the round pebbles. "Marbles. The hardest part of marbles is finding the round pebbles. You could do cat's cradle if you have a piece of string and someone else to play with. There were lots of hand clapping games. Kids *made* play. They didn't just 'turn it on'." She laughs. "Not that kind of 'turn it on'."

"Got it."

Afton is super enthusiastic about this stuff.

"So much of their life was doing chores; from emptying pee pots, starting the stove's fire, hauling water, helping their mom with everything she had to do to get the family through the day that by the time they could finally play, they just played." Her voice gets animated as she moves four plastic people across the diorama platform and puts them in a group with a piece of rope.

"Skipping," I say. "I did a ton of skipping for warmup exercises in karate."

"That's great but do not ever tell kids skipping is good exercise. Did you know it actually started with boys? It was super competitive." She stops and puts her hand over her mouth. "I'm so sorry."

I look around to see what is causing her to apologize but can't see anything. "Sorry for what?"

"I'm boring you to death. My friends in university teased me about being a history geek. It's my thing." She laughs. "I bet you couldn't tell."

"It's...interesting." I nod. "Tomorrow we're going to some old town. Lille?"

"That is such a cool place. Hey, come and find me before you go. I'll be at the front desk in the morning," she says. "There's an old fella, Herb, who lives in a shanty up there. I'll give you a couple of books to give him in case you see him."

"Uh, sure."

"He's a recluse but a great guy. He was in a mine accident and, well," she looks up at the ceiling, "he lost a bit of his face. People freak out when they see him but he's a gem. He knows everything about this area."

The visual of a man with a half missing face is not who I would choose to run into.

"How will I find him?"

"Your group will be in the middle of nowhere making a bit of noise. He'll hear you coming," Afton says. "I usually see him by the ovens."

"Ovens?"

"Not ovens for cooking food. These ovens were used to get the impurities out of the coal and turn it into coke. Coke is a high carbon content with few impurities."

I know I have a dumb expression on my face because what she just said means nothing and the only visual I have is our kitchen stove.

"Coke burns cleaner than coal and gets a lot hotter." Afton lifts both her hands. "Because it burns hotter and cleaner, they use it to turn iron into steel and the end product has fewer impurities."

"Oh, okay." I nod. "Got it."

"Jillian," Mrs. Machuk calls from the hall. "It's time to shut it down for the night."

"Okay." I turn back to Afton. "See you in the morning."

"You can wow your teacher with this piece of information. Tell her, each brick for those fifty coke ovens in Lille was made in

Belgium. They assembled the ovens in Belgium, numbered each brick, disassembled them, and shipped them around South America to Vancouver. They were meant to be reassembled in Frank but then the slide happened, so they took them up to Lille instead. No phones. No internet. No modern technology to make it all happen. You will be impressed when you see how intricate they are. You can even see some of the numbers on the bricks still. Now go, get to your group because I've got lots more I can go on about." She shooshes me away with her hands. "Have a good night. See you tomorrow."

"Bye." I wave over my head. She's got such a positive vibe and energy going on. I bet she's fun to work with.

"Where have you been, Nerd?" Barrett says as he shakes out his sleeping bag in the dimly lit room.

I grab my pillow and swing it at him. "Stop calling me a nerd."

"Pillow fight," someone shouts and the room bursts into bodies flinging pillows. In seconds, the bright overhead lights go on and everyone freezes.

"Okay, class. That's quite enough." Mrs. Machuk stands with her hand on the light switch as she surveys the room. "Save your energy for the hike into Lille because I do not want to hear any complaining. Goodnight."

The lights dim.

"That was your fault," Barrett snickers.

“Was not.”

“Was too.”

I grab my bathroom bag, flannel PJ’s and head to the washroom. When I walk in, two girls jerk their arms behind their back, giggle at each other and ignore eye contact with me. Oh brother. I roll my eyes inside the stall. They better not ruin this trip for all of us. By the time I’m done, the giggling stops and the door slams. When I step out, they’re gone, which is good because I would have skipped brushing my teeth and washing my face to avoid them.

It takes forever to fall asleep. The rustle of sleeping bags, so many types of breathing with a lot of snoring mixed in and the lack of softness to the foamy against the hardwood floor makes it impossible to sleep.

Chapter 10

Before we head out in the morning, I get the books from Afton. She also made Herb cookies. What a sweet thing to do.

"The town of Lille is five kilometers up this road. It was a bustling town from 1901 to 1912 with a population of four hundred people." Mrs. Machuk starts walking up the hard packed, snow-covered trail. "Why do you think they built their town up here?"

"They liked being in the middle of nowhere," someone shouts.

"Next guess," Mrs. Machuk says.

"Coal," Barrett pipes up. "And hopes of gold, but hope ran out. By 1912 the production costs and quality of the coal wasn't worth it anymore."

"You did your homework, Nerd." I elbow him in the ribs, and he sticks his tongue out.

"Oh, aren't you mature."

After the initial chatter, the hike into Lille becomes quiet except for the snow crunching under our footsteps. There are no street signs, or old houses, or any indication anyone lives up here except the packed path we walk on. Forever.

After crossing a few bridges, and so many more corners with endless spruce trees hiding everything from view, I am almost ready to say, "How much further?" when Mrs. Machuk stops.

With her back to us she waves her arm across this huge, snow-packed open field with a handful of bushes and one fire hydrant. Behind the fire hydrant, the clearing runs far off towards the base of a mountain.

She says, "Imagine this...four rows of small, whitewashed houses, outhouses at the end of each street, a big hotel over there." She points to the remains of a partially snow-covered brick foundation. "And the slag pile." This time she points to a huge toboggan style hill with black dirt and rocks peeking out where the sun has melted the snow. "Who knows what a slag pile is?"

"Waste, from after they process the coal," Barrett says.

Mrs. Machuk smiles at him.

I elbow him again and whisper, "Seriously, who's the nerd now?"

"Check out the area and please take the time to read the information board. Meet back here," she taps her hiking stick on the ground, "in one hour. There will be a quiz later. I would appreciate it if you did not groan or roll your eyes until I turn my back."

Barrett makes a snowball and nails Brad in the butt with it. And they're off scooping up handfuls of snow, packing them hard and then lobbing them at anyone in range. A few girls squeal as they get caught in the crossfire. I watch for a bit and then head for the information board where there are lots of black and white pictures of what Lille looked like in 1901. Similar to the town in *Little House on the Prairie* and their pioneer lifestyle. Four hundred people. There were more people living in our apartment complex in Toronto.

All that is left of the fancy hotel is the foundation and a couple of openings where windows or doors might have been. Further beyond the hotel near the slag pile is a wall of bricks. I wander over to see what Afton was talking about.

And she wasn't kidding.

The coke ovens stretch out as far as a tennis court and every section has an oval door I could walk through. I count twenty-three doors but there could have been more since part of the wall has either crumbled or been knocked over. Afton's right. It's amazing they made this happen all the way from Belgium without modern technology. I take a few pictures from different angles.

At the crumbled end, I see a person move. Is it someone trying to avoid getting hit by a snowball? I squint to focus, but they're too far away. After a quick look around, I walk towards them. As I get closer and realize it's no one from our group, I assume it's Herb.

"Hi. Herb?" I swing off my backpack to get the books and box of cookies out. "Afton asked me to give these to you."

I look down at the worn paperback covers of Zane Grey cowboy novels, so it doesn't look like I'm staring at his face. His right eye lid resembles a big blob of pink melted candle wax which dripped down the purple-red, tight skin of his flat cheek. And there's not a whisker on that side of his face. But on the left side, it's hard to see skin for all the beard and moustache and eyebrow he's got growing.

"And she made you these." I put the cookie tin on top of the stack of novels. "She said ginger snaps are your favourite." I look up and hand them to him.

"They are. Please tell her thank you for me." He takes the stuff and tucks it under his arm. "Are you with all those kids?"

"Yes, I am. We're from Banff and are here to learn about the history of the place."

"There's no shortage of that," he says.

The arm of his stained oil-skinned coat lifts and he waves it in front of us. I glance in the direction he points. Usually, homeless people hang out in town or in the park, not in the middle of the woods. But I get why he doesn't want to deal with people's reaction when they see him.

"You kids better not wreck anything," he says. "The place doesn't need any more graffiti or smashed walls or garbage."

I scan the area and avoid making eye contact with him because we're not the kids he's talking about. Besides, Machuk would never let that happen.

"You youngsters have no respect for history."

Okay. That's enough. I turn to face him. "I'm sorry you feel that way sir, but we will not wreck anything. We're here to learn how things were a long time ago."

He lets out a snort and glances over my head. I move beside him to see what he's staring at. Movement in the trees.

A grey shape slinks through the black and white trunks of the aspens and out into the open. The husky again. The one who keeps showing up. What is he doing way out here? *Is he keeping tabs on me? If so, why?*

I glance around.

Behind the husky, two people wearing snowshoes with big packs on and snowboards under their arms wave at us. I look at the old guy and his lips move into a stiff line. He says nothing as they approach.

"Fab day," the first guy says.

"What's happening?" The second guy swings his board out and plunks it in the snow, so it stands up. His face does a quick what-the-fuck expression when he sees Herb's face, but he recovers. I'm sure Herb saw it too and I feel awful for him.

Herb points to the snowy, clear-cut mountain slope in the distance. "Do you fellas plan on going up there?"

"You bet. The snow should be superb to carve a few turns."

"No, it won't be superb. It has melted and frozen too often." Herb shakes his head. "The avalanche hazard is high."

"No way." The other boarder swings around to face the mountain. "The weather's been perfect. It's almost spring snow already."

"Suit yourself." Herb walks off and leaves me standing there. The husky sits at the edge of the ovens and watches Herb leave.

"Your old man?" The boarder who mentioned the conditions are perfect asks me.

"No, just a...someone I met."

"No offense, but he's wrong." The guy laughs. "He just doesn't want us to have fun."

I shrug.

"How far is your group going?" He waves at a few others who've come around to the slag pile.

"This is it. We came up to see the old town site."

"Nice."

"You guys have a good day." I wave and head back to Barrett who's still chucking snowballs.

When I check over my shoulder, I can see the boarders head through the deep untracked snow towards the mountain. From his vantage point at the end of the ovens, the husky watches them leave too.

"Banff students," Mrs. Machuk hollers. "It's time to head back."

I check for the boarders again but they're out of sight and the husky slinks off into the woods. *What is his game?*

"Oma?" I mouth. "Opa?"

He doesn't turn or stop. He disappears, again.

* * *

"How was it?" Afton calls out as I walk towards the information counter inside the Interpretive Centre.

"It was pretty cool." I smile. "Herb says thank you."

"Oh, I'm glad you found him."

"Well, technically, he found me...by the ovens. And you were right, they were impressive. Like putting a massive jigsaw puzzle together."

She pulls a file folder out of the bookshelf behind her. "When you get a chance, this is the paper I wrote about this place. It was for my final mark in a Natural History course."

"Thanks."

Another interpreter calls her over and I open the cover. 'A Comprehensive Review of the People and Mining Industry in the Crowsnest Pass.' A bit of *light* reading. I head back to the group for supper.

"Want to have some fun," Tony whispers as we clean up the tables.

"Pardon?" I lean back. "What kind of fun?"

"You know." He pretends to bring a bottle to his lips and tips his head back.

I mouth, "No."

"Oh, come on. My head hurts from information overload. It's time to lighten up."

I shake my head.

"Come on." He waves his hand at Brad and three others from the cool crowd standing around the end of the table. They wink in unison. "It'll be fine." Tony scopes the room as if he's checking for the bad guy, links arms with me, and pulls me towards an exit. The others follow with whispers and shushing noises as we make our way outside. I feel odd to be included with them but also borderline cool and daring.

"Put the card against the bolt so we can get back in," someone says, as we step out into the night.

I suspect they've done this before.

"What'd you guys bring?" Brad pulls a mickey out of his parka pocket and leans against the brick wall where we're in the shadows of the parking lot lights.

Tony pulls one out too. They all do. Except me. Feeling totally out of place I scuff my runner on the ground as the chatter about sneaking out goes on, how lame this trip is, and some stellar party that is supposed to happen on the weekend. I stare at my feet and shiver.

"Hey," Tony nudges me and passes me his bottle.

I shake my head.

"Come on. We didn't sneak out to be pussies." He laughs.

I look up and watch everyone watching me. Shit. Brad winks. Ugh. I take a sip and the inside of my mouth goes to high alert. It's awful. Like the time I tried to smoke, and all my body functions wanted to eject out my nostrils. But I swallow, let it burn down my throat and pass it back. Then I paste a see-I-did-it-not-a-big-deal smile on my face, and everyone carries on with their chatter.

After a few more sips, a guy pulls out a joint. Great. I remember alcohol and drugs were at the top of the list of items not to bring. The skunk smell saturates the air as the joint gets passed around. I shake my head when it's my turn. Tony passes me his micky and takes the joint. I fake a sip and fake a swallow because I can't do the disgusting taste anymore but don't want to draw attention to myself.

A door slams. Everyone freezes. Caps twist on bottles. Bottles disappear into coats. The joint gets flicked into the snowbank. I glance at Tony, but he's already running for the door. I try to figure out what to do with the bottle since I don't have the cap and when I spin around to catch up to them, I trip. The bottle flies out of my hand. I pick myself up, wincing as my knees and palms sting.

"Miss," a man calls from behind me. "Stay right there."

Fuck.

Mr. Fisher walks up to me and waves his flashlight right in my eyes. Not cool. I turn away and see spots against the wall.

"You lost this?" He waves the flashlight over the bottle and picks it up. "Let's you and I go have a chat with Mrs. Machuk."

Thanks Tony. Thanks a lot, you jerk ass. I follow Mr. Fisher into the building, down the hall and into an office.

"Wait here," he says, and leaves.

Like what else am I going to do? I'm already up shit creek. If I rat anyone out, no one will talk to me. Rats have no friends. I can say I found it. Right? But who would believe that? I doubt Mrs. Machuk will be in any mood for sarcasm or humour.

"Jillian, Jillian, Jillian." Mrs. Machuk sighs as she closes the door.

I want to recite the 'Jillian, Jillian, Jillian Jiggs' kid's story, but from her disappointed expression I don't.

"So," she pauses. "I have to admit, I never thought that you'd be the one to pull a stunt like this."

I remain quiet. No point divulging information she hasn't asked for.

"This is how it's going to go." Mrs. Machuk crosses her arms. "You tell your folks what happened, ask them to call me, and we'll all discuss appropriate discipline and how to go forward."

"Mom is in Europe."

"Then tell your dad."

I force my eyes not to misbehave. "He's in Denver."

"Then you tell whoever signed your permission slip." Her voice has a hint of cranky in it. "Please tell them I expect to get a call by Friday so we can put this matter behind us."

"Yes."

"Now get washed up and straight back into your sleeping bag."

"Yes ma'am."

"Don't ma'am me, Jillian. Mrs. Machuk is good."

"Mrs. Machuk."

She points to the door, and I leave, eyes straight ahead. I hear her exhale as I hit the hallway. Well, that wasn't as painful as I thought it would be. Not totally unscathed, but I didn't squeal on anyone which is huge. Not that they'll ever be on my best friend list though. I have time to figure out how to tell Steph. She knows Tony. Maybe I can come clean with her. Like this is not my fault. But if I tell her Tony was involved, will she tell Machuk?

"What the hell," Barrett hisses as I grab my bathroom bag and PJ's.

"Don't." I give him a grumpy face. "I am *not* in the mood."

When I pass Tony, I shoot stink eyes at him. "Thanks," I mouth.

He looks around then rushes up. "Sorry," he hisses.

I glare at him.

"I can't get suspended again. The old man will...he'll lose it."

"Whatever." I walk away.

The bathroom becomes silent when I walk in, and girls rush to finish up and leave. Figures. No one's got my back. I'm in the wrong. It's all my fault. I want to scream and tell them what *really* happened. But I don't. Because they'll never believe me. I'm not one of them. I bet they're all having a good laugh over it.

I want to go home.

Barrett's sleeping bag crinkles. "Trying to be one of the cool kids?" he whispers. "You want to get kicked out of school?"

"Leave me alone."

"I'm trying to figure out why you'd be that dumb?"

I don't respond because I don't have an answer. So much for feeling cool and daring.

He puts his arm over my shoulder and pats my bag like I'm a baby.

"Get some sleep," he says. "Maybe it won't seem so bad in the morning."

"I doubt it."

Longest night ever. I try a few practise speeches for Steph. And how am I going to tell Greg? He'll be so...I don't know how he'll react. I feel embarrassed even thinking about telling him. And then I feel guilty that I'd keep it from him.

* * *

"Hey," Afton calls out from behind the information desk. "Got a minute?"

I walk over. Bet she heard about last night's debacle. I bet everyone here knows.

"I just wanted to say, if you like this place, and this history stuff, they start accepting applications for summer jobs in March. You should apply," she says."

March is when Greg comes back, and if I'm not grounded for the rest of my life, I have no intention being this far away from him for the whole summer.

"It's a great place to work. They have staff accommodation and there's lots of free time to hike and explore. I think you'd like it."

"Sure." I smile trying to convince her I'm at least a bit interested.

"Think about it. You can apply online. Have a good trip home."

"Okay. For sure. Bye." I head outside.

"Jillian..." Mrs. Machuk ticks a box on her sheet when I get on the bus.

Right now, staying here might be easier than going home to tell Steph. The bus is a lot quieter than on the trip down. Barrett tries to talk, but I have the window seat this time and pretend to sleep.

I smile as the ranch land zips by. Even though I screwed up, I can't wait to tell Greg what a cool place this is. Maybe we can come down and explore it a bit when he's back.

When we hit the Trans-Canada highway, I check my phone and turn off airplane mode. A missed call from the house. Why wouldn't Steph use her cell phone? She is terrible with technology. Almost as bad as Mika. Steph didn't leave a message so, obviously whatever she called about, was not important.

Chapter 11

The house is dark. Steph must have gone to bed early. I enter the code, press down on the doorknob so it doesn't squeak, and drop my pack in the back porch with good intentions to unpack it tomorrow. Tonight, I just want a hot shower and my own bed. My own soft bed in my quiet room.

I flick on the kitchen light and almost jump out of my clothes when I see Steph hunched over the kitchen table, which is scattered with beer cans and a liquor bottle.

What the hell?

While I take in the scene, Bucky comes over and sniffs my pants, my fingers and looks up at me while wandering back to his bed in the corner. He flops down as if it's been a long day for him too.

Steph stares at me. Red eyes. Red face. Ugly girl crying blotches.

I lift my hands in the air. "What's going on?" I whisper, so I don't wake Kyle.

All she does is shake her head. I feel like the angry adult in this conversation, and I don't like it.

Steph's shoulders lift and fall.

"What's. Going. On?" I hiss.

She takes in a slow, long breath before she lifts her head.

"It's over," she says. "I lost him."

"What's over? Tom? You guys broke up?" I wave my hand over the crap on the table. "That doesn't give you any excuse to do this."

"Kyle."

"What?"

"I lost Kyle."

"What do you mean, you lost Kyle?" I rush towards the stairs and his room.

"He's gone. They took him away."

I stop. I am too tired for this but force myself back into the kitchen.

"Who took him away?"

"Family Services."

"Why? What happened?"

Steph does another long, slow, and extremely irritating inhale.

"I had to go to Edmonton today." She stops and her pause irritates the shit out of me.

I'm tired. I want to have a shower. I want to go and sleep in my bed.

"Mrs. Bronigan was going to pick Kyle up from school and bring him here until I got home. I knew I wouldn't be back until after supper."

Steph stops. I bite my cheek as I wait. But patience is not my friend.

"And?" I say.

"Mrs. Bronigan had a heart attack at the lodge. They rushed her to Calgary. Kyle tried to call me. And you."

"Oh no, that was the call from the house. It was Kyle. But he didn't leave a message." I pull out my phone to see if I missed checking voice mail and realize, it's not going to do any good now. I point at Steph. "You were supposed to keep your phone on. Always."

"It was on. I must've been in a dead spot on the highway or in a building. I never heard his call."

"So, what happened?"

"He walked here by himself and when it got dark, he called 911 just like I taught him to." She heckles like a sad witch. "He told them he was home alone."

"Oh, Steph. It'll be okay." I sigh because now it's not a life and death situation. Well, maybe it is for Mrs. Bronigan. But not Kyle. "We'll get him back. They'll understand it was a one off and it won't happen again."

She hangs her head and shakes it.

"Sure they will. How's Mrs. Bronigan?"

"I haven't heard. I called her lodge and the hospital. They said they'd call back when they know anything."

"She'll back us up. She'll tell them this never happens, and we'll make a plan in case something goes wrong again. We'll cover it."

The front doorbell rings. I look at Steph and the mess of stuff on the table in front of her.

"I'll get it." I walk out of the kitchen and hurry past the living room, flick on the outside light and open the door.

"Is Stephanie Meier here?" A lady in a dark going-to-the-office suit hands me a business card.

I stand in the middle of the doorway to block any view to the kitchen. This lady looks important, and she can't see Steph right now.

"She's in the shower. Can I help?"

The lady peers around my shoulder then looks at me with an adult I-don't-believe-you expression.

"Please tell her Kyle is in foster care until we get everything straightened out. He's okay and for a young kid he understands exactly what's going on. It seems this isn't his first rodeo." She gives a lame smile like the rodeo analogy will make this situation a bit humorous and then clears her throat. "I think he's been down this road before so, please let Stephanie know he's fine and I'll keep her in the loop."

I nod.

"Is everything alright?" She glances over my shoulder again. "Are you okay?"

"Yes, I'm fine. You know it wasn't Steph's fault, right? She was out of cell service and so was I. I was on a field trip with school, or I would have been here. I would have been home with Kyle, so he wasn't alone." I know I'm blabbering like an idiot but if I can fix this, I have to try. "It never happens. He's never alone. We've always got Kyle covered."

She stares at me but says nothing.

"Honest. This will never happen again. We'll work out a better plan to *make sure* it doesn't happen again. Ever."

"Do you have to watch Kyle a lot?" She tips her head at me.

"Not a lot. Sometimes. When Steph works, I do, but we both take care of him. And Mrs. Bronigan takes him out sometimes. We all take care of him." I press my lips together to shut the hell up.

"Can you please check and see if Stephanie is out of the shower. I would really like to talk to her."

Shit. She can't see Steph. Not now. I take a step back and lean my head up towards the stairs as if I'm listening.

"Nope, she's still in the shower. I can hear the water running." I nod to convince both of us. "She loves her long showers." *I am the world's worst liar.* "I'll tell her you were here."

"Okay," she says but makes no attempt to leave.

"Bye." I force a smile.

"Have a good night." She finally turns and heads out towards the sidewalk.

I close the door and lean against it. *Have a good night my ass.* Can anything else go wrong?

Poor Kyle. I hope he's okay. I know he'll act tough, but I really hope he's okay and knows we'll get him back. Steph will fix this.

Now is not the time to mention the Frank incident. If Machuk tells Steph I won't have to because either way, I'll be up the fucking creek. And no one will ever pass me a paddle.

I go back to the kitchen and watch Steph clean up the table before I wave the business card at her. "She says she'll be in touch. She says Kyle is okay."

Steph leans on the table and closes her eyes. When she lifts her head, she says, "I may have gone off the rails with her."

"What does that mean?"

"I might have yelled at her."

"Oh, Steph, that's not helpful."

Her eyes water and it scares me. I squeeze her arm. This being *the adult* in a situation sucks. I want to be a teenager. I don't want to have to be the bigger person. But here I am, doing it.

"Hey, Kyle will be okay." I jiggle her arm in hopes it will lighten her up. "You'll see. They'll let him come stay with us again. It will *all* work out."

"Sorry about this." She groans. "I haven't even asked, how was your trip? Did you have fun?"

"It was good." I glance around the kitchen and stop at Oma's cuckoo clock. It makes me wish I could wind it back to last year when she was still alive, and life wasn't a train wreck. "You know what? You've had a crappy day. Let's call it a night. I need the longest, hottest shower ever."

The shower doesn't wash my mood away. I feel awful for Kyle. Is he scared? Or is he being tough like he always is when shit happens to him? How am I going to tell Steph about the incident at Frank with this going on? The timing totally sucks.

I go to my computer. No emails from Greg still. He must be really busy. I hope nothing has changed with Suzanne.

Greg,

Gosh, I wish it was Sunday and we could talk. I miss you. I just got back from the field trip with school. The Crowsnest Pass is a cool place with lots of mountains. Have you climbed there?

How are things? I'm still waiting to hear how great your surfing was. You forgot to send pics. I hope it was the break you needed. Is Suzanne still knocking it out of the park with physio? Are your folks able to catch their breath with her improvement? Look at me using two old people clichés in one paragraph. I must be tired. It's been a long day. Good night.

Chat soon.

Jillian of Banff XO

I shut my laptop, kiss my fingers, tap the lid and sigh. Australia feels so far away.

As I try to fall asleep, tears leak out. It seems Mom is never here when I need her. When is the last time I even had that thought? Forever ago? I've been figuring things out on my own ever since I got to Banff. That thought tumbles into thoughts about Kyle. I hope he knows how much we care about him.

I'll never fall asleep.

* * *

"Can Jillian Meier please come to the office," the voice over the school intercom announces.

Barrett stops in the hallway and looks down at me. "What did you do now?"

I shrug.

"Well, you better go find out." He points towards the principal's office. "I'll see you in class."

Shit. Machuk said I had until Friday. I do not need this. Not today. I force my feet to get me to the office.

"Jillian," the friendly secretary says. "Have a seat. Mr. Little will see you in a few minutes."

I sit with my back against the window so kids can't see me. As I wait, Olivia rolls in with her wheelchair. She looks at me like she has no idea who I am. And I'm totally okay with that.

"Can I see the nurse?" she says to the secretary.

"What seems to be your problem today?"

Olivia glances back at me and then pushes her chair to the end of the counter so she's closer.

"You know, it's that time of the month and I've got cramps and maybe she's got something stronger to make them go away. I took a Tylenol, but it didn't help at all." She emphasizes the *at all* like she's the first girl to ever get cramps.

I stare at the carpet and give myself shit for being such a bitch. The girl was in a car accident. She's in a wheelchair. I tell myself to lighten up, lift my head and give her a sympathetic smile. She gives me stink eyes in return. What the hell? Like I gave her cramps? I go back to being a bitch in my head.

"Hold on," the secretary says. "I'll call and see if the nurse is available."

Mr. Little steps out of his office. "Jillian, right this way please." He waves his arm at me and then gestures back into his room.

It's about Kyle. Maybe Mom. No. Mom would not have me dragged down to the principal's office. If she needs to tell me something she'd tell Steph first.

"So." Mr. Little clasps his hands and puts them on his desk. "How are you today?"

"I'm good, thanks."

"Is there anything going on that I can help you with?"

I shake my head.

"We've been here before Jillian. I'm the good guy. If there's anything at all you need help with, we can figure it out."

"Everything's good."

He looks down at papers on his desk and then back up at me. "So, there's nothing going on with you and your aunt that you would care to talk about?"

"Nope. Aunt Steph's good."

"Are you sure about that?"

"Yup."

He lifts a piece of paper and seems to read it. "Was there an incident yesterday that you might have found upsetting?"

"Are you talking about Kyle? About him having to go to a foster home?" I lean forward and force myself to keep my voice calm. "That wasn't Steph's fault. It was...it just happened. There's no way Steph could've known Mrs. Bronigan was going to have a heart attack and she wouldn't be able to pick him up from school."

"How are you feeling about it?"

"I feel bad for Kyle, but Steph is working on getting him back."

Mr. Little says nothing. I bite the inside of my cheek, so I don't ramble on and make things worse for Steph.

"Do you feel safe at home?" He shakes the paper.

"Yes." I take a breath to keep my voice from sounding pissed off. "And Kyle was safe too."

After forever, he finally says, “Okay, but you know we’re here for you. If you need anything, any help at all, please don’t hesitate to stop by and we can work through the issue."

“Thanks.” I stand and head for the door.

“Have a good day, Jillian.”

I want to run out of the school and scream, but I force myself to walk down the hall to Social Studies class. After a quick knock on the door, Mr. Purkis opens it.

“Nice of you to join us.” He waves his hand from me and then to my desk.

I try to ignore the heat crawling up my face as everyone stares while I walk across the room. When the bell finally rings, I rush out to my locker. Maybe cramps might be a good excuse to get out of here.

“Good morning, Jillian.” Mrs. Machuk smiles as she passes.

“Morning.” I keep walking toward my locker.

Barrett puts a hand on my shoulder. “Is everything okay?”

“No, no it’s not.” I stare inside my locker and blink fast. *Worst day ever*.

“Do we need to ditch class?”

I shake my head. “I don’t need more trouble.”

In mostly monosyllabic words, so I don’t get angry, I explain what happened with Kyle and how Mr. Little thinks there are issues at home with Steph and me.

"That sucks," Barrett says. "But you know your aunt. She knows the right people and she'll figure it out and Kyle will be back before you know it." He gives me a side hug.

After school, I sit down to tell Steph what happened on the field trip and her stupid cell phone *dings*.

"Really?" she stares at the screen.

"Really what?" I lift my hands, not sure if she's referring to her phone or me. Machuk wouldn't text her, would she? No way.

"The Abominable had a bunch of snowboards stolen in the past few weeks." Steph waves a picture of them at me. "Another one today."

I stare at her screen and try to maintain a neutral expression. Fuck, Tony. I totally forgot about his board in the garage. And damned if it's not one of the ones in the picture. No wonder he never came back to get it. I thought he just got busy and forgot. But he stole it.

I do him a favour hanging on to it because I'm a nice person. A stupid, nice person. He's not the fun hanging out, chess playing guy I thought he was. He didn't have my back with the booze. I doubt he'll be there for me if I get caught with the board.

"Isn't finding stolen stuff police work?" I say with every attempt to sound bored.

"We all help out—police, wardens, peace officers. It's a small town and with lots of people coming and going, everyone shares info on what's happening. It's a win-win for all agencies."

"Figures," I mumble.

"Pardon?" Steph says.

"Nothing."

"Are any of your friends sporting shiny new boards or bragging about having one?"

"No." I look at her and hope my eyes don't let me down. I pile my books together to go to my room and figure shit out.

"Hey, don't get mad. I'm just asking. I thought maybe you might have heard something at school."

"I didn't."

All the way up the stairs I worry what Steph will do if she finds that board in the garage. I have to get rid of it. When I have a few moments to think, in the quiet of my room, I realize I have to take the board back. Right now.

With my neck tube pulled up to my nose, my hair tucked inside my toque, I put on a bulky coat I seldom wear and glance in the mirror. Incognito, right?

I press my ear against my bedroom door to listen. When I hear the bathroom door close, I rush down the stairs and shout, "Gotta get something from school. Be back in twenty."

"What?" Steph shouts from behind the bathroom door, but I don't stop.

I duck into the garage, wrestle the board out of the cupboard, wrap an old sheet from Oma's gardening stuff around it, and hurry out to the back alley onto Banff Avenue. Outside the Abominable Ski and Board Shop, I glance at my reflection in the glass. *This better work.*

I walk straight to the till.

"I found this." I lay the board on the counter and pull off the sheet while keeping my head down.

"You found this?" the male clerk says. "You just found it?"

I sink my face further into my neck tube. "It was in the alley behind the school."

"What school?"

What are you, the FBI?

"High school." I talk super fast because I see another clerk coming towards us. "It probably fell out of someone's truck, or off their roof rack or something." I turn and walk towards the door.

"Hey, come back here. Wait a minute."

I hear him open the gate to the checkout and walk faster. When I'm out the door, I book it to the corner.

"Wait! Come back here!"

"Not a chance," I mutter and dodge through the stopped traffic waiting for the green light. My chest heaves as I continue to sprint, zigzagging my way back home in case someone follows me. A block from the house I stand behind a dumpster and peek out onto the sidewalk. I watch it for a few minutes while my heart thumps in my ears. No one. Thank God.

Well, that's obvious...the Abominable is now a store I can no longer go into but at least I didn't get caught, Steph won't ever know, and they have their board back. Stupid Tony. Stupid me for trusting stupid Tony.

Chapter 12

"Did you hear about this?" Steph shakes the pages of the newspaper.

I grab a glass of juice. *Don't tell me they wrote about the stolen boards too. Why can't they just let it go?*

"Hear about what?"

"Two young men were lost in an avalanche on Mist Mountain near Frank, Alberta. That's where you were."

"What?" I catch my breath. "What two guys?"

Could it be the ones I met? Herb said they shouldn't go boarding. He said the slope was unstable.

I check the article she's reading. Their pictures smile out at me. Oh, no. It is them. With everything going on about Kyle and then the stupid snowboard thing, I haven't told Steph anything about the trip, including meeting these two guys.

Steph's chair screeches. She jumps up, grabs me, and squeezes me in a bear hug. What the hell is going on with her? She doesn't know that I saw them. That I talked to them before they disappeared in an avalanche. My mind tries to make sense of her reaction and the reality that Herb was right. Being right is not all it's cracked up to be.

"I don't know what I would do if I lost you too," Steph says.

Oh, now I get it.

We both lost Kyle. The guys got lost in an avalanche. I pat her back and endure her suffocating me while the visual of them walking towards the mountain scrolls across my memory. They were maybe in their twenties. Way too young to die. But maybe they're still alive. They could be. People can survive avalanches. As long as they're not buried for too long.

I quit *enduring* Steph's hug and squeeze her back like I don't want her to let go of me. *It's all been a bit much.* When did life get so complicated? For both of us? I feel Steph's response to me hugging her hard and she starts rocking sideways ever so slowly.

The house phone rings and startles us. I pull away from Steph to answer it.

"Hello."

"Jillian? Jillian Meier? Is that you?"

"Yeees." I don't recognize the voice, but she definitely has an Aussie accent. I press the phone harder against my ear. "Who is this?"

Silence.

I watch Steph watch me.

"Jillian, this is," another pause, and then, "this is Greg's mom, Mrs. Patterson. From Australia."

"Mrs. Patterson." I smile. "Hi."

Silence again. Someone coughs and I hear a bunch of muffled voices. *What's going on? Why would she call? Where's Greg?*

"Hello Jillian," a man says, but it's not Greg's voice.

"Hi. Hello. Is Greg there?"

"No. No, he's not." I hear a loud gasp. "I'm sorry. We thought you should know. We know Greg would want us to tell you. He talked about you all the time." A throat clearing.

What's wrong? Why isn't Greg on the phone?

Steph walks up to me. Her eyes are funny, a concerned funny, which freaks me out even more.

"Jillian, Greg was surfing."

"Yup, he told me he was going." I laugh but it's not a ha-ha funny laugh. It's squeaky and nervous. "He told me he was going with a bunch of friends. He was so jacked to hit the waves again."

Nothing.

"Hello?" I say.

"They..." another gasp. "Two of them, they never came back. They found Chris's board but not Greg's. It's been eight days."

My heart sinks when I recall how annoyed I was that Greg didn't send any emails and he missed our video chat on Sunday.

"They've searched everywhere. The ocean is rough right now."

I slide down the wall and press the phone hard against my ear. Steph crouches in front of me and puts her hands on my knees.

"He'll be okay," I whisper.

"I'm sorry. They've done everything. They've looked everywhere. There were riptides in the area, and they have decided to call off the search today. They feel there's no chance they could have survived."

"No, no, no," I mumble.

"I'm so sorry dear. We had to tell you. We didn't want you to hear it from someone else when word gets around to his mates in Banff. We wanted to be sure you heard it from us."

"Uh-huh," is all I can manage to get out between the sobs I swallow.

"You were so important to Greg. Your messages and chats, they kept him going during Suzanne's ordeal. Thank you for being there for him."

I squish my eyes shut.

"We're planning a small family service, but we probably won't have it until July. Maybe we'll have it at one of Greg's favourite spots. We don't know yet. It's still all such a shock."

"Uh-huh," I say again and feel stupid for not being able to make a sentence, but I can't. I feel broken.

"When you're ready, if you want, we'd love it if you would share your stories of Greg with us. I want to give you our number. Do you have a pen and paper?"

"Just a minute." I pull myself off the floor and mime writing on a piece of paper to Steph. She rushes to the office and comes back with a pen and pad of paper. "I'm ready."

Greg's dad spiels out a bunch of numbers and I repeat them, so I know I have them right.

"Goodbye, Jillian."

"Bye."

I hang up the phone.

"What happened?" Steph says, in a soft voice.

"Greg was surfing. With friends. They can't find him." My chest shakes. "They called off the search."

Steph wraps me up in her arms as I sob.

"Oh, Hon," she whispers.

The night runs into the day and then it's dark again. My throat is raw. My eyes burn. The hiccups are fucking exhausting, and they hurt like hell. Steph cooks and makes me eat, and talks quietly, and whispers when she's on the phone.

I'm in a horrible dream. A dream I try to pull out of. But every time I do, I remember it's not a dream. It's real. And the hurt starts again. It's relentless.

At some point, I pull out of the nightmare and there's Mika, sitting on the edge of my bed. I have nothing to say.

Neither does she. The next time I open my eyes, she's gone, and Barrett is there.

"Hey," he says in the quietest voice.

I close my eyes and listen to him punch his fist into his palm. When I wake up, there's no one there. I'm all alone again.

* * *

"I'm sorry," Steph says.

The light blinds me, and I yank the covers over my head.

"I know your heart feels like it's busted. I get it. And telling you you'll get through this is probably unimaginable, but *it will happen*. Now come on. Let's get you out of bed and back into life." Steph tugs my blankets off.

Four days ago, my heart broke and now I can barely feel it at all. I move in auto pilot mode. I shower. Put clothes on. Eat. Walk to school.

"Hey," I hear a quiet Barret voice from behind my locker door. I don't shut the door to see Barrett's face because I'll start to cry. "I'm so sorry, Jillian." My door moves, and I feel Barrett watching me.

I shake my head. "I can't talk. Don't talk." I close my locker, look up at his sad eyes and walk away. I can't do this. I can't have other people be sad too. It's hard enough to deal with my sad. They have to take care of their own.

Everyone except Barrett and the chess club avoids me. I feel people stare at me but when I look up, their heads turn. I get it. *My boyfriend died.* They have no idea what to say. Almost like when Opa died and everyone at school avoided me for days and then it's like they thought I was over losing him, and life was back to normal. But it wasn't. I pretended it was when I was out of the house because it was easier than watching everyone put on sorry faces every time they saw me.

As I debate walking home for lunch to avoid having to go to the lunchroom and see Tony, Derrick grabs my elbow in the hallway.

"Hi." He gives me a solid hug. Right there. In the hallway. In front of all the kids walking by.

I rest my head on his coat's fuzzy collar and squeeze my eyes shut.

"I'm so sorry," he says, then pushes me out at arm's length. "I can't make the hurt go away, but you don't have to be alone with it." He swings an arm over my shoulder and pulls me towards the lunchroom.

We walk in silence. It's nice not to have to talk. Tony and Gary are already playing a game, so Derrick grabs me a chair and sits next to me. And we watch the game. I stare at the top of Tony's head. Jerk ass. I haven't forgiven him for the field trip fiasco, and I haven't told him I brought the snowboard back. I'm not in the mood to discuss either and, from his quick glance at me, I assume he's uncomfortable with me there. Too bad.

School takes forever to end. I step off the curb and head to the elementary school before I remember Kyle won't be waiting for me to pick him up. He's gone too. Not dead gone, but not here with us anymore. Life sucks.

"How'd it go?" Steph pulls a casserole dish out of the oven. Her cooking to overcompensate for stress is becoming a habit and her overcompensating today smells like Shepherd's Pie.

I drop my backpack of missed assignments on the floor. "I got through it."

She flips off the oven mitts, comes over and puts her hands on my shoulders. "I know you won't believe this, but it will get easier."

While we eat, I say, "Any word about Kyle? Mrs. Bronigan?"

Silence.

"Steph?"

"Mrs. Bronigan has a long road to hoe."

"Pardon?"

She puts her fork down. "She can't move her right side and has limited speech. It'll be a long time before she's out of the hospital." She looks down at the table and then at me. "All the physio in the world may not help her get back to where she was before the heart attack."

"Oh no. What about Kyle then? Can he come back to us? Can she vouch for us so he can live here?"

Steph shakes her head.

"That's not fair. It was one mistake. It'll never happen again."

"There is an upside." She gives me a shitty attempt at a fake smile. "He has an aunt. His mom's sister."

It's my turn to shake my head. "Did we know he had one?"

"No. No, we didn't. She and his mom didn't see eye to eye...on a lot of things. Especially childrearing and choice of lifestyles."

"What's she like?"

"She apparently checks all the boxes according to Family Services and is now his temporary guardian."

"Does she live in town? Can we go see him?"

"No and no. She lives in Lloydminster which is six hundred kilometers northeast of here. They don't want us to see Kyle for a while, if at all. It depends on his aunt and how he settles in."

"Do you know how Kyle is? Have they said anything at all?"

"They say he's a super star. He's apparently doing amazingly well considering what's going on in his life."

"Yup, that's Kyle. Roll with whatever shit the world throws at him."

We sigh together.

“Enough of this,” Steph says. “Life has been crappy. Very crappy. I don’t want any more of it happening under this roof.”

“Me either.” I make a note to tell her about the field trip another day since Machuk hasn’t been on my back about it. The upside to a death I suppose.

In my room, I glance at my computer. I want to reread every one of Greg’s emails again, but I don’t need to because I’ve memorized them all. If I do read them, I’ll only end up crying again.

“No more crappy,” I whisper. “Homework. That is sure to cure crappy.” I let out a sarcastic snort laugh, look around the room and am thankful no one heard the noise.

* * *

Just outside the Cascade Mall, after Tony and Gary go through the doors, Derrick stops and turns to me.

“Happy birthday.” He steps in front of me and kisses me. On the lips.

His moustache tickles and for the briefest second, my lips almost return the kiss. But I pull back. What the fuck? *My lips, they’re traitors*. And what the hell is Derrick doing?

He taps his finger under my chin and smiles.

"It's not my birthday," I whisper.

"I know." He winks and walks away.

Like nothing just happened.

I stand on the sidewalk like a dolt. My brain recaps the kiss. It didn't feel like a birthday kiss even though it's nowhere near my birthday. It was a real kiss. A serious kiss. Like it meant something to him. I shake my head. And it sort of felt okay. To me. Definitely not as good as Greg's kisses, but it was okay.

Immediately, my face is on broil and my heart wants to jump out and run away. I miss Greg like crazy every minute of every day. When I'm alone, my heart shatters just thinking about him.

So why did Derrick's kiss feel okay? And why did he kiss me in the first place? My heart is messed up enough. I don't need this.

I force myself to walk through the mall's doors, take the escalator down and join the others at the chess table. Derrick doesn't look up and carries on like he didn't just throw my life into total chaos. I sit and say nothing. It's not like anyone notices because I have been quiet all week. They tolerate it and don't push for me to talk. And honestly, it doesn't even feel uncomfortable to be here. What is that all about?

What is wrong with me?

I hate myself for not stopping Derrick from kissing me. But I had no idea he was going to do that. Even if I had known, I don't know what I would have done but *I should have done something*. Anything. It was wrong. Totally wrong. What would Greg think? And that thought alone crushes my heart. I focus on breathing and stare at the chess pieces. I am so mad at myself. I am the world's worst girlfriend ever.

* * *

"Hi Babe," Derrick's voice whispers through my phone.

"Morning." I'm not sure my answer is a question or statement. I know they all have my number, but he's never called before. And he certainly has *never* called me Babe. Is this about the kiss? I try to sound normal. Not confused or worried. "What's up?"

"Just checking to see what you're wearing."

I look in the mirror. Beige sweater, Khaki pants. Toe socks.

"Clothes."

He laughs. "Are you wearing my favourite colour?"

"Uh, I don't know what your favourite colour is."

"Pink. I like pink. See you at school." *Click*.

What the heck was that about? Creepy? Cute? Is there such a thing as creepy-cute? Personally, I don't like pink. In fact, I don't even own anything pink.

When I get to my locker, Derrick comes over and runs his fingers up the side of my ribs. I pull away.

"I guess your pink cheeks will have to do."

He kisses me. On the lips. Again. The blush heats my face as he leaves to join a group of grade twelve guys. I glance around to make sure no one saw it. Unless they looked away quickly, it seems everyone else is going about their own business and not mine. Thank God.

This is too fast. And much too soon. What's he doing? There is no way he can just step in and take over for Greg. It's not going to happen. I have to tell him to stop kissing me.

As I grab my binder from my locker, there's a solid tap on my back.

"I'll grab the board after school," Tony says.

Crap. I guess I may as well get this over with.

I clench my binder and face him. "No, you won't."

Tony pulls his head back and gives me a puzzled eye expression. "Why not?"

"I took it back to the store." I close my locker.

"What store?" he says.

"The one you stole it from."

"It was my brother's for his girlfriend's birthday, which is today." His eyes squint. "I was hiding it for him so she wouldn't see it. Why would you think I stole it?"

"Because Steph showed me a picture of the boards which were stolen from Abominable."

"Well, your aunt is a misled narc."

"She's not a narc." I glare at him. "She's doing her job."

"Well, she's got the wrong guy." Tony puffs out his chest and crosses his arms. "I didn't steal it."

"If you didn't, then your brother did."

"Why would he steal it?" His voice isn't quite as snarky. "He's got cash."

"Apparently, he didn't use it. It doesn't really matter anymore. Problem solved. Stolen board returned to shop. Done."

"You know he'll beat the shit out of me when I show up without his board. You know that, right?"

"Not my problem." I turn and head to class feeling not nearly as brave as I hope my walking-away-body looks. And I don't want Tony's brother to hurt him, but I also don't want to deal with this ever again.

When Tony doesn't try to catch up, I walk slower. That wasn't so hard, right? Easy-peasy. I clench my fingers together to encourage them to stop shaking. Steph never found out. And now Tony knows. He'll probably never talk to me again. Why do I care? Because I do. I hate it when people are mad at me.

I'm thankful classes go on forever. It makes it easier not to worry about Derrick and Tony.

* * *

There's a tap on my shoulder and I turn so fast I skim my locker door with my cheek.

"Hi Babe," Derrick says.

I close my locker and work my face into a normal glad-to-see-you smile before I turn to him. "Hi."

"There's a dance next Friday. We should go together."

I turn my head to the side a bit so there is no chance of a kissing opportunity while I try to figure out how to say 'no.'

Derrick grabs my hand, lifts it, and kisses my fingers. "Later, Love." And away he walks down the hallway.

What? Whoa. The 'l' word. Shit. No. No. No. This can't happen. None of this can happen. And he can't 'l' me. Not now. Not ever. Love is way more complicated than like *and right now even like is getting complicated.*

"So." Barrett throws his books into his locker. "What was that about?"

"What?" I instantly regret the defensiveness in my tone. "Sorry. What was *what* about?"

He grabs my hand and gives it an exaggerated kiss. “Seems you’ve gotten over Greg awful fast.”

“Stop it.” I slam my locker door and do not regret that people turn and stare.

Barrett’s supposed to be my friend. He’s supposed to be on my side.

I poke him in the chest. “It’s *not* what you think.”

“Really? And what do you think I’m thinking?”

“You think it’s something. It’s not. It’s just...I don’t know what it is but it’s nothing. I *don’t want it* to be anything.”

“Sure.” He pauses then sticks his chin out. “You tell yourself that. I told you before. Derrick’s the marrying kind.”

“Quit it.”

“Don’t say I didn’t warn you.” He slams his locker as hard as I did and walks away.

All the way home I fume about Barrett and then get pissed at Derrick and how he thinks I am into him and just...just kisses me whenever he wants to. I have enough going on right now. I do not need either one of them making assumptions about me which complicates my life.

I pull out my phone and text Mika to see if she’s around for a chat. I need to talk to someone who will be brutally honest and help me work my way through this mess.

A text from her comes back instantly—*Come on over*. Wow. That’s unreal. Mika usually takes days to respond. I turn up the next street and head over to her place.

"Jillian." She grabs me and gives me a solid hug. Totally not a Mika move. "How are you doing? I have wanted to talk to you to see if there's anything I can do to help you...with missing Greg."

I nod. Right. *We haven't had that talk yet.* At first it was too hard to have the conversation about Greg with anyone but Steph and then it was just never the right time. There's nothing like ruining people's good moods with talk about death.

"I'm okay." I say as she pulls me towards her room.

She puts her hands on my shoulders and backs me up until I'm sitting on her bed. Then she brings a chair over, sits down and leans forward like this is an interrogation. It's kind of funny how intense she's being.

"I'm sorry I didn't come over more. I have no excuse. None at all. You didn't reach out and I didn't want to invade your space. I didn't know what the right thing was to do so I stayed away. I'm really sorry."

"Hey, no biggie," I say. "I get it. No one wants to talk about it if they don't have to. It doesn't make it go away for me, but I do get it. You have nothing to be sorry about."

Mika grabs my hands. "How are you?"

I shrug. "I try to be okay. But it's hard and exhausting. It gets all awkward when I...slip up and get sad or cry, so I just avoid it altogether when I'm around people. It makes it easier for everyone. After Kyle and then Greg..."

"Uh-huh, your life kind of blew up."

I sigh. "That's one way of putting it."

"How can I help? I'll do anything. You just have to ask."

"I wish Greg was here." I swallow hard to keep the lump down. "Sometimes it never seems real. Sometimes I know he's going to knock on the door, and we'll be *us* again and...but it won't happen. Ever."

She squeezes my fingers hard and closes her eyes.

"His parents want me to tell them about the things we did together."

"Wow. That won't be easy. How do you feel about telling them?"

"I kind of want to keep him to myself right now, you know, I don't want to share him with anyone. Is that selfish?"

"No. Not at all. You need to deal with it in your own way. Whatever that looks like."

"I'll get back to them, but not yet."

"Give it time." She jiggles my hands. "You'll know when you're ready to talk to them about him."

"Hey," I say. "Change of topic." I give her a quick run-down on the whole Derrick kissing, Babe, 'l' word incidents.

Mika leans back and crosses her arms. "Wow. That's a bit intense. Who *is* this guy?"

"Grade twelve. Barrett says he's the marrying kind and I need to be careful."

"Well." She exhales. "I hate to admit it, but he does read people pretty good."

"I know. And I don't want to go out with Derrick. I'm not ready for that. Yet. Maybe never."

"Well, then, tell him that." Mika puts her hands up like she's stopping traffic. "Tell him it's too soon. Too fast. Thanks, but no thanks. You don't owe him anything so be upfront and be honest."

"That's what I was thinking. I just hate being mean."

She shakes her head. "You're not being mean at all. You're being honest and if he can't take honest, girl, you don't want to be with him even, if and when, the time is right."

After a few seconds of silence, I cuff her on the shoulder. "Enough about whoa-always-me. How are you? How's the gig working at the Information Office? Do you still like it?"

She explodes with enthusiasm about how fabulous her job is and all the doors it's opening for her career. It's a relief to have an energetic conversation about good stuff happening to someone.

Chapter 13

When the house phone rings, I ignore it. It's a bad news phone and I'm not in the mood, so I check out the contents of the fridge for supper options.

Steph shouts as she stomps down the stairs, "You got a piano tied to your ass?" She gives me her do-I-have-to-do-everything-around-this-place grumpy face as she picks up the phone.

"Jillian?" Her face squishes up as if she's trying to figure out who she's talking to. "Yes, she's here. Just a minute please. I'll get her."

She waves the phone in the air as she walks towards me. I lift my hands and mouth, "Who?" She shrugs and hands me the phone.

I stick my tongue out at her before I say, "Hello."

"Hey, Jillian."

I press the phone so hard to my head it digs into my ear. "Greg? Is that you?" My heart stops.

"Yes. Yes, it is." His soft laugh gives me goose bumps. "It's me."

I swallow. Try to breathe. I put my hand on the wall to hold myself up as I stare at

Steph. Her lips move but she doesn't make a sound.

"I can't believe...Greg, it's really you?" I whisper. "I thought you, I thought..."

"I know. Everyone did. But I'm not. I'm here. I'm a whole lot skinnier and hairier but I'm here."

Tears fall and I know my voice shakes. "I can't believe it's you." A sob sneaks out and I put my hand over my mouth.

"I thought about you every day. You got me through this. When I didn't think I had any gas left to get through another hour, I thought about boarding with you, or hiking, even playing Mario Cart." His voice gets quiet. "I thought about kissing you."

So many tears. Solid, happy sobs.

"Hey, it's okay," he says. "I'm okay."

"How?"

"Luck. Pure luck. Someone was watching over us, and you know I don't believe in that malarkey. We ended up a long way from anywhere and Chris was hurt. This hermit of a fisherman found us and took care of us." He stops and is quiet for a few seconds. "It took forever to flag down a chopper, but it doesn't matter now. I can't wait to see you."

"You're coming back? Back to Banff?"

"Of course. It's my forever place and I can't wait to be with you."

"When?"

"A week maybe. The doc wants to do blood work to make sure things are normal and I want a few days with Suzanne and my folks."

Guilt, shame and embarrassment tumble into each other and railroad my initial relief that Greg's not dead. He's alive. And he's coming back.

"Jillian? Are you there? I didn't want to tell you in an email. I thought that might be too bizarre."

"Yeah." I laugh a nervous laugh. "That would've been bizarre."

I hear a guy in the background, call Greg's name.

"I'll be right there, Pop." I hear Greg tell him something, and then he says to me, "I have to say bye for now. Pop and I have a list of things to do for Mom. It is *so* good to hear your voice. Can we video chat on Sunday?"

"Yes, for sure." I blurt out, "I can't wait."

"Me too. Bye, Jillian of Banff."

I listen to the dial tone for a few seconds then hang up the phone.

Steph leans against the counter, arms crossed, unblinking eyes, shaking her head. "He's alive," she says. "That guy's got horseshoes up his ass. His folks have been through hell with him and his sister. They should buy a lottery ticket."

"What?" I stare at her. "Why?"

"Because his sister pulled through getting shot and he's alive when they thought he died. No one saw either of those outcomes."

"I'm sure they'll rush out and buy tickets."

Total happiness tries to ignore the guilt. *How many times has Derrick kissed me? Why didn't I listen to Barrett?*

Steph puts her hands on my shoulders.

"Are you okay?" She squeezes them and I stiffen.

"I can't believe it."

Greg's coming back to Banff. I, me...I helped keep him alive. It's hard to breathe on so many levels while I try to take it all in, everything, at once. Steph pulls me into a hug, stiff at first but then we kind of melt into each other and I don't fight it.

"I am so happy for you," she says in a soft voice.

"Thanks. Right now, I need to...I don't know, take it in, make it real. It is real, right?"

"Yes, it's real."

I head to my room. Once inside I lean against the closed door and the tears start. I gasp as my feet get me to the edge of the bed. Face down, I drop into my pillow. My thoughts flip from all the nights of crying after his folks called. The intense sadness. My heart hurt like it was on fire. Like the hurt would never end. But it did. Faster than I thought it would. I have Steph to thank for that. She made me get up and face the world. And I hate to admit it, so I check around my room quickly to make sure no one can hear my thought, I think Derrick might have helped me get through it too.

Derrick and his kiss in front of the Cascade. Comparing it to Greg's. Actually comparing it, knowing I would never feel a kiss from Greg again. And after Derrick's kiss, I can't remember if I hurt as badly as before the kiss. *I hate that part of it. I hate it.* I know I still missed Greg like crazy but did my heart hurt as badly after?

Barrett was right. I got over Greg too fast.

But not for one second did I think Greg was alive. Not once. I blame Greg's parents. They were the ones who said it's been too long. He couldn't have survived. They were the ones preparing a memorial to say goodbye. If they thought he was gone, why would *I* think differently?

Yes, it's their fault I was not totally freaked out with Derrick's first kiss.

"Stupid," I hiss. Grow up. It's *my* fault. And I'll take care of it. I'll tell Derrick there is nothing going on between us. And there never was. At the time, I just didn't know how to deal with it, how to tell him I was not ready to start something new.

I sit up and swipe the itchiness off my cheeks.

"He's alive," I whisper. "Greg is alive."

And I am the world's worst girlfriend ever.

I'm sure Derrick will understand. Why wouldn't he? It's not like we're officially going out or anything. He just randomly kisses me. I recap the kisses and I know I did not kiss back. That almost takes a tinge of the guilt away—the not kissing him back part.

I have to fix this right away.

My door busts open and Mika and Barrett are there. Huge smiles. I stand and Mika lunges at me and hugs me so hard. Steph obviously told Tom.

"I'm so happy," Mika shrieks.

Barrett stands behind her giving me stink eyes.

I stop my eye roll at him and face Mika. "I can't believe it. I really can't."

"Tell all," Mika says. "How'd it happen? What happened?"

"I don't know much. Something about how a fisherman found them, but he didn't have any way of getting them home. Greg is going to email me the details." I don't tell them he said thinking about me kept him alive, because it makes me want to cry. And because, well, fuck, thoughts of me kept him alive. Like WOW. That's unbloody believable. But I totally don't deserve it.

"When's he coming back?" Mika pulls me out of my pity party.

"In a week maybe." I sigh.

"I have to use your can. Don't say anything until I get back." Mika heads down the hall to the bathroom.

"I told you," Barrett says in a super-serious, quiet voice.

"Stop it. How was I supposed to know?"

"You could have believed in Greg."

"Thanks a lot. Like everyone in Australia thought he was dead, and I should have doubted them?"

Barrett shrugs. "Just saying."

"What'd I miss?" Mika steps back into the room.

"Barrett's being a nob." I laugh to lighten the mood, so she doesn't sense the tension.

"I leave the room for a minute, and you can't be nice?" she says.

By the time they leave, my head hurts. It's all I can do to close my door and fall onto my bed again. It burns to keep my eyes open, but I can't fall asleep when they're closed.

"It'll be okay," I whisper. "I'll make it okay when I see Derrick at school tomorrow."

* * *

Today was the longest day ever at school. Probably because the whole Derrick thing was creating havoc in my head, and I wasn't looking forward to dealing with it. Barrett was also on my case about just *getting it over with.*

And I did try. I watched for Derrick at breaks. He never showed up at noon for chess. I checked the halls all through lunch and after school. But he wasn't around. I even called once but it went straight to voice mail. Leaving that type of message seemed mean and texting also seemed wrong. So, I didn't get a chance to tell him.

What does Mom always say? 'Tomorrow is another day.' I guess tomorrow will be my day to *get it over with.*

After supper, I curl up on the couch and watch TV for a bit before tackling my homework. My cellphone rings. Derrick. Shit. Figures. Just when I think I don't have to deal with it, there he is.

I might as well get it over with right now.

"Hey, Babe. I'm swinging by in five to pick you up." Before I can say anything there's a *click.*

I won't go with him. I'll tell him at the door.

"Who the hell is outside honking their horn?" Steph yells.

Dammit. I run and grab my parka, slip on boots, and say, "Be back in a bit."

"Where are you..."

I close the door before she finishes, then rush down the stairs and out the back gate. With a quick inhale and a mini speech ready, I get in the passenger seat and say, "You weren't at school today?"

Derrick doesn't even look at me. "That is correct."

Before I can say anything else the car pulls away and heads down the back alley. I put on my seatbelt and mumble, "I have a ton of homework. I can't be out long."

He nods as the car bumps over the train tracks, and we head out of town. Lights from the recreation centre flash by.

What's going on? Where are we going? My inside voice panics but my outside voice says nothing while my brain tries to scramble words together to tell him.

Derrick signals and turns off on the Vermillion Lakes Road. Uh-oh. He wants to make out. Oh, no. How do I slip Greg into the conversation when all Derrick wants to do is kiss? Shit. I should have called him. Or texted. I should have said something already. Stupid me. I bite my bottom lip to stop from freaking out.

He pulls into the deserted parking lot at the third lake. The silhouette of Mount Rundle, with a black sky and twinkling stars behind it, shines through the windshield. *The perfect spot to make out if Derrick were Greg.*

Derrick turns the car off, undoes his seat belt, swings his arm over and drapes it against my head rest. He taps my shoulder and when I look at him, his shadowed face looks so serious. Damn. I hate to do this, but I have to tell him. Right now.

As he leans towards me, I say, "Hey, there's something I need to tell you."

Derrick pulls back and lets out this long, slow sigh. "You mean the news that your old boyfriend is alive?"

I nod and realize my smile is super cheesy, but I don't know what expression to use in this awkwardness. "He's coming back to Banff."

Derrick stares at me for a few seconds before he says, "I thought you were different, Jillian. I had no idea you were playing me."

"I wasn't. I'm not..."

He interrupts before I can even finish, "I'm not sitting around pretending to be your boyfriend just so you can punt me when he gets back. You have to pick who you want to be with."

"You're not my boyfriend...we're not..."

"You kissed me." He coils a few strands of my hair around his finger.

"No. No, I didn't." I shake my head and my hair slips out of his grasp. "*You* kissed me."

"You liked it. I could tell."

What do I say? 'Yeah, I kind of did like it, but only for a second until I had a reality check. Then it was not okay.'

We watch each other in silence as I try to figure out what to say to make this right. To get us back to being just friends. If that's even possible.

"Were you going to tell me he's coming back?" He taps my shoulder. "Or were you going to let the school whisper about what an idiot I am?"

Before I can even answer, he continues with, "So, I'm out? He's in? Is that the deal?"

What the hell? You were never in. You made all the moves. And they surprised me. Yes, I should have said something, but I didn't want to be mean. I don't want to be mean. *Mika said be honest. Just be honest.*

"Thanks. Thanks a lot." Derrick's voice is so quiet. "Here I was being nice to you because you were so sad, and this is what I get for it?"

"I *am* sorry." I take a deep breath and pull my chin up so I can look right at his eyes. *It takes a lot to be this honest.* "I should have said something right away. My bad. I should have told you to stop..."

"In all honesty Jillian, I don't think you wanted me to stop, did you?" he says.

"Yes. Yes, I really did. I just didn't know how to tell you."

He rests his hand on my shoulder, and I pull away from it.

"Are you *positive* you want to be with him and not me?" He points at himself. "Because if you change your mind after, I will not be sitting around waiting for you."

Trust me, I do not want you sitting around waiting for me. Ever.

I stare out at the dark trees and twinkling stars. *Why is he making this into such a huge deal? He is the only one who thought we were a thing.* We're not a thing. Barrett was right. Derrick is the marrying type.

"I really like you, Jillian." He drops his head and shakes it. "I thought we were good together. I thought you liked me."

"I like you as a friend. That's all." I grab the door handle and get out of the car. I don't want to be a part of Derrick's sad. I want to be happy. Greg is alive. That's my happy. Not this. Whatever this is.

"Come on, don't do that. Get back in the car. I'll drive you home."

"No. I'm good. I need air. I'll walk."

"Jillian don't be stupid. It's dark. Get in the car."

I lean inside. "I'm okay. Really. It's not far." I shut the door and start to walk. Shit. It *is* dark. Really dark. Maybe this isn't my smartest moment.

The car's headlights flick off and on.

"Jillian." I hear him call but keep walking. "Suit yourself." A bit of gravel spits out as he pulls away.

I stare at the tail lights, pull my coat tight and curse the fact I didn't bring gloves. I shove my hands in my pockets and press my arms against my sides. If I walk fast, I'll get home sooner and keep warm.

The sky is humungous with zillions of pin prick stars, some brighter, some blinking, some ever so slowly, moving. There's a hue of light above town that filters across the base of Mount Rundle. Not really light pollution. It looks almost magical. Unfortunately, nothing else feels magical right now.

In the dark, Rundle's iconic shape is more defined than in daylight. How many people take pictures of it? Are there more pictures of Mount Rundle than Cascade Mountain? I shake my head. Sometimes the stuff my brain comes up with makes me wonder who I am.

As I round the corner to the second lake, a shadow moves across the aspen trunks near the edge of the road. It can't be a bear. They're sleeping. It's not big enough for a moose—thank God, because I don't know how to react to a moose encounter. I cross the road and scan the trees to find a good one to climb in case I need it.

And there he is. The husky. The look alike to Dog. Again.

"What're you doing here?" Saying it out loud makes me feel in control.

The husky moves onto the road across from me and walks in the same direction but doesn't even glance my way. It does make me feel less alone but now the creep factor heightens. The last time I saw him was when I met those two guys in Lille. The ones who went missing in the avalanche. Is he foreshadowing my demise? No. He can't be. I've seen him quite a few times and I've never woken up dead.

"Are you with Oma? Opa?" I feel silly saying it out loud but what the hell. It's not like anyone can hear me or that I'll get an answer back. "Thanks for the company."

The ice on the second lake is glazed black and shimmers. It would be good skating ice if I was in a skating mood. I chuckle at my sarcasm. The husky keeps his distance and moves along at my pace.

"Thanks," I say again.

Headlights blind me. I step into the ditch and put my arm above my head to block the glare. Please don't be Derrick. I can't do sad Derrick again. And please don't be a crazy person. I step further into the shadows.

"Jillian!" The truck's passenger window rolls down. "Get in the truck. Now."

Yikes. I'm not sure if wandering out here alone is better than getting in the truck with a mad Steph. *How did she know where I was? Did she put a tracker app on my phone?* I debate asking her, but she looks too pissed to push that button. I'll check my phone later.

The truck whips a U-turn and I press into the door. The only noise comes from the motor and the tires on the gravel. She says nothing, which is worse than yelling. At the house we get out and I follow her inside.

In the kitchen, she says, "What happened? Why did you get out of Derrick's car?"

Well, that explains how she knew where I was. *Cancel checking my phone for the tracker app.*

How do I make this less painful? *For me.* I squeeze the back of the kitchen chair while I think of what to say.

"Have you totally lost your mind?" Steph marches to the fridge and grabs a beer. "It's dark. There are lunatics everywhere. Why would you do something so irresponsible?"

"He found out about Greg," I say.

"What do you mean, he found out? What's the big deal?"

"He used the 'l' word a few days ago."

"The 'l' word?" Steph gives me a confused look.

I open my eyes wide like *come on Steph don't be so dumb* and mouth love.

"Oh. That word. He used it in relationship to him and you?" She twists the beer cap off.

I nod.

"Yes, I guess that could make it a bit prickly."

"A bit prickly?" I snort.

"I didn't know you were going out with him."

"I'm not. I wasn't going out with him. Or anyone."

She takes a long swallow, sets the bottle on the table, and says, "Then, again, I have to ask, what's the big deal?"

"He thought we were a thing."

"You should have told him to back off."

"Right." I roll my eyes. "Because that's so easy to do."

"When Derrick came by, he told me you wouldn't get back in his car. What was that about?"

"I didn't think the whole thing through. I knew it was stupid as soon as he drove away."

"So? Why did you get out of the car?"

I close my eyes for a second and then open them and say, "It got awkward trying to convince him there was nothing going on with us when he thought there was."

Steph points at me. "Did he try anything?"

"No." I shake my head. "No, nothing like that. He was just sad, and it was my fault so I thought it would be easier to walk home than stay in the car."

"Don't do it again." Steph takes her beer and marches up the stairs.

That's it? That's all? I totally expected a bigger scene with some yelling. Why is she letting me off so easy?

* * *

My feet slow down as I get closer to school. I miss Kyle. I miss his seven-year-old chill outlook on life. Even though his life has been shitty, he still smiles, and I could use his optimistic attitude right now. I have no idea what Derrick will say to people. I shouldn't care but I do. And I don't know how to act if I see him.

Greg cannot get back to town soon enough, so I have something to smile about.

On my way to class, someone taps my shoulder.

"What's up Barr..." I turn around. It's not Barrett.

Holy crap. Tony's eye is swollen shut and his bottom lip is purple and cracked.

"What the hell?" I know my eyes are huge.

"I told you. Big brother was not happy. I hope you are." He turns and disappears into the crowd.

No. No. Shit. Tony was telling the truth when he said his stepbrother would beat the crap out of him if he showed up without the snowboard. I thought he was joking. Being a jerk. His face must hurt like hell. I feel awful. I didn't return the board so he'd get beat up, I did it so I wouldn't get caught with it. I'm glad Steph stopped going out with his stepbrother. He sounds like a piece of work. Poor Tony.

This day can only get better.

As I walk towards class, I convince myself I did the right thing. I took the board back. Between Derrick and Tony being pissed at me, I will not be joining the chess club at noon.

"Jillian." Mrs. Machuk flags me down as I head into Social Studies class.

Shit. I haven't told Steph yet about the Frank thing.

"I'm expecting a call from your aunt." She hands me a slip of paper. "I know she works all day, so here's my cell number."

"Sure. Thanks."

"There's a field trip to the Glenbow Museum in Calgary in a few weeks." She hands me another piece of paper. "Pull up your socks and you can come along. I think you'd enjoy it. It'll have a display about the Crowsnest Pass and Frank Slide disaster."

Pull up my socks from where? I glance at the paper so she cannot see my face's response to her expression.

"Let me know if you're interested in coming." She walks away.

I have to tell Steph tonight but maybe I can soften the blow with this—tell her even though I screwed up the teacher invited me to go on another field trip. I'll start with the bad news, and then slip in the good news. That might work. Hopefully.

"Where are you going?" Barrett calls, as I head out the front doors of the school.

"So, you're talking to me now?"

He swings an arm over my shoulder. "I figured you could use a friend."

"You have no idea." There's something about Barrett that when he's around things seem a bit better even when they aren't. "Want sandwiches for lunch?"

"You bet."

While I dig through the fridge for fixings, Barrett grabs plates and glasses.

"Grilled cheese?" I wave plastic-wrapped cheese slices in the air.

"Sure. Hey, we need to plan a big shindig for Greg when he gets back."

"I don't know any of his friends. Besides, do you think he'd want a big thing? Or do you think he'd want just an *us* thing?"

As we dip our sandwiches in ketchup, we discuss our welcome home options and I realize it's been forever since Barrett and I have hung out. How'd I get so caught up in the chess club? Oh, right. Barrett. New Year's Eve. That was the start of it. And then we never went back to normal, even after he told me what happened. *Life's funny.*

* * *

When I hear Steph's truck door slam, I put the garlic toast in the oven to broil and take the lid off the pot of leftover chili.

"What's cooking?" she calls from the back porch.

"Leftovers."

"Good smelling leftovers." She glances at the set table and then at me. "What's going on? What happened?" Her eyes squint.

"Nothing. I just thought I'd have supper ready for you."

She shakes her head. "Nope, something's up. What happened?"

"I can't even do a nice thing and you think I'm in trouble?"

Hands on hips, she says, "Tell me first. Then I'll eat."

Seriously? I'm that easy to read?

"Fine." I pull the browned toast out of the oven. "There was this incident on the field trip."

I give a brief rundown of what happened, leaving out names. Facts only. Steph's expression remains expressionless. I could be giving her a weather report. When I'm done, I tell her she needs to call Mrs. Machuk. Steph fills a bowl with chili, grabs a piece of toast and sits down.

"I don't think she's mad at me anymore," I say, to break the quiet. "She asked if I wanted to go to the Glenbow Museum on another field trip."

"What's her number?"

"Pardon?"

"I have to call her. What's her number?"

"I'll get it." I run up to my room. I'll never figure Steph out. No yelling again. Not even a lecture. Nothing. *Does that mean she's mad at me? Done with me? Doesn't care?* Or what if she's adding up my misadventures to decide about Waterton? I can't believe I haven't thought about her job offer in a long time.

"Here." I pass her the slip of paper.

She waves it in the air. "Is there anything else I should know before I call?"

"No." I shake my head. "Nothing."

"Good. I don't want any surprises." She heads to the office and closes the door.

Wow. That was too easy. She must be distracted. She hasn't mentioned Kyle in a few days. I sure hope the whole Frank fiasco doesn't chalk up points against me to make moving seem more appealing to her. There's been no job offer discussion and now that I think about it, Tom hasn't been at the house in over a week. I glance at Bucky.

“Did Steph and Tom break up?” I whisper. No response. Bucky doesn’t even lift his head. “Not helpful at all.”

Chapter 14

"Greg," I say as I reach out and touch the monitor.

Sweetest smile ever.

"Hey," he says.

We stare at each other for a few seconds as my stomach does flips. I still can't believe he's alive.

"How's things?" he says.

"Good. The real question is, how are *you*? Holy moly. How? What happened?" My words blurt out.

"It was pretty much a miracle. We tried to keep the group together, but the waves got too wild, and I lost sight of my mates and had to focus on keeping myself going. I crashed into the shore but not the shore we took off from. I thought I was alone, but I found Chris down a ways on the beach. She was in rough shape. A broken leg and arm and beat up pretty badly." He takes a big breath. "Then the weather turned to crap. It was hard to stay dry and there was no way to get any attention from boats or planes."

I am so glad I know the story has a happy ending but the details to get there are frightening. *And is this the same Chris who is his old friend from school?* The one helping him out at the hospital with Suzanne?

"We were lucky. That's all I can chalk it up to. I lost count of the days. Pretty much lost count of getting off the island until I spotted this old fishing boat." He laughs. "I got his attention by waving and screaming. He picked us up and took us to his side of the island. The fella lived off the grid. No communication with the outside world. He fed us for days until we were able to flag down a chopper." Greg sighs and closes his eyes for a few seconds. When he opens them, he says, "Enough about me. Tell me what you've been up to."

"In comparison, nothing much." I give him a quick rundown of the field trip, minus the incident, and finish off with a low-key version of why Kyle is not here anymore. "How's Suzanne? Your folks?"

"They said we've given them enough gray hair to last a lifetime. Suzanne can get around with a walker. The physio saps her strength, but she toughs it out. She will be months in rehab, but she's got this. Mom and Pop are catching up with each other and just enjoying day to day stuff again." He nods. "It's been a rough go. But hang on, I have a news flash. I booked a flight."

"What? No way. When?"

"It'll be a surprise."

"No, come on. You can't do that. I can't wait to see you."

“Soon.” He winks, puts his fingers to his lips, and taps the screen.

“You brat.”

“See you in Banff, Jillian.”

I tap my monitor. “I can’t wait.” And the screen goes black.

When is soon? How soon is soon? *Best news day ever.*

* * *

The days blur into each other with school. Barrett seems as excited as me for Greg to get back. It’s pretty cute. I’m not sure why I don’t let myself get totally caught up in his enthusiasm. Maybe it has a bit to do with this overwhelming feeling of dread which creeps in once in a while and I have to shut it off or I find myself heading down the sad rabbit hole of losing Greg again. I mean, how is he going to feel when I tell him about Derrick? Does it count as cheating because I didn’t put a stop to it right away? What if he says goodbye because of it?

When I get myself so wound up, I literally have to stop what I’m doing, and think of something else to get into a better head space.

Maybe that is why I keep my emotion meter in check—so the fall won’t hurt as much if it happens. Silly maybe. I don’t know. The endless nights of tears are still vivid. Maybe it's a new superpower. My protective layer to keep the hurt out if it's incoming. And the reality that at some point I do have to tell him about Derrick.

I cringe. How do I even start a conversation about it…'you know when everyone thought you were dead? I kind of sort of let this guy kiss me…a few times, but when I found out you were alive, I told him he had to stop.' The fact I hung around with him, embarrasses me now that I know what he was after. At the time though, it was nice not to be alone.

One thing at a time. Let Greg get home first.

"You're not going to school today," Steph says. "Go put something fancy on and be ready to leave in twenty minutes."

"What?" I pull my head back. "Who are you and what have you done with Steph?"

She puts her hands on my shoulders, turns me towards the stairs and says, "Go."

"Greg's coming today?" I squeal.

"Maybe," she drawls.

I screech, as I race up the stairs and rip my closet open. Fuzzy sweater. Skinny jeans. Messy pony. Lip gloss. I jiggle his bracelet on my wrist and screech again.

Barrett and Mika are standing in the back porch when I step into the kitchen. I glance at Steph, who waves her keys in the air.

"There's more room for all of you in my truck." She tosses the keys to Barrett. "And there will be no eating in my vehicle," she calls out as we race out the back gate.

"Shotgun," Mika shouts.

I cringe at the expression but only because of Suzanne and I know Mika didn't say it for any other reason than that's what you say when you want the front passenger seat. I shake the words off and climb into the backseat. My heart thumps. I run my tongue across my teeth. Yes, they're brushed.

"Why am I the last to know?" I tap their shoulders.

Mika turns around. "Greg wanted to surprise you. He planned the whole thing with Steph."

"No way." I push back in the seat. "Steph was in on this?"

Mika gives me an uber-smile and faces the front again. The music blasts and even though it's country, I do not care. We're off to the Calgary airport. The mountains disappear and the Morley Flats take over the landscape as the kilometers click away and we get closer to the city.

Mika and I duck as Barrett pulls into the underground parking at the airport. How does he know how high the truck is? It must be a guy thing because the roof doesn't scrape the concrete ceiling.

The three of us line up against the half wall that separates us from the international travellers coming from customs. My eyes hurt from staring because I don't want to miss seeing him. There are so many people.

So many colours of jackets. Hats and hairdos. Suitcases on trollies. And a lot of suntans.

And there he is. With his huge red backpack on. That's what I see first in the crowd, the backpack.

"Greg!" I jump up and down and wave.

Mika and Barrett join in. Greg sees us and I see that smile, his smile—my heart melts. The three of us work our way through other excited people waiting for their arrivals. I dodge them but do not lose sight of Greg.

He is so tanned. A bit thinner. And his longer hair bounces as he walks faster. In a flash, I am in his hug. I can't get my arms around him because of the pack so I tuck them in front of me. He pulls me out of the people traffic towards a wall, lifts my chin and my heart stops. The world stops. All the tough stuff of the last few months disappears. The warmth. The softness. The quiet intensity of his kiss. My body sighs. I'm lucky he holds me up. When it's over I bury my face in the collar of his jacket to catch my breath.

"Bro," Barrett shouts and thumps Greg's pack. "Missed you, buddy."

Barrett pushes me aside, grabs Greg's hand, lifts it to do a manshake, combined with a shoulder bump. I glance at Mika, who's mouth is a perfect O, and her eyes are as big as owl's. She nods her head ever so slightly at me and gives me the cutest grin.

"What?" I lift my hands at her while Greg and Barrett wrestle with who's carrying what.

"That was *some* kiss," Mika whispers as she passes me to give Greg a hug.

Barrett pulls the suitcase and he and Mika lead the way through the crowd to the parking lot. Greg swings an arm over my shoulder and pulls me in tightly. I look up. He kisses my forehead. Perma-grin on my face.

"It is so good to be back," he says as we head outside.

Barrett turns the radio off and both he and Mika fire questions at Greg about the flight, the weather in Australia, his sister and the surfing incident. Greg answers every question. I sit next to him, content to listen. It seems like forever ago, and just yesterday, that he was here. He's been through so much. Around the Nakiska Ski Resort turnoff, almost halfway home, Greg's head bobs and he blinks to stay awake. I put my jacket on my shoulder and pull his head onto it.

"Thanks," he mumbles and closes his eyes.

I tap Mika's shoulder. When she turns around, I point to sleeping Greg.

She mouths, "Okay," and turns the radio on, but not as loud as it was on our trip into Calgary.

The smooth ice on Lac des Arcs shimmers as the dome of the cement plant behind it gives the view an unnatural industrial look against the mountainous background. I can never figure out why people pull off at the viewpoint to take pictures. The massive concrete structures obscure the views of the mountains, yet even today, people lean over the railing with their iPhones taking selfies. Wait until they see what the Rockies are really all about.

"You might want to wake him up," Barrett says as we slow down to enter Banff's townsite.

"Hey, sleepyhead." I tap his cheek. "Time to wake up."

Greg lurches forward and pushes his arms out in front of him.

"Whoa. Sorry about that." He rubs his eyes. "I didn't mean to fall asleep."

"You've been on a plane forever and the eighteen-hour time difference might do it to you." Barrett laughs. "Should we go to your place and dump off your stuff?"

"Sure." Greg grabs my hand and squeezes it. "I want to see if my car will start."

When Barrett parks at the staff accommodations, Greg sighs.

I tap his arm. "Are you okay?"

"Yup. I've never been better." He gets out, stretches and walks over to his car. When he starts it, all we hear is a *click*.

"I'll give you a boost." Barrett gets back in Steph's truck and pulls in front of the car while Greg brushes the snow off.

"We can take your stuff into your room," I say, since I don't have car boosting talents.

Greg gives me his key and Mika and I wrestle the heavy backpack and suitcase up the stairs. His room is relatively tidy considering he left in such a rush. The blankets are on the bed but they're not straight, the floor is bare, but books and papers are stacked in unruly piles. I glance at the climbing and snowboarding posters in his cozy man cave and lean his pack against the bed.

"I *am* super jealous," Mika says.

"About what?" I look around the room. "This?"

"No." She smacks my arm. "About that kiss. At the airport."

"You're jealous because *you* wanted to kiss Greg?" I step back and give her a suspicious eye stare.

"No. Don't be stupid. I'm jealous of the kiss you guys had."

"Okay. I give up. You and Barrett kiss all the time. What's the big deal?"

"We don't kiss that way, ever. That was an 'in love' kiss."

"No, it wasn't. It was a 'happy to see you' kiss. An 'in like' kiss."

"No way." Mika shakes her head. "Nope. Do not let that kiss get you into trouble."

"Stop it."

"I'm serious.

"Would you quit already." I put my hands over my face. "You sound like a mom."

"The car is officially operational," Barrett calls out as they come into the room. "I've got to switch trucks with Steph and get to work. Do you want a ride home, Jillian?"

Wow. Perfect timing. *Gosh, Mika.* I give her an eye roll. What the heck was that about? Who does she think I am? Maybe she and Steph are in cahoots to make sure I don't become a pregnant teen statistic.

"I can take Jillian back," Greg says.

"Right. Later." Barrett and Greg do their bro hug.

"Glad to have you back." Mika gives him a typical 'Mika hug' and they're gone.

I pull the suitcase beside his pack while Greg stands at the door and checks out his room. It's quiet. I follow his eyes, wondering what he's thinking.

"There were hours, even days, I thought I would never see this place again."

I don't know what to say so I continue to watch him take in the room. He walks over, pulls me into a hug and rests his chin on my head. Even though he's been enroute for over twenty-four hours, he smells so good.

"And there were times I never thought I'd see you again," he says.

He pushes me back and we're kissing. Calm. Quiet. My whole body sighs. Happy to be here with him. When it's over I press my cheek against his chest and the world feels perfect.

"I better get you home before your aunt gets ideas we're up to something."

"What?" I pull away and give him a puzzled look. "Why would she do that?"

"We're here." He points at his bed. "Alone together. I don't want to do anything to get you in trouble with Steph *or* get myself in her bad books."

"She's not so tough." I laugh.

"Oh, yes she is." He puts his arm around my shoulder, and we head out to his car.

"Greg, my man." A guy carrying a snowboard thumps up to us in his heavy boots, leans the board on the hallway wall and grabs Greg. They spin in a crazy circle laughing. "So good to have you back. Work's been nuts. We need you, man. We need you bad."

"Thanks, Ty. The boss said I can have tomorrow off and then it's back at it."

"Great. See you then. Later, Jillian." He waves, grabs his board and is off.

I point at him. "I think I might have met him on Norquay."

"Probably. When he's not ice climbing, he's boarding."

Bucky goes nuts when we step into the back porch. Nuts for Greg. Not for me. What a traitor. Greg wrestles with him a bit before he pushes his butt outside.

"Pizza is almost ready. Greg," Steph comes over and gives him a hug, "it is so good to have you back in one piece."

Through supper, Steph grills Greg with almost the same questions as Mika and Barrett did on the drive home. They chat away as if I'm not there. It's funny in the sense I've never been sure how Steph feels about Greg. But then she was in on the whole surprise of picking him up. She even let us use her truck. And now she's being uber-sociable with him. Cool.

"I'm knackered," Greg says as he pushes back from the table.

"Go turn on the TV and relax. You've had a day of it. Jillian and I will tidy up."

I want to say, '*we will?*', but she's got an odd tone in her voice, so I don't. Greg heads to the living room.

"Now that you two are official, we need to chat." Steph leans against the counter. "I don't want..."

"Shhh," I cut her off, tiptoe to the hall, and see Greg's feet hanging over the edge of the couch. Thank God he didn't hear that. I go back to Steph. "We don't need to chat. I'm good."

"I'm sorry but yes, we do need to talk."

"Look, quit worrying," I whisper. "Nothing will happen."

"Yup, that's exactly what I thought. I also thought I knew it all, but it does happen, and the consequences last a lifetime."

"Tell me about it." I sock her in the shoulder to lighten her serious expression. "It's also not genetic so it won't happen to me just because it happened to you."

"That's not funny."

"It kind of is. Relax."

She crosses her arms. "I'll go to the doctor with you if you want to go on the pill or get some contraceptive advice."

I put my hands over my ears. "Stop. I'm not twelve. I can take care of myself."

"Your Oma wasn't receptive to this type of conversation. She preferred to 'put her head in the sand'."

"Stop talking about Oma like that."

"I'm being honest with you because I want you to have the most amazing future, the best opportunities for education, and I want you to be able to explore the world without any baggage."

"Oh, so now I'm baggage?" I give her an expression feigning comical surprise. "Thanks."

"That's not what I meant, and you know it. Think about it. I'm here for you, always." She grabs my shoulders. "You know that, right?"

"Yes, and sometimes it's kind of annoying."

"Good." She heads upstairs.

After I shake off the gross feeling of almost having *that* conversation with Steph, I go to join Greg. The TV is on. He's snoring. Quiet snoring, but snoring nonetheless. Poor guy. I grab a blanket and put it over him. He doesn't flinch or budge. Oh well, tomorrow we can catch up. For now, he's here. He's back in Banff. And I couldn't be happier.

I lock the back door and turn off the downstairs' lights. One last peek at Greg and I head upstairs to knock on Steph's door.

"Yes."

"Hey." I open her door a crack. "Greg fell asleep on the couch. I don't want to wake him up. So," I point down the hall, "I'm going to my room. You don't have to stand guard. I will not go back downstairs."

"Promise?"

I scrunch my eyebrows. "Seriously? You're making me promise?"

"Yes."

"I promise." I almost shut her door too hard but catch it just in time.

No more checking my computer to see how Greg is. Lucky me.

* * *

My alarm goes off and I groan. And then I remember Greg is on the couch. I get ready for school and rush downstairs. Before the last few steps, I hear voices and stop. Greg and Steph are in the kitchen. Talking. Oh, my God. She wouldn't. I hurry into the room.

"Morning." I smile at Greg to avoid giving Steph the look. "How'd you sleep?"

He comes over and puts his hands on my shoulders. "I'm sorry I crashed."

"No problem." I grin at his messy hair and uber-adorable smile. "You were in transit for a whole day."

"Greg, here," Steph interrupts, "asked if he could take you to Skoki on a ski trip in a few weeks. He's apparently been planning it for a while."

"Where's Skoki?" I grab a coffee.

"It's this back country lodge behind the Lake Louise Ski Resort," Greg says. "We'll splitboard in, carve turns down Deception Pass, and stay overnight in the dorm rooms. The place is awesome. Out of this world phenomenal."

"Cool your jets." I cringe at Steph's aggressive tone. "I told him I'll castrate him with a rusty tin can lid and pour salt on his genitals if he tries any hanky-panky."

I lift my hands to my face as the heat runs across my cheeks. *God, Steph. Why do you think I'm going to be a pregnant teen like you were?* I peek through my fingers at her. "You really did just say that didn't you?"

"She did and I'm pretty sure she means it." Greg laughs. "I've got to go back to my place. I need to hit the shower and then catch up with my boss to see what I've missed."

"Yeah, for sure." Bucky and I walk him to the back door. "Catch you later?"

"I have to see how the day goes. I may need to hustle a few ski trips to catch up on bills. I'll text you." He leans in. A quick kiss. And he's gone.

Bucky rushes around the corner of the house as I watch Greg walk out the back gate to his car. It gives me a few minutes to let the kiss subside before I have to face Steph.

With a bowl of cereal in hand, I join her at the table.

"You be careful, okay?" She waves the butter knife at me.

"Stop. It's too early."

The house phone rings, and we stare at it. It's still the bad news, good news phone and we are both a bit afraid of it. On the third ring I scowl at Steph and get up.

"Jillian?" a lady asks.

"Yes, this is Jillian." I don't recognize her voice.

Steph stares at me.

"This is Sensei Geri. I hope you don't mind but I got this number from Kyle's registration sheet."

"Okay." I lift a hand in the air at Steph. Maybe Sensei knows something about Kyle.

"I was wondering if you'd be interested in helping me out with classes on Tuesday and Thursday nights. I would pay you fifteen dollars an hour. We have more tournaments coming up and I could use an extra person to help the class get ready for them."

"Can you please hold on for a minute so I can ask my Aunt Steph?"

"Of course."

I cover the mouthpiece and tell Steph.

"I don't see why not," she says. "As long as it doesn't affect your schoolwork."

I roll my eyes at her. Seriously? What does my life consist of? School work. Forever. And now Greg too. I can handle it. Besides, it'll be nice to have cash, so I don't have to ask Steph for money all the time.

"Yes, I can," I say to Sensei.

"That's great. I'll see you at six forty-five tonight. I have a Gi I think will fit you. Have a good day."

Click.

I stare at the phone.

"Wow. That's kind of an honour, isn't it?" Steph says. "To have a Sensei ask you to help teach?"

"Yup, it is. It's a huge honour." I glance at the cuckoo clock. "I have to get going."

"I'm going into Calgary after work to see Mrs. Bronigan. I was going to see if you wanted to come but I guess you'll be kicking butt." She feigns a poor front kick.

"That's sad." I point at her leg. "You need to lift your knee up first, then pop out the ball of your foot to penetrate the kick." I demonstrate the proper way.

"Look at you, a mini sensei."

Bucky whines at the back door and Steph lets him in. His snowy face indicates he attempted to snuff out sleeping mice. Steph grabs an old towel and tussles with him to dry him off.

"Do you know how Mrs. Bronigan is doing?"

"I talked to one of her nurses the other day." She hangs the towel over the sink.

"Poor Mrs. Bronigan hasn't had any visitors at all. They say she's bedridden. I thought I'd bring flowers to cheer her up."

"Does she know about Kyle?"

"I don't know and if she does, I'm not sure how much she'd retain. The nurse said her short-term memory is somewhat scattered."

"Say hi for me."

"I will." Steph shakes a finger at me. "Trust me, we will be talking about Skoki before you go on the trip."

"Stop it."

Chapter 15

The walk to school feels easy today. Like the world doesn't weigh so much anymore. Except for Kyle not being here, life is good. It's really good. As long as Steph lays off lecturing about Greg and me doing *it*, life will only get better.

"Jillian." Mrs. Machuk waves at me from down the hall.

Uh-oh. Steph said she called her, but she never said anything about the conversation. She didn't get mad at me, so I assumed their chat was amiable. I didn't push Steph for details in case she'd already filed it in her non-issue category. There is no point upsetting her now that Greg is back. It would only affect my personal time with him. Besides, Machuk would enlighten me if there was anything more I need to do to get past the incident. *Right?*

So, why does she want to talk to me now?

Wait a minute. What if Steph said something derogatory to her? Did she get me into more trouble by yelling at Machuk like she did at the Family Services lady about Kyle? Different situation. She wouldn't yell at my teacher. Would she? My brain runs mini scenarios as I get closer to Mrs. Machuk.

"I got an email from Afton, from the Frank Interpretive Centre," she says. "She asked if she could get your contact info to get in touch with you to send you an application link."

"Oh, okay." Phew. That was painless. I rip out a sheet of paper and put my email and phone number down and hand it to her.

"Thanks." She folds the paper in half. "Are you looking at a summer job there?"

"I'd thought about it." I don't mention that there is *no way* I'm leaving Banff now that Greg's back.

"It would be a great opportunity." She taps the paper in her hand. "Oh, you haven't signed up for the Glenbow trip yet. Did you plan on coming?"

"Yes. Right. I'll get to that."

"Great." She turns and heads to her class.

"Yo." Barrett hip checks me. "We should go boarding Saturday. The four of us, like old times. Sunshine Resort is getting pounded with snow."

"I don't know. Greg has to figure stuff out about his job."

"My man would not turn down an opportunity to board in champagne powder, trust me." Barrett grins like a huge goof and then winks. "I'll mention it to him."

"You do that." I say to the back of his head as he walks away. Honing in on my time with Greg. What a guy.

Oh, crap. Derrick is coming towards me. It's the first time I've seen him since the Vermillion Lakes night. I can't hide. That would be too obvious. Besides, why should I? I pull my shoulders back and keep walking. As he gets closer, his lips turn into a slight smile. Panic sets in. What's he up to? He puts two fingers to his temple, does sort of a salute, and passes on by. Well, wasn't that easy? Possibly I make a bigger deal out of things that aren't that big a deal.

"You missed the pop quiz yesterday." Mr. Purkis puts a sheet on my desk. "I want it back by tomorrow. I trust you not to check resources while you answer the questions. I'm sure you'll ace it."

Damn. It figures the one day I skip, he'd spring a test on the class. I tuck it inside my textbook.

When school finally ends, I check my phone. A message from Greg—*Working late. You free tomorrow night?* Well, that's disappointing but not a surprise. Karate class will make the evening pass quicker.

I text Greg back—*You bet.*

I stare at the screen for a few seconds, waiting for his response, until I realize chances are pretty good he's not sitting around waiting for messages to pop up on his phone. Gosh. Will I figure out this boyfriend-girlfriend thing sooner, rather than later?

Wow. I catch my breath. *It's the first time I've called us boyfriend-girlfriend.*

* * *

"Sensei." I put my arms straight down my sides and bow at the waist.

"I'm glad you can help out." She hands me a stiff white Gi and a white belt.

Ouch. That hurts my ego a smidge. I was a blue belt at my dojo in Toronto.

"Go get changed and then we'll run through what I have planned for tonight."

"Yes, Sensei." I bow again and then head to the change room.

The uniform fits baggy and loose like all Gis. After two tries I finally get the stiff belt tied properly. It feels weird being here without Kyle. I hope he gets to keep up his karate in Lloyd-where-ever he is.

The kids come into the gym as Sensei walks me through the drills and katas she has planned for the night.

"If you can, walk up and down the rows, help anyone with their foot positions, their arms, and their body posture." While she talks, she drops into front stance and then a back stance, running her arms down her body, pointing to her legs. "Be tough on them. No smiling."

"Yes, Sensei."

"Good. Thank you."

"Jillian," a few kids call out. "Where's Kyle?"

I didn't expect them to ask, which is dumb, because of course they would. Kyle and I always came together.

"He's not in Banff right now," I say. "So, he can't be here."

"Where'd he go?"

"Lines," Sensei calls.

Totally saved by the sensei.

I do the warm-up drills with the rest of the class and then Sensei explains to them how I'll be helping them perfect their techniques while she demonstrates at the front. Their heads turn and twenty little people give me an interrogating look as if I'm not in any position to question their skills. It would be intimidating if they weren't so darn cute.

The little stinkers are a workout. Between holding the kick shields, walking through their forms with them, and joining in on the relay races, the armpits of my Gi are scratchy damp. It feels good to exercise until I sweat. It's been a while.

The next morning, I'm actually stiff when I get out of bed. Boy, am I out of shape. It's a bit embarrassing, but I resolve to fix it. I'll work harder with the karate kids.

"Your quiz paper?" Mr. Purkis puts his hand out as I step into the Social Studies class.

Crap. I forgot to do it last night. Damn it.

"I left it at home," I say, as I try to meet his look and not give away my lie.

"Then you can get it at noon and hand it in."

"Sure." I walk to my desk. Great. I didn't even look at it and have no idea how many questions there are. I will be speed writing through lunch hour.

The morning drags on and the classes take forever as I have a few mini panic attacks about doing the test. When the noon bell rings, I rush to my locker.

"Whoa, where's the fire?" Barrett asks.

"I forgot to do a test." I wave over my head, as I hurry down the hallway fighting with my coat to get the sleeves to co-operate.

"Later," I hear him call.

The bright sun on fresh snow blinds me. Five minutes to get home. Thirty minutes to write. Five minutes back. The chess club is ahead of me. Derrick and Tony each hold hands with a girl. In an ironic and funny way, it makes me smile for them. I take a shortcut through the alley, so I don't have to race by them like a moron.

Give three examples of federal government systems practised globally.

Great. I check around the kitchen. I know there's no one home but the guilt of the fact I'm going to cheat bothers me. Hello Google.

What is one reason to adopt a federal system of government?

Have I been sleeping through class? Why don't I know the answer? I struggle with the questions, but Google saves my ass on most of them. *I promise I will never get in this predicament again.* I'm not a cheater. The cuckoo clock *cuckoos*, and I scribble the answer to the last question, grab a handful of cookies, and hurry back to school.

Mr. Purkis isn't in the classroom, so I fold the paper and drop it on his desk. With fingers crossed, I leave the room without running into him and head to English class.

Barrett pokes me in the shoulder after I sit down. "You okay?"

"Sure." I leave it at that. No point explaining.

As I head out the school doors Friday afternoon, my phone *dings*. Please be Greg. I know he's got stuff to do with work and he's only been home a few days, but it's almost harder having him in town and only texting. He said we'd do something tonight, but I have no idea what it is, and I don't want to be in his face texting, so I haven't asked.

Greg—*Pick u up at 6 dress warm.*

Hmmm. Dress warm? Are we going night skiing at Norquay? That wouldn't surprise me. Fun. I hurry home.

"How's Mrs. Bronigan?" I ask Steph as I grab some chips for a quick snack.

"Not very good. She didn't recognize me. I talked, but it was hard to tell if she was comprehending what I was saying because she didn't respond often and then she fell asleep."

"I'm sorry." I turn to her. Her lips are doing a scrunchy sad thing. "That's rough."

"I don't think she'll be coming back to Banff any time soon."

"No news about Kyle?"

Steph shakes her head.

"I'm sure he's doing okay. You know Kyle. He's tougher than we give him credit for. He'll be okay."

"Well look at you all full of optimism and sunshine." Steph laughs. "Greg is a great influence on you."

"What do you mean?" I put my hand over my mouth to keep the chip in. "I haven't even seen him for a few days. This sunshine and optimism is me. Just me."

"What are you doing tonight?"

"Greg is picking me up at six."

"Bingo. I called it. Sunshine and optimism in the form of a handsome Aussie."

"Stop it."

"Where're you going?"

"I'm not sure. He said to dress warmly." I lift my hands in the air and shrug.

"Night skiing?"

"Maybe."

The doorbell rings and Bucky beats me to the back porch.

"Hey, hi." Greg steps aside so Bucky can get out.

"Hi." I try to sound calm but seeing him here like it's an ordinary thing to come by and pick me up makes me catch my breath. "How *warm* am I dressing?"

"In many layers," Steph calls out.

I turn and give her double stink eyes.

"We're going on a picnic supper," Greg says.

I turn back and tip my head at him. "A picnic? You do realize you're not in Australia, right?"

He laughs. "Yup."

"I'll go and get changed."

As I pass Steph to go to my room, I make my eyes big, hoping she gets the expression and *doesn't* say anything dumb. I change into thick fleece pants and a turtleneck, grab a heavy sweater and run back down the stairs in record time.

"Ready," I say.

"Just watch the road. It may be a bit slick on the hill after today's melt and freeze," Steph says to Greg. "You two have fun."

No finger wagging or Mom tone to her voice. Thank God.

I grab the rest of my snowboard gear, minus the snowboard, to stay warm on the picnic and put my stuff in the back seat.

"Where are we going?"

"It's a surprise."

"Do I have to close my eyes or anything?" I have a flashback of the drive to the surprise Christmas bowling party Steph had for me last year.

"Nope." He squeezes my hand as we head up the road to Tunnel Mountain. "Nothing creepy like that."

He pulls into the Hoodoo parking lot, winks at me and gets out. While I put on my parka and snow pants, he hauls his pack out of the trunk and from the way he puts it on, I can tell it weighs a ton.

"What's in there?" I laugh. "A baby elephant?"

"Weights." He cinches up the hip strap.

"Why?"

"I've got to get used to it again. I'm taking out a group of Europeans next week and they want an overnighter, so we're cross-country skiing into Egypt Lake."

"Fun, I guess."

"Oh, it will be. I'm out of shape though, so I need to get back at it."

He shakes the pack and I hear the solid *thunk* of the weights as they hit each other. Wow, that's dedication. I feel guilty not carrying anything.

Greg passes me a headlamp and I follow him along the frozen snow and dirt covered trail which overlooks the Bow River and parallels Mount Rundle. It takes a few minutes to figure out where to position my head so the light shines on the path and not across the trees.

"How's it feel to be back at work? I bet they missed you."

"There are a few new faces, but most of the staff have been there since I started.

They're running flat out with tours, so everyone is scrambling." Greg stops and spins around so fast I almost bump into his back. "Barrett said we're going boarding tomorrow."

"He did, did he?" I knew Barrett would wrangle his way into an outing with Greg.

"Which is great." Greg turns and continues walking. "I'm going to Lake Louise on Monday with a few guests to show them around the resort and I haven't been on my board since I left."

"I seriously doubt you need practice."

He steps off the main path and we head onto a narrow animal trail. The branches slap against his pack, so I don't follow as close to avoid getting one in the face.

When we break out of the woods, my light shines across a deep gorge to the base of Mount Rundle. Below, the beam flickers off the Bow River. Where my light doesn't shine are endless black tree shapes and above them, the dark sky is full of stars.

Greg drops his pack onto the snow and starts pulling gear out. "Reservation for two." He passes me a fleece blanket.

"You paid extra for the view I bet." I shake it out and spread it near the edge but not too close. Falling to the bottom of the ravine would ruin the evening. My internal humour makes me grin in the dark.

"Can you collect dry sticks as big as your index finger?" He holds up a canister the size of a large thermos. "This is our stove, mini-heater, light and, if you need your phone charged, it can do that too. All it needs is fuel and a match."

"Impressive gadget." Shining my headlamp on the ground, I scour under spruce trees for sticks and bring them back to Greg.

He's got tin plates, metal cutlery, ketchup and a pack of hotdogs set out on the blanket.

"Perfect." He grabs the twigs.

I sit on the blanket, wrap an end over my legs to stay warm, and watch Greg snap and stuff the sticks into the base of the canister. Within minutes, there's crackling and a steady flame. He plugs a cable in, and a tiny reading-like lamp illuminates the space around us as he prepares supper. Roasting hot dog smells fill the air. When they're cooked, he turns the light off and we sit side by side on the blanket eating supper, while the moon brightens the horizon east of us towards Canmore.

"Wow," I whisper. "It's almost a full moon."

"Pretty cool, hey."

"It is. Did you know it would be?"

He chuckles, puts his arm around me, pulls me in close and our heads touch as clouds drift across the moon and float towards the peaks.

The only sound is us breathing as we watch the night sky. It comes as a surprise that we don't chat about the day, about life, or anything. It's been months since we've been able to talk in person. But it feels right not to disturb the evening.

I wiggle to snuggle in closer and absorb some of Greg's body heat.

"Are you getting cold?" He grabs the blanket on his side, drapes it over our legs and tucks it under me.

I'm wrapped in this warm blanket with Greg. Nothing can get in to hurt me here.

He rocks against my shoulder. "How was your day?"

"School. You know," I twirl a gloved finger in the air, "yippee."

We make plans for boarding tomorrow at Sunshine with Mika and Barrett, I tell him about helping with the karate class, then he runs through his schedule for the next week with clients and trips. He'll be gone a few nights. Light, comfortable chatter.

And then he leans in for a kiss. I don't know why, but it catches me off guard. Not that I didn't think we'd kiss but damn, he is such a good kisser. Before I know it, we're lying on the blanket and after a playful tussle, I'm on top of him, grateful for all the layers of clothes between us. I initiate the kiss this time. And apply the pressure on his lips. I listen to his breath when I stop.

He rolls me over and supports himself, so he doesn't squish me. The moon silhouettes his head, as he leans in. My heart stops with the intensity. The feeling. My body parts do what they have never done before. A surge of tingles and heat.

Greg pulls back. Almost pants. Which makes me think he might be feeling the same as me. I'm disappointed and relieved and disappointed that he stops.

He lets out a quiet laugh. "I better get you home."

"Yeah. I think so." I pull him back for a quick kiss and then tickle his sides. More playful banter and then we put everything together and head home.

"I'll pick you up at eight so we can get first tracks."

"That early?" I groan. "It's Saturday."

"Yup, that early. We'll beat the keeners to the hill."

"No." I poke his chest. "We'll be the keeners."

At the house, he grabs my hand before we go up the back steps and pulls me into the shadows. "Just in case she's on high alert," he whispers and points to the light on in the back porch.

His hands cup my face as he leans in for another awesome kiss. Slow. Deliberate. A pause. He presses harder on my lips before he pulls back.

And the kiss is over.

He sighs. He actually sighs. I love that he does that. We stand there holding hands and watch each other for a few seconds. His kiss scares me, in a good way.

"Thanks for tonight," I whisper.

"You bet. See you tomorrow." He waves from the gate, and I wait until I see his headlights leave the alley before I head inside.

"Jillian," Tom calls out.

"Tom, hi." I hang my stuff up in the porch. "It's been forever. Where have you been?"

"You know the government. They're slave drivers." He walks over and gives me a quick hug.

Odd. Maybe he did miss me. Nope. Tom is a lot like Mika. Neither one of them are huggers. So, what's going on then? Steph is wearing a huge smile that looks genuine. I glance at her hands on the kitchen table. No ring. Phew. Okay. I go back to *what's going on*?

"How was the picnic?"

"Really good. Hot dogs on a stick. Great view." I pull off my sweater. "And you guys, what're you up to?"

"Talking," Steph says.

"Right." I nod. "Talking."

Tom and Steph do this eye check with each other, and they both have grins on now. What the heck? *Are they scheming about how to move me out of Banff and drag me to Waterton*? No way. I can't. I won't. It's all I can do to not blurt out shit I won't be able to take back.

"Nice seeing you Jillian, but I have to run," Tom says. "Mika needs her snowboard tuned for tomorrow."

Steph gets up from the table. I move into the kitchen as they step into the porch. It's not like I want to eavesdrop, but I do. I feign getting a glass from the cupboard and out of the corner of my eye I see them kiss. They whisper stuff, but even leaning my head in their direction doesn't help me hear what they're saying.

After Tom's gone, the suspense drives me mental while Steph tidies up the table.

When I can't stand it anymore, and it's obvious she's not going to offer any information, I say, "What's going on?"

"I do not want you to panic. Please don't start panicking. We were just running through various scenarios."

I put my hands on my hips. "When you use panic twice in a row, what do you expect me to do?"

"Don't panic. They're being really flexible with when I have to be in the position because they like the optics of a female taking it on."

"So." I set the glass down. "You *are* taking the job?"

"Yes. I accepted it today."

Steph steps in front of me and puts her hands on my shoulders. "Please don't worry and *do not* let this upset you. It will not happen until the summer and by then, we'll figure out how to make it work for both of us. I promise you that."

"Eddy can come live here," I blurt out. I have a vague recollection of thinking about him checking in on me, but living here would work even better to convince Steph I don't have to move. *I am a certified genius.* He's an adult. And he's cool. "You always said he's like a brother to you. He could be my guardian. Look after the house and stuff. And even Mom likes him."

Steph's lips pucker and move side to side. She's thinking about it, I can tell.

"That's an option I hadn't considered."

"It's a good one. It would work. Then I don't have to leave Banff and you can go do your thing in Waterton with Tom."

"My thing?" Steph's eyebrows lift and wrinkles run across her forehead. "My thing is a career. It's my job and I enjoy it. You make it sound flippant like it's some sort of pastime."

"Sorry. I didn't mean it that way." I give her an uber-sweet smile, hopeful my Eddy idea sticks with her, and she loses the edge to my shot about her job.

I grab a few cookies. "I've got homework and I'm going boarding early. Goodnight."

Steph's conversation put a huge damper on the picnic mood, and now I'm totally unmotivated to do schoolwork.

My phone *dings*. Greg? Nope. Afton. Afton from Frank Slide Interpretive Centre—*check your email.*

Great timing for a distraction. I flip on my monitor and open email. Junk, junk, junk. Clicking through my inbox reminds me of all the times I rushed into my room to check if there was anything from Greg. Big sigh. I'm grateful that's not part of my routine anymore.

I open Afton's email first and a picture of her and Herb pop up.

I snowshoed into Lille today. Yes, I said snowshoed. We got a dump of snow overnight. It's a winter wonderland here again until the next wind blows through, or a chinook melts it. Anyway, I thought I'd send you the pic. I also replenished Herb's cookie supply and brought him more books.

Remember the summer job posting I told you about? The link to apply is at the bottom of this email. I hope you consider it. The Crowsnest Pass is an amazing place to work. You'd like it.

I'm off to spend the weekend with a bunch of Beavers and Sparks—kids who want to be Scouts and Girl Guides. I'm helping them put together a play for their Easter pageant about the days of old in the Pass. Exhausting, crazy fun I expect.

Take care. Keep in touch. Here's the link.

Afton

How sweet of her but I'll find a job in Banff for the summer. I can save up money to pay for my stuff when Steph is gone, and I can be close to Greg. It's kind of exciting and a bit scary to think of being responsible for myself. It's not like Steph and I are in each other's face but to not have her around will be different.

Tomorrow, I'll take a picture of us boarding and send it to Afton. She'll get why I don't want to leave town.

There's a short email from Mom. So typical. The shortness of it. No surprise though. Sometimes I imagine she won a lottery and instead of telling me, she created this job in Europe so she can travel without me and catch up on all the stuff she missed being my mom now that she's got Steph looking after me. Creative Imagination 101. I send Mom a note with a quick review about good marks and tell her I'm going boarding. I'll send her a boarding picture tomorrow. I wonder if she'll even notice there are guys in it. I know she'll recognize Mika and maybe Barrett, but will she ask anything about Greg?

I Google the Sunshine Ski Resort to refamiliarize myself with the hill. So many runs. So many lifts. When Steph and I went, I followed her the whole day, so I didn't pay attention to where anything is located.

After that, I check out this Skoki Lodge Greg talks about. Wow. Eleven kilometers to ski in. That's far. *Grueling uphill into the pass, rum drinking, poker playing ghosts along the way, delicious food.* Well, I'm good with the delicious food. Not so good for the uphill or ghosts. I better get into shape. I'll train harder with the karate kids. That should help.

I almost go down the Google rabbit hole again about the rights of a sixteen-year-old but am confident Steph liked my Eddy idea.

Chapter 16

"They said they'd meet us at the bottom of the Angel Chair." Greg grabs both our boards off the gondola rack and we head to the lift.

"Greg, my man," a red-coated boarding instructor calls out and rushes towards us.

Greg puts our boards on the snow before the man grabs him in a thumping man-hug. They're both laughing, almost falling over with their big boots on.

"Glad you're back."

Other instructors join the hug-fest.

Someone bumps my shoulder. When I turn, Mika says, "Hi."

"Hey, hi," I respond and the three of us watch the instructors surround Greg.

"I feel like we're hanging with a rock star," she laughs.

"Yeah," I say. "I guess they all know him."

"Everyone knows Greg." Barrett holds their boards. "He's the youngest rock and snow legend here."

I pull my head back, totally doubting what Barrett said. "Legend? How did he get legend status?"

"You come back from death. You have more talent than a lot of locals and you don't brag about it. Legend material."

We stand there like unused utensils at a meal and watch them carry on with their greetings. A bell rings, and just like that, the group of red-suited instructors wave and take off up the hill to the Ski School sign.

"Wow, I think they missed you." I poke Greg in the shoulder.

He picks up his board. "To the top?" He grins, totally ignoring what just happened.

"Can we start on a shorter run?" Mika asks. "You know, for those of us who are not rock stars. I need to do a few warm-up runs first."

"You bet. To the Strawberry Chair."

We hike up the small hill, strap on our boards and in seconds we are on the lift. Barrett and Greg point out and argue over the best runs, tell over-the-top stories of spectacular wipeouts and powder days. Mika and I listen. Someday I'll be able to join in. Until then I'll work on my speed, so I don't hold the guys up.

"What're they doing?" I point to a group of boarders with an instructor. Everyone in the group has one arm out as they're making their turns down a run.

"It's a technique to commit to your turn. You pretend you have a flashlight in the lead foot hand. When you want to turn, you swing the flashlight in the direction of the turn and your body follows."

"Does it work?"

"Yup, lots of teachers use that method. It's more a mind game, but your body has to follow your arm so its effective."

"Cool."

After we're all buckled up, Barrett shouts, "To the Dell."

Greg swings his shoulders and upper body like he's dancing as he glides in beside me.

"Go." I point down the hill. "I'll meet you at the bottom."

He waves but stays right by me. Too sweet.

The Dell run is the shape of a half pipe. I slide up one side, use the pretend flashlight in my lead hand to initiate a turn, and it happens. It just happens. Who knew? I don't care if it's a mind game. It works.

Snow sluffs on my board as I slide up the other side. I wave my flashlight where I want to turn and, bam, it happens again. Easy-peasy. I wish I'd known this trick sooner.

Greg swooshes in front of me, rides up the other side, and pulls a 360 before I catch up. I chase him down the run. Best run ever. No wipe outs. And it feels good.

We wait for Mika and Barrett at the bottom and up we go again. And again.

"We should try Angel," Greg says. "You gals are crushing it."

"Right." Mika laughs. "Whatever."

The chair bumps over the tower as colourful skiers and boarders pass underneath us. What a day. Blue, cloudless sky. Sunshine and endless runs. I lean into Greg, and he swings his arm over my shoulder.

It takes longer to get to the bottom now, but the guys pick the green beginner runs so it's easy riding. I had to take my board off once because I got stuck on a flat spot and Greg was too far ahead to pull me. I unstrapped my bindings and did the walk of shame until I got to the next downhill pitch. But on the next run, I knew it was coming, and I kept up my speed to make it across without stopping. Huge improvement.

"Are you ready to try going from the top?" Greg taps my helmet.

I glance at Mika. "We can do it, girl." I fist pump the air.

Steph never took me to the top lift. Oh, well. Worst case scenario, it will take the rest of the morning to get down.

The sign on one of the last towers says, *Welcome to BC.*

"What?"

"Cool, hey?" Greg turns and points down the slope. "Alberta." Then he points up the hill. "British Columbia. And that's Quartz Ridge." He points at a mountain on the horizon and tells us about the different trails and trips he has led beyond Quartz and on towards the impressive peak of Mount Assiniboine.

We get off the lift and traverse across the hill. What a view. All around me. And tiny black dots of people move down the numerous runs. The four of us sit side by side as we do up our bindings.

I pull my phone out and set the camera for a selfie. "Who's got the longest arm?"

Barrett grabs the phone. We tuck our heads together and he snaps a few shots.

Another boarder stops right in front of us.

"Greg?" He stares at Greg.

"That's me."

"Bro, it's me. Todd."

Greg jumps up and they do an awkward hug-wrestle greeting complete with a few hoots.

"I have an extra beacon. We're doing Delirium Dive," Todd says. "Join us. It'll be like old times."

"No, thanks though. I'm with my gal and friends." He waves at us.

"You gotta go," Barrett says. "I'll get these two down. We'll meet you at the Goat."

Greg shakes his head.

"Listen to me." Barrett takes his board off and sticks it in the snow. He grabs Greg's shoulders. "Waist deep powder. Few tracks. If you don't do it for yourself, do the run for me."

They have this stare down and then Greg looks at me.

"Would you be okay if I took a run with them?"

"Sure. Go for it." I smile. I have no idea what this is all about, but I get the gist. It's more than Mika and I are capable of doing.

"I'm coming." Greg gives me a quick kiss and follows a group of boarders up a packed trail.

We watch as they hike up a snow-trenched path which leads to a gate.

"You can't go into Delirium Dive without a partner and a beacon in case there's an avalanche," Barrett says. "They're registering their beacon at the gate." He points as each person waves a small black device at a box, and then the gate opens.

The gate in the middle of the snow-covered hill looks out of place and a tad ominous. Almost like it's making a statement: *'those who pass are willingly going into a known avalanche area.'* But it's on a legit ski hill, right? They all have beacons. And there is a group of them. I cross my fingers, just in case, to keep Greg safe.

After they're all through the gate, they hike up to the top in single file and then their heads disappear.

"Okay, gals. Follow the blue diamonds down the run." Barrett points to a line of tall poles in the snow with wooden, blue diamonds on top.

"That's a blue run. Where's the green one?" I scan the hill looking for green circles.

"Sorry. No beginner runs up here."

"What?" Mika and I say in unison.

"So, who wants to lead? I'll bring up the rear in case there are any crashes."

"We do not crash," Mika says. "We fall with grace."

"Right." He taps her helmet. "Let's go."

I point my board down the slope, get my pretend flashlight ready, and away I go. Across the slope, swing flashlight, turn, across again, pick up speed, turn, turn, angle a bit uphill to slow down, turn. I am tempted to check behind to make sure Mika is following but multi-tasking right now could be disastrous, so I just hope she's there.

A steady stream of people come across the traverse from Angel, and I don't want to chance merging in case I misjudge and run into someone, so I stop and sit down. My legs are Jello. Mika plops down beside me and snow sprays us from behind.

"Nice work ladies," Barrett says. "We'll work our way down to Jack Rabbit and the Goat Chair."

He carves around in front of us and points out the route he wants us to take. More blue diamond runs.

"You lead this time," I say to Mika.

She shakes her head. "I like following you. Then I don't have to decide where to turn."

I push myself up, wait for a break in the people traversing and start again. The run is busier so, not only do I have my flashlight ready, but I also need to dodge boarders and skiers. The first couple of turns are smooth and it flows. But when I have to abort and turn in a different direction than I planned to, it takes time to get my rhythm back.

The run forks off and Barrett glides by, like it's nothing to catch us, and he points to the one we need to follow. My breathing comes in puffs, but I get to the bottom where there is a flat stretch. It's a comfort to see other boarders taking off their boards, tucking them under their arm and walking the stretch. Of course, skiers pass me because they can pole. Maybe there are benefits to skiing.

We take the Jack Rabbit lift up and at the top, Barrett points to the Banff Avenue run. Yay. A green one.

"To the Goat," he shouts and away he goes, with Mika pushing off behind him.

Well, be that way. Now she's okay to go ahead of me. I laugh to myself. Oh well, we're almost down. The first part has a gentle slope to it but ends in a flat spot. The only reason I know this is I see Mika with one foot out pushing to catch up to Barrett. I crouch and ride flat, fingers crossed I don't catch an edge and biff it.

Damn. Not enough speed. My board stops short of the next downhill pitch. I unstrap my back foot and push myself along. If Greg were here, he would glide next to me, grab a hand and slingshot me further ahead so I don't have to do the walk of shame.

When I sit to strap in again, I hear what sounds like a kid crying. Mika and Barrett are halfway down but there is no one else on the run. I listen again and turn towards the trees. Uh-oh. It sounds like a little kid. I glide to the edge.

"Hey," I call out to a small figure hunched over in the snow next to a tree. One ski tip pokes out of the snow. "Are you okay?"

No response.

I take my board off, stick it in the snow and follow his ski tracks through the trees. Each step, I sink up to my crotch.

"I'm coming," I pant. "You must be a really good skier to get in here."

The little person doesn't look up but says in a sobby voice, "I'm not supposed to talk to strangers."

"That's a good rule."

With my boots, I pack the snow in front of him, so I don't sink. One ski is off. I can't tell if the other one released. The strap from a ski pole pulled off their glove. The exposed wrist is blue. Bruised from getting the strap yanked off? Or from the cold?

"I'm Jillian." I crouch down. "What's your name?"

Nothing.

"I can get the ski patrol to come and help you. They're like the police on the ski hill."

The helmet lifts and a snotty, with goggles on crooked, red face looks up at me. I move the goggles up onto his helmet.

"There are police here?" his tiny voice says.

"Yes, they're the ski patrol." I smile. "They help people who're in trouble on the hill. What's your name?"

"Carl."

"Carl who?"

"Carl McAndrew."

"Nice to meet you, Carl." I take my jacket off and wrap it around him without moving him at all. "Do you hurt anywhere?"

"My arm hurts and my leg is stuck."

"Okay, you stay put." *Like he's going anywhere*. Poor guy. The expression on his face reminds me of Kyle when he was having a bad day. "I'm just going to go back and ask someone to get help."

"Don't go," he whines.

"I'll only be ten seconds. I promise. Okay?"

The helmet drops and there's a muffled, "'kay."

Following the same steps I took to get in, I lunge back to the edge of the Banff Avenue run.

"Hey," I holler and wave at two boarders.

"What's up?" The boarder sprays snow beside me when she stops.

"Can you please get the ski patrol? There's a little kid stuck in the trees." I point to him. "I think he might be hurt."

"You bet." Off they go, straight down the hill.

I retrace my steps back to Carl.

"Help is on the way," I tell him.

"Really?"

“Hey, do I look like I would lie to you?” I sit down close to him. “How’d you manage to get in here?”

“I tried to keep up to my class,” he starts to cry. “And my tits crossed.”

I stifle a giggle before I say, “You mean your tips crossed?”

“That’s what I said.”

He looks at me like I’m hearing impaired, which is cute and funny, but I don’t smile. “So, you were with a ski lesson group?”

“No, my class from school. I told Mrs. Andison I could ski good.” He looks down. “I’m not very good.”

I pump information out of him that might be helpful to find his people.

“Guess what?” I look out through the trees. “I hear the ski police’s skidoo.”

“They drive a skidoo?”

“They sure do. I’m going to go out and tell them where you are. Don’t you go anywhere.”

“You’re not funny.”

Man, tough audience.

“He’s in there,” I point to the patroller who stops by my board. “I didn’t want to move him. He says his arm hurts and his leg is stuck. I can’t tell if his ski is off or not. He buried himself pretty good. His name is Carl McAndrew.”

Two more patrollers take off their skis and we head back to him.

"Hey Carl. You are quite the hot dog skier to get in here," the first patroller says in a serious proud-of-you voice.

"Yup," Carl says. "I'm pretty good."

What a kid. I watch them dig around him and pop his other ski off. While one of them assesses Carl, another patroller goes back to get the toboggan. So I'm not in the way, I go back to the edge of the run and wait for them to pull him out.

"Jillian," I hear Greg and Barrett yell.

Oh, shit. I totally forgot about them. I forgot about meeting at the Goat. I should've called or something.

Greg whips his board off and runs to me. "Are you okay?" His goggles are up, and his eyes are huge. "I thought something happened to you." He grabs me in a bear hug. Not an ordinary bear hug. This one's grizzly bear status.

"I'm good." I put my hands on his chest. "I found this kid." I point towards all the activity in the trees. "He's stuck. Maybe a bit hurt."

Greg kisses my cheek and squeezes me again.

The patrollers hook the toboggan onto the back of the skidoo.

"It's a short ride to the Ski Patrol hut," one of them tells Carl. "I'm going to pull this cover over your head, so we don't get snow in your face."

"Jillian," Carl calls. "I get to ride in a toboggan."

"You bet, buddy. You sure do." I wave. "Have fun."

Barrett and Greg stand beside me as a patroller asks my name. I tell them what Carl told me about his class and teacher.

"I'm going to go meet Mika, so she doesn't worry." Barrett straps on his board. "Meet you at the Goat."

Greg puts his hands on my shoulders. "When you didn't come down the run and we waited and waited, and then we checked the lodge and washrooms in case you went in ahead of us and we called, and you didn't answer..." He stops to catch his breath. "Well, Mika checked the washrooms, but I would have." He winks. "I should have known you'd be out saving the world."

"What?"

"Remember that Outward Bound trip to Aylmer in the fall when you untangled the deer caught in fishing line?" He points at me. "You save the world. One piece at a time."

"Right." I laugh. "That's me. Wrong place at the right time. Hey, how was your run?"

"It was epic." The biggest grin replaces the worried face he was wearing. "I'll tell you about it later. I'm starved. Let's go. I'll follow you."

"Yes, sir." I push off and we carve down the slope to the Goat.

"Over here," Barrett calls from the ski racks.

“So, Miss Jillian Meier, our superhero.” Mika puts her hands on her hips. “You’re out there being a hero while I’m down here worrying about you.”

“I’m sorry.”

“For what? Rescuing a kid?” She hugs me. Not a Mika move. Feels cool though.

We settle in at a lunch table, with trays of the best smelling fast food in front of us.

“So, before you lost Jillian, how’d you guys do?” Greg looks up from his hamburger.

“Good.” I nod. “Blue runs. We nailed it didn’t we?” I glance at Mika.

“They’re shredder material.” Barrett fist bumps the air.

“Whatever.” Mika laughs.

Barrett points at Greg. “Tell me more, bro. Which route did you take?”

They almost talk a foreign language with formidable, Bre-X, scope a line, goofy foot. They’re so animated with hand gestures and verbal versions of *wow*. And then they’re quiet, like they have to digest both their food and Greg’s run. It’s sweet to watch.

My phone *dings* in my pocket.

“Now I see your call.” I wave it at them. “Sorry I didn’t hear it before. Steph wants everyone to come for supper tonight.”

They all nod.

* * *

The back porch smells like fried onion and hamburger and oregano. Steph must be making lasagna.

"How was it?" She calls from the kitchen, as Bucky races towards us.

Greg holds the outside door open for him, but Bucky shoves his muzzle into Greg's hand for a quick scratch first.

"Epic," Greg says again. "And Jillian here is kind of a hero."

"A what? Why?" Steph tosses the dishcloth in the sink and Tom gets up from the table.

"Well." Greg puts his hands on my shoulders and marches me towards them. I try to duck out of his grip, but he's insistent on making this an issue. "She saved a kid on the hill."

"Go on." Steph puts her hands on her hips.

Greg gives them a rundown of the event. His voice has this *you-go-girl* tone to it, and it feels awesome that he's this proud of me. My face blazes with the attention, but in a good way.

"That's quite the story. I'm glad I cooked enough for a heroine's supper." Steph hugs me. "Way to go Wonder Woman."

"Wonder who?" I wiggle out of her arms.

"You know, the sexy lady in the tight suit who flies through the air."

I roll my eyes at her.

"Never mind. There's a lot of food. I hope you're hungry."

"Do not say no." Tom puts his hands up. "She's been cooking all afternoon."

Steph looks behind us. "Where are Mika and Barrett?"

"They went to drop off their gear first," I say. "They'll be over in a bit."

"You two go in the living room. Eddy will be here shortly, too." She shooshes us out of the kitchen. "Supper will be served in an hour. Relax. It sounds like you've had a busy day."

"She's in a great mood." Greg settles on the couch. "What do you want to watch?"

"I'm going to grab a shower." I hand him the remote. "Be right back."

Maybe Eddy is coming over to talk about staying with me. But would Steph do that with everyone else here? I doubt it. Regardless, the fact that Eddy's coming over gives me hope Steph is considering my suggestion. Which is a good thing because I don't have a Plan B yet.

Supper is delicious and there's so much of everything. When Eddy finds out about my heroine rescue, there's a bit more Wonder Woman teasing, but for the rest of it, the chatter is light and easy and constant.

Tom, Steph and Eddy ask Greg about his Delirium Dive run. Apparently, they've all done it at one time or another. How did I not know Eddy skied? Always full of surprises, that guy.

I keep waiting for an indication as to why we're all together. Nothing. Not one word of any topic which gets extra attention. We're like one big happy family having an ordinary supper together. Cool. I can get used to this.

Everyone pitches in to clean up and before I know it, they all leave except Greg.

"I've got a group to take out tomorrow," he says as he slips into his parka. "I don't know when I'll be back, but I'll text you when I find out."

"Okay. Thanks for today. It was fun."

"It really was." He leans in.

"I'm right here," Steph calls out.

A quick kiss on the lips, a wink, and he's gone.

"Really?" I turn to Steph and give her a you've-got-to-be-kidding-me expression.

"Really." She heads to the living room.

I follow her and stand in the archway as she grabs the remote.

"Is everything okay?"

She looks up. "What do you mean?"

"You're cooking again. You invited people over. You used to hate cooking for a crowd. Is there anything going on I should worry about?"

"Nope. I had the day off and thought you guys might want a big meal after boarding."

"That's all?"

"Yup." She turns on the TV.

"Thanks for supper and feeding everyone," I say. "Goodnight."

It *is* possible she just wanted to do something nice for us. I stare at the ceiling. What a day. My legs may never be the same. I poke a quad. Yup. It hurts. A lot. With Greg working tomorrow I can do homework and let my legs recover.

It bothers me that I haven't told Greg about Derrick yet. Today didn't seem like the right time. There has not been a *right* moment since he's been back. Will there ever be one? But I have to tell him before he finds out from someone else. That would be awful. Crap. I will do it. Soon. I groan. Now there's no way I can fall asleep.

I get out of bed and open my computer. First, I send the selfie we took today at the top of Continental to Afton and Mom and tell them what a great day it was. Then I go down the Google rabbit hole—*how to tell a boyfriend bad news.*

Find the right time.

Be calm.

Do not mix emotion with facts.

Start out with a positive statement.

What the hell? How is any of that even possible? Let alone helpful?

'Hey Greg. It sure is a nice day (*opening positive comment*). By the way, I need to tell you this guy kissed me...a few times.'

I turn my computer off, crawl back into bed and try to fall asleep again.

Chapter 17

My room is full of bright sunshine. Wow. I must have finally fallen asleep. And I slept hard. I crawl out of the warm covers and head downstairs. Pancake smells come from the kitchen.

"Morning," I say.

Bucky lifts his head and grins at me.

"Where's Steph?"

He drops his head back onto his bed.

"Not helpful."

A sheet of paper in the middle of the table with Steph's writing on it says—*Gone jogging. Breakfast is in the fridge.*

"Exactly when did Steph take up jogging?" I shake the paper at Bucky. No response again.

A plate of thin, Oma-style, German pancakes sits in the fridge. One of my favourites. Oh, Oma. I miss you. A lot. And Opa. It hasn't even been a year, but sometimes it feels like you've been gone forever.

I heat up a pancake, melt butter on top, lather it with strawberry jam and head to the living room to watch TV. I'll get into homework mode later. I feel like I haven't had any down time in the last few days. And it feels pretty good to just chill for a bit.

Laundry. Done. My turn to clean the bathroom. Check. Tidy kitchen. Complete. Nothing left to procrastinate with, so I head upstairs to do homework.

I could do this. I could live here and take care of myself. It's not a big deal.

Karate classes and a summer job will help with my expenses, but Mom will have to cough up more cash.

I can't remember the last time I sent Dale, I mean Dad—no I don't mean Dad, Dale—an email. But he hasn't sent me any either. We have both been negligent in keeping in touch. I remember when my world revolved around finding him and making him a part of my life. I don't know when that changed.

Just in case I need him as an ally in my future, I almost duplicate the email I sent Mom, attach the picture and send it off to him. It can't hurt to stay in his good books.

Then down the Google rabbit hole I go, searching for articles on 'rights of a sixteen-year-old in Alberta.' It says I have the right to leave home and to parental care. Well, technically I don't want to leave home. I want to stay here. I just might not have an adult under the same roof.

Incoming squirrel-attention span. Homework. I need to get it done. But after a quick nap.

* * *

“Jillian,” I hear Steph calling in my sleep, but the dream is so good I ignore her and roll over.

“Are you sick?”

It’s now impossible to sink back into my dream with Steph poking me.

“No. I’m sleeping.” I pull the covers over my head. “I *was* sleeping.”

“Supper is ready.”

I sit straight up. “What time is it?”

“Six.”

Holy crap. I slept the whole afternoon away.

“When did you start jogging?” I sit down in front of a large plate of leftover lasagna.

“I’ve always jogged.”

“Nope. Never seen it.”

“Okay, I jog intermittently, and I felt like it this morning.” She waves her fork at me. “Did I mention your teacher wanted to talk to you about joining a group?”

I stare at her. “What teacher and what group?”

“The drinking issue teacher from the field trip. It’s a history group.”

“Mrs. Machuk?” I keep my voice even, so this conversation doesn’t get confrontational. “Why would she want me to join a history group?” As much as I enjoyed the field trip to Frank, joining an after-school history group is right up there with the chess club right now. Not something I want to participate in.

"She says you're a good egg."

"A good egg?"

"Those were her words, not mine," Steph says. "You're a good student, and she said you seemed to appreciate the Frank field trip. She thought you might want to expand your horizons and get more acquainted with the topic."

I look down at my plate, so Steph doesn't see my eye roll. Just what I need. To be a teacher's pet in an after-school club.

My phone *dings*. It's from Greg—*back home*.

"Can I go see Greg for a bit tonight?"

"Sure. Have you finished all your homework?"

"Yes." I cross my fingers in my lap and promise myself I'll do it later. No point ruining Steph's mood by telling her it's not done.

"Home by ten."

"Got it."

There are a few guys with Greg in the TV room of the staff residence.

"Congratulations." One of them slaps Greg on the back. "You'll be on that trip."

"Jillian." Greg walks towards me. "Hi."

He kisses me. My face heats up but how cool is it that he did this? That he kissed me right in front of his friends?

"Hey." I feel awkward with everyone staring, so I wave. And then I feel stupid for waving.

Greg grabs my hand and introduces me. I try to remember all their names but I'm so nervous, I only remember Todd's, and that's because I met him on Sunshine.

"Later," Greg says to them, and we head to his room.

"How was your day?" He moves stuff off the chair so I can sit down.

"Lazy. I even napped. How was yours?"

"I skied with a family into Shadow Lake and showed them a few places to go while they're there." He laughs. "I stayed for supper and then had a fast ski out so I would get back to the car before it got dark."

I smile while I try to figure out how to tell him about Derrick and the kisses. How do I even start? *I wish I could remember Google's suggestions.*

"What's wrong?" He pulls a chair across from me and sits on the edge of it.

"I have to tell you something." I lock my fingers in my lap. "When...you know when everyone, when we thought you were...when your folks called and told me you were gone?"

"It's kind of hard to forget. What's going on?"

"This guy I am...I *was* friends with, he kissed me," I blurt out. "A few times. But when you called and you weren't, you know, dead, I told him we weren't a thing and he had to stop." I press my lips together because I said it, he knows and there is no point in, what would Mom say, 'adding more fuel to the fire' by telling him how I felt about it. "I'm sorry."

We stare at each other. Maybe stare isn't the right word. We watch each other. TV noise and the guys talking muffles through the door. I bite my bottom lip.

Greg grabs my hands and shakes them gently.

"Chris and I kissed," he whispers.

I tip my head. I *did not* see that coming. And I'm not sure how I feel about it. Which is pretty hypocritical, considering.

"It was a few days in, and the weather was getting worse. We knew they wouldn't be able to look for us."

I nod. He said thinking about me kept him alive during his ordeal. Maybe he meant Chris kept him alive.

"She didn't want me to come back to Banff. She thought we'd be good together." He shakes his head. "I wanted to be here with you."

I feel myself breathe. My chest moves. But I have no idea what to say. I mean, I feel like he cheated, but so did I. For a while, he thought he would never get home. And I thought he was dead.

Greg looks at our hands and continues to swing them side to side.

"Are we okay?" He squeezes my fingers.

"Yes, we are."

He pulls me up and then into a hug. A quiet, solid, safe hug.

I did it. I told him. And I try not to let thoughts of him and Chris ruin this moment. Our first issue. And we got through it. Unscathed, almost. And now it's behind us.

"My Mom called," Greg says. "Suzanne got to leave the hospital for the day and go home."

He tells me about the phone call, and I listen for any change in his voice but there isn't any. It's just Greg.

"I have to get back to the shop and fill out some paperwork." He stands and pulls me up. "I'll give you a ride home."

The heater in the car blows cold air and I zip up my parka. "What was that guy congratulating you about when I came in?"

"Oh, nothing. The boss put my name in for this climb up Mount Logan, but I doubt I'll get it. There are way more experienced people in the game." He shrugs. "I'm going to be out of reception for a few days this week. Can you believe guests are paying to trek out into the wilderness to winter camp instead of checking into the Fairmont Hotel? I can't complain though because it pays the bills."

"For all your sakes, I hope it doesn't get any colder."

Greg walks me to the bottom step and pulls me into the shadows again. I pay attention to the kiss to see if it changed because of our talk. Nope. It's still the same.

Soft. Warm. An unrushed Greg kiss. Right up until Bucky bounds down the stairs.

"Is that you out there?" Steph shouts.

Greg and I laugh. Steph and her timing. Right up there with *very bad*. Another quick kiss and Bucky races him to the back gate.

* * *

A substitute teacher in English class reads a passage about the Great Depression. Her voice is shaky, as if she's afraid of us but as she gets into the story, she becomes dramatic with hand and body gestures, almost like she's on a stage. I get caught up in the tale although I see a few heads nod off.

"Your assignment for this reading is to create a presentation of the scene. Art, music, writing. Be creative. Think out of the box," she says. "Before you ask, no you can't work in groups."

A number of groans.

"The assignment will be worth twenty percent of your final mark."

More groans.

The week ticks by. There are only two texts from Greg but our times don't jive with karate class so we can't hang out. Frustrating. Annoying. But our reality, I guess.

Look at me being all grown up about it.

Greg is off on the weekend and asked if I can keep it open to do something together. *Yeah.*

I bet we go boarding again. That will be fun.

Maybe I can make a diorama for the English assignment. After supper on Friday night, I send a quick message to Afton to get ideas on how to pull it off and then search in the attic for possible props and miniature toys I can use. A few of Kyle's miniature characters and building blocks are the perfect size. I bring the items into the office. Cardboard. I need a big piece for the base. I check in the closet and pull out a box.

With everything set out on the desk, I position pieces to get an idea on the spacing and how it is all going to fit into the scene. Totally focused, I draw lines for the school's walls and where the doors are going to be.

"Hi," Greg says, and I almost jump out of my skin.

"Sorry, I didn't mean to scare you. Steph let me in." He pulls me in for a kiss and hug. "I missed seeing you this week."

He smells so good. Shower fresh. And warm. I press my head against his flannel covered chest and we just stand there in the hug for a few seconds.

Gosh it feels good.

"What are you working on?" He puts an arm over my shoulder as he looks down at my assortment of stuff.

"It's for an English assignment. I'm trying to make a diorama of a scene about an old schoolhouse during the Depression. This stuff is too new though. I need old props to make it look authentic."

"You could make the furniture out of twigs and twine." He moves a few pieces around. "Maybe use some moss and lichen for the ground."

"You've done this before?"

"No, but there were displays at the airport and that's what they used in some of them."

I look up at him. Impressive.

"Yup, that would work." I grab his hand and pull him into the living room. "What's on the agenda for the weekend?"

Ah...about the weekend," he groans.

"What's wrong?"

"One of the guides is down with a flu," he says. "I have to fill his spot, so I have to bail on doing anything this weekend."

He sits on the couch and pulls me onto his lap.

I fake a smile. "That sucks."

"It does. I'm sorry." He tickles my cheek, then glances over my shoulder. "Do you think she's busy?"

I hear clinking dishes—the sound of Steph unloading the dishwasher.

"For a few minutes."

We just start to kiss, and Steph calls out, "I'll be coming into the living room in five, four, three..."

I move off Greg's lap and snuggle beside him before I grab the remote.

She stands in the archway. "What're you two doing tonight?"

"This." I point the remote at the TV and turn it on. "You?"

"I'm going upstairs to read." She lifts her hand as if she is going to point a finger at me, but it stops halfway.

I wave at her and watch her leave before I snuggle in closer to Greg.

"I have to be at the shop at seven AM," he says. "Pick something short and funny to watch."

I flick through channels. Within minutes I hear quiet snoring. I turn my head slowly. Yup. Greg's head is back on the couch. Mouth a bit open. Sound asleep. Wow. I'm not sure if I should be offended, or pleased he's so comfortable he can fall asleep here. I turn the volume down and surf the channels, only watching minutes of each show before I move on to the next.

After about an hour, I realize Greg is out. No hint he'll wake up. Since he has to be up early, I slip out from under his arm and lift his legs onto the couch.

"What?" he mumbles.

"I'll get you up at six thirty." I grab a blanket and lay it over him.

"Thanks. Sorry." He stretches full out and pulls the cover under his chin.

Hot date Friday night. I kiss the top of his head before I go upstairs.

“Steph.” I tap on her door.

“Yeeeess,” she answers like a witch.

I open the door a crack. “Greg’s asleep on the couch. He has to be up early, so I’ll set my alarm.” I point down the hallway to my room. “I’m going to my bedroom.”

Not exactly how I thought I’d be spending my evening. Or my weekend for that matter.

Chapter 18

The days run into each other with school and karate. Again, I only get a few texts from Greg. When I respond it takes hours, sometimes days, for him to say he has read them. Obviously, cell reception is sketchy wherever he is. Barrett and Mika invite me to a movie one night but the third wheel status, sitting in a dark theatre, is not what I want to do.

After karate, I walk by Greg's place, but his car isn't there. Darn.

My phone *dings* Friday afternoon. *Pick u up Sat 8 AM sleeping bag warm clothes pack for 1 overnight.*

No way. But shoot. Steph will never let me do an overnighter with Greg. *I'm not sure I'm comfortable doing an overnighter.* I mean, I want to. I do. I just don't know if I'm ready for that.

Why do I always go to the worst-case scenario first?

Spending a night with Greg is not a big deal. I know how to say '*no*' now after the whole Derrick fiasco and besides, Greg would never push the issue. I'm sure of it.

After supper I put my sleeping bag and clothes on my bed. I decided not to tell Steph about Greg's text while we were eating and debated saying I was going to spend Saturday night at Mika's to avoid having to deal with her lecture. But then I'd have to get Mika on board with the lie and it would get complicated, so I didn't.

As I stuff everything in my backpack, I stop myself. Is this the trip to the Skoki Lodge Greg talked about a while ago? He said something about sleeping in dorm rooms, which means other people will be there. I relax. And Steph already approved it even though she threatened to castrate him. I chuckle. Subtle is not Steph's go-to spiel.

The next morning, Steph waves a frying pan at me when I step into the kitchen. "You need nourishment, lots of it."

"What?" I shove my backpack against the stairwell so she can't see it just in case we are not going to Skoki. "What's going on?"

"Greg stopped at the office yesterday to check avalanche conditions for Skoki." She loads a plate with bacon and eggs and hands it to me. "You will appreciate my culinary skills when you are puking your lungs out going up the pass."

"Wow, not a great sales pitch for the trip," I say.

"I'm just kidding. Well, no, I'm not kidding, but you'll be fine."

To kill time after breakfast while I wait, I putz around with my diorama. I'm impressed with how well it's turning out. Greg's idea to build furniture out of little sticks was painstakingly slow and the blister on the tip of my index finger from the glue gun verifies my technique needs work.

"Wow," Greg says. "Look at you go."

"Hey, there you are. Hi."

He wraps his arms around my waist and rests his chin on my head as he looks at my work.

"It's kind of fun," I say. "The research is even cool but there's no way I would've survived in those days."

"Well, you will ace this assignment." He turns me around. Quick kiss. "I missed you."

Another kiss. Deeper. Like he *did* miss me. A lot. My stomach flutters as his tongue presses on my teeth until I let him in. Oh my. Weak legs. I hug him hard. And when it's over, we are both breathless. *Thank God we're staying in a dorm.*

"We should hit the road," he says. "Where's your gear?"

I grab my pack from the hallway, and we head through the kitchen.

"See you Sunday." I wave at Steph. "Don't miss me."

She raises her hand again, like the other night and I cringe waiting for her to drop a bomb on the moment. But she doesn't. I have to say, I *am* pretty impressed she didn't force *the talk* on me before the trip. Maybe she trusts me. A bit.

"Be safe and have fun," she says.

I stare at her for a second. She's biting her cheek. I walk back and give her a quick hug. It totally takes her by surprise.

"Don't worry," I whisper.

"Right."

The westbound Trans-Canada is busy with weekend ski traffic. We chatter about the week. Not much to report in mine other than school, karate and home. Greg's week sounds way more interesting. He takes the coolest people out on trips.

A solid line of traffic turns off at the Lake Louise Ski Resort and snakes up the hill. Greg pulls into the Skoki parking lot. After we have our winter gear on, and the packs lean against the car, Greg passes me two fat skis with snowboard bindings on them. I wave them side to side.

"Super fat cross-country skis?"

"Sort of. This is a splitboard. You use them like cross-country skis for the flats and uphill." He takes them from me, puts them together, flicks a few levers, rotates the binding and it is a solid snowboard.

"Sweet."

He undoes it and passes the two planks back to me with a pair of ski poles. I put my pack on, pick up the boards and poles, and follow Greg to the trailhead.

Step. Slide. Step. Slide. It takes a few minutes to get into the same rhythm as him but once we are in sync it feels natural. The only sound is the swish of our boards as they skim across the snow and the squeak of our poles when they dig into the packed base.

"Is this an old road?" I ask, as I glance at the solid bank of trees on both sides. Lazy clouds float across the blue sky.

"Yup. They use it in the summer. It's also the ski out back to the base."

Step. Slide. Step. Slide.

A few skiers whoosh by us. I'm jealous. It's a gradual uphill slog and I unzip my coat to cool off. We pass under a chairlift. I could use a ride up to anywhere right now. A lot of skiers and boarders wait in the lift line, but Greg ignores them and keeps heading up the hill. Darn.

"Need a pit stop? This is the last flush toilet until we come back tomorrow." Greg points at a large, dark brown log structure. "This is the Temple Lodge."

"No. I'm good."

He checks up the busy ski run as we cross the slope.

"Say goodbye to civilization." Greg veers off into the woods and onto a narrow trail.

Tall spruce trees hug the edge of the path now and it seems darker. Step. Slide. Step. Slide. Up and up and up. Forever.

Greg looks over his shoulder. "How're you doing?"

I try not to pant when I say, "Good."

"It opens up soon and we'll be able to see forever."

I hope I can see the Skoki lodge at the end of forever.

And just like that the trees thin and we're in the base of a valley with peaks all around us. Big mountains. In your face mountains. I'm not sure why they surprise me. For Pete's sake, I live in Banff. There are mountains everywhere. But these are different. They look rougher and they don't go straight up. They have a gradual incline with clumps of short trees and bushes sticking out of the snow randomly. These mountains look more desolate than Rundle or Cascade Mountain. Beautiful nonetheless—but different.

"Wow," slips out.

Greg turns and smiles. "Pretty impressive, isn't it?"

"It really is."

We ski side by side again.

"It gets even better," he says.

I try to take in all the views as we ski in silence. Comfortable, awesome silence. It feels intrusive to interrupt the quiet with talking.

Greg stops and points.

"What?"

He leans into me. and I follow where his gloved hand is pointing.

"Are those wolves?"

"Yup."

"They're huge."

Six wolves. Almost black in colour.

"They see us but they're moving fast in that direction." He waves his hand away from us. "I doubt they care we're here."

I stay as near to him as possible without stepping on his equipment.

"We'll stop at Halfway Hut for a break."

I search ahead but I don't see anything hut-tish looking. I glance at the wolves, who continue to parallel us, and hope Little Red Riding Hood is not on their menu.

"Over here." Greg cuts off the main trail and voilà, there is an opening behind a bank of trees where the snow-covered roof of a tiny log building stands.

"Halfway Hut." He does a grand arm gesture as if I'm entering the grounds of a palace. Kind of cute considering it's a cabin in the woods. "Beware of the ghosts."

"Ghosts?" As I undo my bindings and drop my pack into the snow, I check around. No wolves. No visible ghosts. But when I open the door, I pinch my nose. Still no ghosts but mega packrat stink. I let my eyes adjust to the dim room. There's an old wooden table, two canvas, partially chewed, camping chairs and a wood stove with the door wide open.

"Beware of the cards you hold," Greg whispers from behind me.

Goose bumps run up my neck.

"What?" I shake the feeling off as we head back to our packs and settle onto the snow seats which Greg kicked out for us against the cabin wall.

"There's an urban legend about two brothers who played cards in the cabin the night before they went missing. All they ever found were the last hands they played, face up on the table."

"I read something about that. What happened to them?"

Greg tips his face towards the sun and closes his eyes. "They were never seen again."

I sock him in the shoulder. "Quit freaking me out."

"Then there's the story about a painter who died in the cabin waiting for the perfect sunset."

"Stop it."

He swings his arm around my shoulders. "Not to worry. I'll protect you from ghosts."

We soak up the rays as we munch on trail mix and sip water.

"Now the hard part." Greg gets up, puts his hands out and pulls me up. He stops when I am in front of him and kisses me.

All my girl parts hum. In a nice, but scary way. It's so quiet. I feel his breath on my face, and we kiss again before he puts his hands on my shoulders and gives me a super serious expression.

"The next stop is the top of Boulder Pass," he says. "It will be a grunt but well worth it."

"Great." I roll my eyes but am both relieved and disappointed we have moved on from kissing. "It sounds like more uphill."

Once we are back on the trail, Greg points out the wolf pack again. They are further ahead and moving a lot faster. Certainly not as intimidating.

And what a grunt. Sweat trickles down my face. I take off my toque and stuff it inside my parka. Step. Minimal slide. Step. Step. We zig zag up the slope to keep from sliding backwards.

"Almost there," Greg calls back.

I stop and look up.

"Liar." I laugh.

"Boosting morale," he says. "You're doing great."

I don't feel like I'm doing great. My quads are on fire. My heart thumps in my sweaty ears. Who knew ears sweat?

"Here on your right, we have Ptarmigan Lake." Greg sounds like a tour guide as he points to the small, snow-covered surface of said lake.

"Where are the Ptarmigan?" I try to sound funny-sarcastic without panting as I look for any sign of the furry-footed white birds.

"I can honestly say I've never seen one here in the winter or summer. We'll take off a layer to get up Deception Pass." He drops his pack, takes his parka off and stuffs it inside.

I peel mine off and stuff it into my pack with my gloves and toque. It feels fabulous to stop.

"Keep your toque on. Even though we're sweating and climbing, it'll keep you from getting chilled if the wind picks up."

I dig it out, pull my hair back and put it on again.

"Perfect."

Greg leans over and kisses my sticky, sweaty face. What a guy. I wonder if it disgusts him because right now, everything about myself disgusts me. And there are no showers where we're going. It's probably a bit late to wonder if I used enough deodorant. I sneak a smell. Yup. Seems okay.

"This is the last uphill," he says. "I promise."

I refuse to look farther ahead than Greg's feet because the top seems so freaking far away. Endless up. Endless zigzag. I don't think I'll make it. I have to consciously control my breathing, so I don't hyperventilate. And it's all I can do not to scream '*enough already*.' I guess I should have done more jumping jacks with the karate kids. Maybe I should have taken up jogging with Steph.

"Knock, knock," Greg calls out.

"What?"

"Knock, knock."

I roll my eyes at the snow and smile at his distraction tactic. "Who's there?"

"Banana."

"Banana who?"

"Knock, knock," he says again.

"Who's there?"

"Banana."

I groan. "Banana who?"

Greg laughs. "Knock, knock."

"If it's another banana..."

"Knock, knock." He's pretty insistent.

"Who the fuck is there?"

He laughs. "Orange."

What happened to the banana?

"Orange who?" I say.

"Orange you glad I didn't say banana?"

"Funny." I snort. "Not funny."

Greg points his poles in the air and shouts, "We made it." The echo bounces and fades.

All I can do is smile because I *did* make it. Without dying.

"This...this here," I point at the mountains ahead of us, "deserves a selfie."

Greg takes my phone, and we pose in numerous directions to take in the entire landscape.

"Okay, now for the fun part of the trip." Greg undoes his bindings.

My mind goes to a roll in the snow and a lot of kissing, and I instantly regret that I probably taste like salt. *But making out is not what Greg has in mind.* He fiddles with our splitboards and in seconds they look like ordinary snowboards again. Then he collapses our ski poles and tucks them in his pack.

Sitting on the snow with our boards on, Greg points down the slope.

"Follow me. We're going to sweep over and across, and back and forth. Don't get close to the big trees. They could trip you up and you might get caught in a tree well."

"Tree well?"

"It's a deep tunnel which runs down the base of the trunk."

"Got it. Stay away from trees."

He hops up and slowly heads down at an angle. Snow sprays up behind him in a big arc. I follow and after I get some speed, the momentum pulls me from one turn to the next. Almost as if I'm floating.

"Woohoo," I shout.

Turn after turn. Effortless. Greg carves wide around the trees. When I get out of his track, my board slows down, so I angle back onto his path. The slope ends and we glide across a flat spot which ends in front of a long-gabled log building. Lazy smoke drifts straight up out of the rock chimney. White trimmed windows. Huge antlers over the door. The building is similar to the Cascade cabin I spent the summer in with Steph, but this one is a lot bigger.

We take our gear off, drop our packs outside the door, and head into the wood fire and fresh baked cookie smelling room.

"Greg Patterson. As I live and breathe." A large, brightly coloured apron clad lady rushes up, grabs him and kisses his cheeks numerous times. "You made it."

I squish my lips together to contain my grin. When she lets go of him, she walks up to me with her hand out.

"You must be Jillian." She pumps my arm like she's doing reps with a light barbell.

"Yes, I am."

"Sonya Batchki."

"Nice to meet you."

Greg stands behind her and winks at me as she pulls me towards a long table close to a blazing fireplace.

"You two settle in. I'll get something for you to eat and drink. How was the trip?" she calls out as she disappears behind a curtained off doorway.

"Fantastic. There was a lot of untracked powder for us," Greg says in an uber-loud voice then whispers to me, "She's a gem. An enthusiastic gem."

In minutes she's back with a tray of sweets and two cups of coffee. While Greg and Sonya catch up on their current events, I grab a Nanaimo square and check out the old black and white pictures hanging off the walls. Some go back to 1930. Long, skinny cross-country skis and people dressed in wool outfits. I'll have to remember to check into the type of clothing they wore for my diorama.

I try not to eavesdrop, as I read the comments in the guest register, but they're both so excited with catching up that I hear most of their conversation. It's pretty cute. Almost like she's a favourite aunt.

"Hey, Jillian," Sonya says. "I have an empty cabin tonight. It's ready and I want you two to take it, so you don't have to stay in the dorm. I've heard the snoring in there almost lifted the roof last night."

"No, that's okay," Greg says. "We're fine staying upstairs."

"I insist. It's my treat and there's no extra charge. I'll go get you the key." She hustles off behind the curtain again.

Greg lifts his hands in the air and scrunches up his lips. I think he mouths, "Sorry."

"Here you go." She hands him a tiny key which is attached to a long chain and a square piece of wood.

It'll be difficult to scan that and get any door to open. I grin. Welcome to the rustic outdoors.

I try to stay neutral about the change in sleeping arrangements, but panic creeps in. What the hell? This should not be a big deal. I slept next to Ray on the side of a mountain for a whole night. Big difference though. Ray was injured in the helicopter crash, he's as old as Steph, and Tom told me to keep him warm until he hiked out to get help. Greg is not even eighteen yet. He's not injured. Nor are we stuck on the side of some mountain. I smile at Sonya, who seems happy to be getting us out of the snoring dorm room, and try not to let my face show I'm a bit freaked out about the change.

Steph will also freak out when she hears about this. *If* she hears about this.

"It's the first cabin after the path to the outhouse." Sonya ushers us towards the door.

Greg thanks her but the expression on his face is not as exuberant as hers. Maybe he's having second thoughts about this too. After we've put our packs on, he grabs my hand and we head down the path.

At the same time as I am about to say, "I can't," Greg says, "Don't worry." We stop and look at each other. He chuckles.

"I vividly...very vividly remember Steph's rusty tin can threat which I believe she would follow through on." He puts his hands up. "I promise nothing will happen."

I hope he doesn't hear me sigh as we make our way to the cabin. *Did Dale make Steph the same promise when she got pregnant?*

Greg unlocks the door with the giant key and pushes it open. It's sauna warm inside, and a huge box of firewood sits next to the stove. There's a large old-fashioned rod iron bed with no blankets. Right. Sleeping bags. We brought sleeping bags. My panic mode reduces another notch.

But there's nowhere to change, and my clothes feel damp.

"Hey, you face the stove," I tell Greg. "I'm going to change into something dry."

"Got it." Greg faces the stove like a marching soldier.

I toss my sleeping bag on the bed, check to make sure he's still facing the stove and change.

"Done." I drape my damp clothes over a chair and push it closer to the fire.

"My turn." Greg spins me towards the stove.

I grin at the shiny silver brackets trying to imagine Greg in his underwear. Briefs? Boxers? Please not commando.

We spend the afternoon walking on the packed trails around the site and Greg points out all the peaks he has climbed.

I stare at one of the mountains, which looks almost vertical. "Does it scare you? Ever?"

"No. Not in the sense that I'm scared when I climb. It's more an adrenaline rush, which gets me over the tough pitches. I can teach you."

"No thanks. I'm good. I'm more of a two-feet-on-the ground kind of person. The scramble you took me up Mount Rundle was my limit."

"That's okay. Climbing isn't for everyone."

At supper time, the long table is full on both sides with couples, older Oma and Opa type people, and a few younger families with kids. Loud. Noisy. And the food is amazing. In reality, I'm so hungry Sonya could have served stew, and I would've inhaled it.

After we help the staff tidy up, a Steph-aged-lady pulls out a guitar and a singsong starts around the fire. I sit next to Greg on a bench at the back and relax against the wall to watch the entertainment. Country songs, ballads—none are familiar, but they're fun to listen to. A couple of kids even get up and sing. After a while, people start to disperse.

"Goodnight." Greg waves at Sonya and we head to the cabin with a flashlight.

"Outhouse trip." I take the light from Greg and climb the small hill to the can.

Once inside, I talk myself off the cliff. *This is going to be okay*. Everything will be okay.

When I get back, Greg turns off the light and after our eyes adjust, we walk the rest of the way to the cabin in the moonlight. So many pinprick stars. No clouds. The snow on the mountains seems fluorescent against the black sky. We stand outside for a few minutes, pointing out possible satellites and I watch for a falling star so I can make a wish. But there are no falling stars.

Once inside, there's a repeat of the changing ritual except after I change, I jump into my sleeping bag and face the wall, so Greg has his privacy. When he's done, he stokes the fire, climbs over my sleeping bag and crawls into his. We lie on our backs. In silence. For a few seconds.

"We can kiss, right?" Greg says. "And canoodle?"

"What exactly is a canoodle?"

"A cuddle with no sex."

The blunt way he says it makes me laugh out loud. "Yes. We can canoodle."

Greg and his sleeping bag rollover to face me. "I had a great day."

"Me too."

And the kissing starts. Just light and tickly at first. But then, more intense. The breathless, heart-thumping kind of intense.

"Can I sneak under your top?" Greg whispers.

"What part of canoodling is that?"

"The non-intrusive, get to know you better kind."

I slip my hand under his shirt first. His back is warm. Tight. Muscle tight. I run my fingers down his spine as he runs his lightly up my ribs. I try not to squirm because I'm super ticklish. When he circles under a boob I gasp.

"Is that okay?" he whispers again.

I nod in the dark as my warmth and body parts' hum increases. To levels I have never felt before. Ever. My hand rests on his side, afraid to move. Afraid to miss a second. His fingers...they skim across my chest and back again. I know what's pressing against my crotch, but two sleeping bags have to be better than one condom.

His fingers circle my nipples until they are hard. And then his touching moves down and stops at the waistband of my panties.

"Is this okay?"

"Uh-huh."

I catch my breath as he sneaks down and works his way towards *you know who*. He touches and presses and rubs. His finger moves inside and stops.

"Still okay?"

I can only nod in the dark room as my pulse thumps in my ears. He moves in and out, slow at first and then he speeds up, comes out, rubs the outside and goes back in. Faster. Slow. Faster. Until my body shakes. Every. Part. Of. Me. Quivers. I close my lips tightly but even I hear my gasp. And the sigh.

Greg runs his finger up my side and pulls my shirt down, then props himself up on his elbow. I feel him watch me.

"Hi," is all I can think to say.

"Hi, yourself." He kisses me, rolls onto his back, puts his arm under my shoulders and pulls me against his side.

I snuggle in, totally wide awake. An orgasm. My first. And he did it without a penis. Wow. Just wow. They never discussed this in Sex Ed. I stare into the darkness as my body parts settle down. The feeling lingers in a really nice way. How in the world did he get so good at that? I want to credit Google because the other option would take my smile away. *Thank you, Google.*

When I wake up, the cabin is cool. I'm in the same spot I was when I fell asleep. Safe. Cozy. Happy. I don't want to wake Greg, so I lie still and enjoy being this close to him. I have to make a doctor's appointment and check into birth control.

"You're awake," Greg whispers.

"How could you tell?"

"Your breathing changed." He turns towards me.

Morning breath be damned. Kissing turns into horseplay and tickling and a pillow fight and then we are both hopping around the cold floor looking for socks. I love it.

A loud clanging bell interrupts our fun.

"Breakfast call. You get dressed first," Greg says. "I'll start the fire."

The pancake and bacon smelling dining room is noisy as people surround the buffet table. Sonya waves and smiles as she dishes food out.

"You know what a slug it was getting here?" Greg waves a spoon of fruit at me.

"How could I forget the endless uphill?"

"Today, there's only one steady up." He points out the window at the slope we carved down yesterday. "The rest of it is pretty much downhill. We'll leave early, so the snow doesn't get soft and sticky. Then we'll be able to slide across some of the flat parts."

"I sure don't remember any flat parts." I shake my head.

"There were. Trust me. We'll grab a bagged lunch after breakfast and head out."

Sonya gives us both bear hugs.

"You two come back anytime." She kisses Greg's cheek and pinches mine, a bit hard. "I can always make room for you."

"Bye."

I look back a few times as we start to climb Deception Pass. Other people shuffle around the outside of the lodge getting their gear ready. The chimney smoke still goes straight up into the blue sky. *What a great place. What a great memory.*

The slug up the slope doesn't seem as bad today. Or maybe the happy in me makes it easier this time. Anyways, it's over before I know it and the downhill begins. I follow Greg's tracks on the open slope but once we get to Ptarmigan Lake, he passes me my poles.

"Stay in the packed trail and use the poles when you feel yourself slowing down." He puts the pole's straps around his wrists. "Let's see how far we can go before we have to break the board down again."

If I stay in the hard packed, almost iced over track, my board rides on top and it doesn't take much of a push to get going when I slow down. Greg does goofy pendulum movements to slide further without poling. I copy him but find using the poles is easier for me to get momentum. Greg crouches really low, pops straight up and spins a 180. He's riding down the hill looking at me.

"Show off," I shout.

He repeats the move and faces downhill again. It will be years before I attempt that move.

At the Temple Lodge, a lot of people eat lunch outside in the sun. Skiers and boarders race down the hill. We pass under the Larch lift and onto the ski out. I know why they call it a ski out. Because it's a bugger on a board. A lot of poling required because there are so many flat spots. How did I not notice them on the way up?

And before I know it, we're back at the parking lot. We pack the gear into the car, and I sigh.

"Thanks for taking me." I hug Greg.

"Told you you'd like it." He winks.

Kiss. Lingering kisses. Double sigh. Bigger hugs. A perfect weekend. I turn the radio up on the ride home and hum along.

Steph shouts as we drop my gear in the back porch. "How was it?"

"Fabulous." Greg swings his arm over my shoulder as we step into the kitchen. "We couldn't have had better conditions. The snow was perfect."

"Good." Steph nods her head but gives me the we-will-talk-as-soon-as-he-leaves look.

"I have to get to the shop and see what the week's schedule looks like." He raises a hand at Steph. "See you."

He gives me a quick kiss on the lips right in front of her.

"You brat," I whisper.

Gorgeous, cute, mischievous smile. And then he leaves. I watch the back of him go down the steps and out the gate as I put on a chill expression for Steph.

"So, how was it?" Steph waves a tea towel in front of her.

"It was amazing. What a cool place." I unpack the clothes I need to wash. "Sonya is quite the character and can she cook. I ate a million calories. There were so many people there. They had a big singsong last night. And the outhouse smelled like cinnamon. I prefer your vanilla scent at the Cascade. I need a shower. And," I stop in front of her, "you were right. There is a lot of uphill."

Steph doesn't say anything. I can't read her face and am not sure if that is a good thing or not. *Can she tell? Does she know?*

I point at her and switch topics. "How was your weekend?"

She flicks the towel. "Good. I cleaned the house. I went to the office and did a bunch of paperwork I've been procrastinating about and then went for a jog. You know, same old, same old."

"No Tom?"

"He went to Lethbridge with Mika and Barrett. Mika wants to check out the university."

"Right. She starts in the fall."

Poor Barrett. How is he going to deal with their long-distance relationship?

"I got an unexpected call from Kyle's case worker," Steph says slowly.

I freeze. I even stop breathing.

"She said there is a possibility we can see him once school is out. Kyle's aunt told her Kyle asks about us and worries we miss him too much."

"Oh, my God." I grab her arms, jump up and down just like Kyle did when he was excited. "That's fabulous."

“Don’t get your hopes up too much.” Steph tightens her arms to stop my bouncing. “Just in case they change their mind.”

“Wow, way to put a downer on good news.” I shake my head. “Don’t worry. They won’t change their minds. Kyle won’t let them.”

* * *

On Monday, in the corner of the foyer at school, there is a group singing an old Beatles’ song. Olivia is with them and she’s on crutches now instead of in a wheelchair. I stop to listen. They’re pretty good. All smiles. Having fun. The ones in the front do a few old school jive-like steps to the song and Olivia rocks back and forth on her crutches. It’s nice to see her enjoying herself.

“How was the trip?” Barrett shuts his locker door.

“It was great. How was Lethbridge?”

“Lethbridge. The city that blows.”

“Pardon?”

“The wind blows there all the time, and it blows that Mika will be there in September.” He snorts.

“Hey, you two will figure it out. It’s not that far.”

“Not that far?” He gives me a how-dumb-are-you look. “Who’re you kidding?”

“Come on. Shake it off.” I link arms with him and haul him towards class. “She doesn’t start until September. Don’t be so glum already.”

Chapter 19

The whole week rushes by with only a heart emoji, and an *I miss you* text from Greg. I keep busy to avoid missing him while he's off working.

Sensei Geri asks me to help at the tournament on Saturday. My initial reaction was to say no, but if Greg is gone all weekend, it'll make Saturday go by faster, so I say yes. The kids are jacked to do their patterns and spar, but a few are nervous. It takes me back to when I used to compete in Toronto. I understand how stressful it is to stand in front of a line of stern-faced senseis to perform their pattern. I stay after class to help a few practise. Kyle will be uber-proud of me when he finds out how much I'm helping Sensei teach the kids.

Afton sends more ideas for my project. She says she uses a Styrofoam base or clay to keep the items in place, none of which I can find in the house. But I do have Kyle's stash of play dough and use it instead of clay. It adds colour and pizazz to the scene.

Early Saturday morning, after breakfast, I call up the stairs to Steph, "See you later. I'm going to the tournament."

"Bye."

At the gym my phone *dings*. Of course it would be from Greg—*I have a few hours got time to catch up?*

Karate tournament all day sorry—I add a heart emoji.

Darn it. I wish I could ditch the tournament, but I promised the kids and Sensei.

Greg—*Can I stop by?*

Sure.

I look down at my Gi. Not exactly flattering apparel.

A couple of kids from our karate class rush up to me, all chatter and bounce. I herd them back towards Sensei to hear the schedule for each age group. She sends four kids with me to the seven-and-under kata ring. They walk with me, but all their chatter and bounce disappear. Now they look terrified.

When we get to the competition ring, I crouch in front of them.

"This is just like we practised in class." I point to the three stern-faced senseis sitting in chairs across the front of the ring. "When it's your turn, bow before you enter the ring, march up to them, bow again, assume neutral stance, tell them your name and the kata you will be doing. Then you..."

"Bow again and walk backwards to the centre of the ring before you start," a pigtailed girl finishes for me.

"That's right. You all know the routine." I tap them on the back. "Let's do this."

The kids sit cross-legged on the floor with the other competitors. Kata after kata, different clubs go through their routine, and everyone claps when they finish. One of our students goes up, I hold my breath, wish them the best in my head and clap loudly when they make it all the way through.

"You guys did great," I say when they're done and herd them back towards Sensei's corner. Someone grabs my waist from behind and I turn.

"Greg." I can't stop the uber-smile which takes over my face. "Hi."

"Hi." He grabs my hand and whispers, "Is kissing allowed in here?"

"Not really."

"Dang."

"Who's he?"

"Where's his Gi?"

"Is he your boyfriend?"

The kids bombard me with questions.

"This is Greg Patterson. He's not here to compete," I say. "And yes, he's my boyfriend."

"Jillian has a boyfriend," one of them shouts and runs off towards Sensei.

"Look what you started." I laugh and give him a quick kiss.

Greg follows us around as I escort kids to their rings.

"They kind of like you." He winks. "Should I be jealous?"

He puts his hand on my hip while we watch, and it feels so good. Way too soon, he looks at his watch.

"I have to run into Calgary. There's a meeting I need to attend for the shop. Can I stop by tonight?"

"Yup," I say. "I should be done here by five."

A quick kiss and I watch him walk out of the gym. And sigh.

"He's cute." Pigtailed girl grabs my hand. "Do you like him?" She looks up at me with serious kid eyes.

"Yes, I do," I say. "Very much."

After the medal presentations, the kids gather up their gear and Sensei Geri shakes my hand.

"Thank you," she says. "The kids did great, and I appreciate the time you spent with them. It was a good tournament. Thanks again for coming."

"You bet."

I walk home feeling pretty darn proud of the kids and really good about being there with them. It's early, and I have time to get cleaned up before Greg arrives. Steph heads over to Tom's after supper and I curl up on the couch and channel surf.

And I wait. And wait.

No text. No call. *Maybe the meeting went longer. Why was the meeting in Calgary and not Banff?* Bucky barks in the middle of my thought and his nails scratch the floor as he rushes to the door. *Finally*. I run my fingers through my hair and head to answer it.

"Hey," I say. "Hi."

Greg pushes Bucky away and takes his boots off. When he looks up, there's something going on with his expression. Something is off. I grab his hand and pull him into the kitchen.

"Want something to eat or drink?"

He sits down at the table. "No. I just ate. Thanks though."

"Want to watch TV?"

Why does he look so serious?

He shakes his head.

"Okay." I pull a chair out and sit across from him. "Why so glum, chum?" I grab his hands and shake them to break through his sad aura. "Everything okay at home?"

"Oh yeah. Suzanne is amazing the doctors with her improvement every day and my folks are good." He looks up and forces a smile. It's still a sweet smile but it's not the easy, casual one he usually wears.

He takes the longest inhale and with it I sense a piece of my world about to fall apart.

"Remember I told you about the climb up Mount Logan? The one my boss put my name in for back in the fall?"

"Yup. You said you didn't think you stood a chance of getting on with them."

"That's what the meeting was about in Calgary." He alternates squeezing my fingers. "They want me to be a part of it and the shop wants to sponsor me."

I stay quiet because his tone scares me, and I can't tell why he's not over-the-moon ecstatic about this.

"The group got permission to do the climb. It's the highest mountain in Canada. Second highest in North America." A pause, and then his head does these little nods.

"That's fantastic Greg." I grab his shoulders. "Wow. That's huge. Congratulations. You must be jacked."

Still no happy in his face. *What the hell?*

"The training and the trip will take six months. Maybe more. It depends what the weather is like on the mountain when we get there. And after, when the climb is done, I don't know what after will look like, or where it will take me."

"Wow. That sounds intense." This time I jiggle his shoulders to get him to look at me. "But you know you can handle it."

"I know." He drops his head again. When he lifts it, he says, "They want the team to live together. Train together. Breathe together. We have to rely on each other all the way up and down, so we have to be totally in sync." He stares at me. "I have to move to Edmonton in two weeks."

What? No. He'll be gone for six months. Maybe more. That's like forever. We barely did two months, and it was hell. Right. For a small part of that I thought he was dead. That was the worst. *But six months?* Now I know why he's bummed. But he loves climbing. It's his jam. Even more than snowboarding and hiking.

"What an opportunity." I try to make my smile not feel like my heart hurts. "What an amazing opportunity. And experience. This is a chance of a lifetime. For you." I try to put words and a sentence together, but it sounds like gibberish.

Greg stares at our hands. "It *is* a huge deal but when I agreed to be signed up for it, I didn't know you and now..." he runs out of words.

I struggle to find an option to give him an out. To take away his sadness and make him happy to have this opportunity to do what he loves.

So, I throw myself under the bus.

"Hey, you know what?" I say in a quiet voice and hope I can gain courage and momentum to make him believe me. "I'm thinking about working at the Frank Interpretive Centre this summer."

He looks up with a puzzled expression.

"Yeah," I convince myself and him. "It's pretty cool there. And it will give Steph time to figure out her life, and Tom, and the Waterton gig. Frank is close to Waterton. It'll make life easier with her new job."

Greg stares back at our hands and squeezes my fingers again. I'm so glad he's not looking at me. I'm so glad he can't hear my heart break. For both of us.

"So," I say a bit louder, so my voice doesn't shake. "You know. You'll be gone. I'll be gone. Life will go on. We'll just be doing it...not together anymore." I pause so I don't gasp out loud. It surprises me how convincing I hear myself sounding. Almost. "Who knows." I stand and snap my fingers in the air to feign happy. "I might even tell Mom I'm coming to Europe to go to school. That would rattle her world." I let out a high-pitched laugh.

Greg stands. His eyes are borderline teary. He pulls me into a tight hug, and I blink fast and bury my face in his collar, his smell, his warmth.

"You got me through some of the ugliest days of my life," he says. "I wouldn't have made it without knowing you were here."

"Yes, you would've." My voice is a few octaves higher. I swallow and bite the inside of my cheek.

"Nope, no I wouldn't have. What's that old saying?" He pulls his head back and looks at me. His lips are in a tight line.

I shrug because I'm out of words, and I don't want to let go of him, but I know I have too. Soon.

"You know, the sappy one about love...setting it free...if it comes back." He stops talking and watches me watch him.

I know which one he means now but I can't say it out loud because my throat burns. Besides, I don't know anything about setting love free. I didn't think I knew anything about love, at all. Until right now, I thought this was only like.

If like is this hard I don't ever want to be in love.

"Can we be friends? Not right away," he says. "I know that would be too tough, but after, can we? In time? Please? It would mean the world to me."

I nod.

He rocks us side to side as we continue to watch each other. I still don't trust myself to talk. He pulls me in close and kisses me. The deepest, softest, saddest kiss ever and I kiss him back as my heart breaks into a gazillion shards.

"Remember, I am ever always here. Regardless. Don't you ever forget that." He taps me under the chin and lifts it, so we're looking in each other's eyes. "If you ever need me."

"Ditto," I whisper.

We hug. Hard. And long.

"I wish for you a happy ending," he murmurs in my ear.

And when he lets go, it takes everything I've got not to pull him back. I want to pull him back. But I don't.

"I'm sorry," I say.

"Sorry for what? For meeting? For having a fabulous time getting to know each other? Don't ever be. I wouldn't have missed it for the world." He presses a kiss on my forehead and holds it there for a few seconds. "You are my first love, Jillian Meier. Wherever that mountain takes me, I will not forget you."

I can't form a single word in response.

"Are you okay?" he says.

I shake my head. "But..." big breath, "...I will be. We both will be."

He squeezes my shoulders. "Who knows, maybe our paths will cross again." And then he leaves.

I can't say goodbye out loud. I lift my hand and wave, shut my eyes and when I open them the back door closes without a sound. I watch him go down the steps and out the gate.

The cuckoo clock ticks. My breath comes in short bursts, and I force myself to take deep, long ones, so I can focus on breathing instead of falling apart. It doesn't work. I grab a chair and sink into it, hold my head and let the tears fall. My chest hurts like someone hit it with a shovel. Sobs run into each other and then the hiccups. Fucking, stupid hiccups. Endless tears. I press my arms on the table and put my head on them.

I want to run after Greg and tell him we can make long-distance work. I want to tell him we can hang out until he leaves. I want to tell him I don't want *us* not to be *us*. But that's not fair. We can't be *us*. Not right now. Quite possibly never. He has too much ahead of him.

"Jillian?"

I pull my head off the table and the kitchen light blinds me.

"Jillian." Steph rushes to me. "What's the matter? What happened? Are you okay?"

"Greg and I, we...he...us..." I stand up and Steph pulls me into a hug and the sobs return. "There's no more *us*."

"Oh, girl, I'm so sorry. So, so sorry." She rubs my back. "I'm here. I'm here for you always. Love is hard. It's so hard."

"Even *like* is hard." I hug her back, as if I'll never let go.

"What happened?"

"Life. Life happened," I blurt out. And then mumble about his climb, and the team, and the commitment and moving. She doesn't interrupt. She just keeps rubbing my back.

When I stop babbling, she says, "It's hard to watch someone you love move on without you."

"I didn't know I *loved* him until he was gone." The tears start again.

At some point I go to bed. And I cry some more. Sunday, I wander around the house. I try to work on my project. Homework. Laundry is a distraction. But only for a few minutes. Steph makes suggestions to go boarding or to go for a walk.

"Thanks. No." I shake my head and end up on the couch channel surfing.

At school, Barrett peeks out from behind his locker door. "Hi," he says in the quietest voice.

"Don't talk."

"Got it. No talking." He throws his arm over my shoulder, and we head to class.

After karate I walk to Greg's place. His car is there, and I see his reflection in the window. I watch him. I want so badly to knock on his door and say, '*let's hang out until you have to leave*' but I don't. It would be like ripping the band aid off every time we say goodbye. That's not fair. To him. Or me.

But I want to.

I take the long way home. It hurt so much when I thought he was dead. This hurt, it's different, but it still hurts like crazy, like it will never stop.

Chapter 20

Saturday morning all I want to do is stay in bed, and be sad and alone, without having to smile, or be normal, or act like nothing happened. But there's so much noise downstairs that sleep is impossible.

"What the heck is going on?" I snap, as I pull my housecoat shut and step into the kitchen.

In the middle of the floor is a black garbage bag overflowing with take-out food wrappers, newspapers and garbage.

"What's all this?"

"I need a big box." Steph slams the miscellaneous drawer so hard the cuckoo cuckoos and Bucky barks.

"You won't find one in there." I keep emotion out of my voice because Steph is pissed about something and until I can figure out what, or who, or why, I don't want to get her madder. "How big of a box do you need?"

"I don't know." She waves her hands in random dimensions of a box—presumably the size she wants.

"And *why* do you need *this* box?"

"I went for a jog this morning and at the end of the alley, some asshole opened their car door and threw their junk out. Too damn lazy to find a garbage can." She makes stabbing-pointing gestures at *our* garbage can.

"Okay."

"But I found this." She waves a pink piece of paper and an envelope at me. "Their address is on it."

"Okay," I say again because I have no idea where this is going but want to be supportive to her sudden outburst of craziness.

"I'm going to box up their shit, send it to them and leave a note inside to tell them they left it in Banff."

Her tone is not losing its energy, so I say nothing.

"Don't look at me like that," she says.

"I'm not."

"Yes, you are. You're judging me. You think I'm nuts," her voice gets louder.

It takes courage, but I walk up to her, put my hands up like I surrender and say, "Steph, are you okay? Is everything okay?"

She glares at me, throws the pieces of paper on the table and stomps up the stairs to her room.

What the hell is going on?

I should go talk to her. Or maybe I should give her a few minutes to settle down first and then try. This cannot just be about garbage. She has to deal with stupid people all the time. It usually doesn't get her this wound up. I glance at Bucky for suggestions. His paw is over his snout. His eyes are closed.

"Not helpful at all," I tell him then head upstairs and knock on Steph's door. "Hey, can I come in?"

Silence.

"Steph?"

The door handle turns, the door opens, and Steph comes out.

"Sorry about that." She walks by me and heads back downstairs.

I follow her.

"Is everything okay?"

"Yes. Maybe. I don't know." She puts her hands on her hips.

I'm certainly not going to point out the differences in those responses, so I stay quiet and wait for her to realize it herself.

Steph blinks a few times before she says, "Everything is fucked."

My eyes totally give me away. Steph *never* drops the 'f' bomb.

"Kyle, Tom, Waterton, Greg," she says. "Your mom is being vague. Oh, and the clinic called to remind you about your doctor's appointment."

That stops me short. I totally forgot I made the appointment after Skoki. At the time it was such a huge deal. I wanted to be ready for the next time. And now, I don't think I'll ever be close enough to be that ready again. With anyone.

"Is that what this is all about?" I point at the garbage mess. "The call from the clinic?"

"No." She shakes her head. "Maybe it was initially. Your mom's call after, that had more of an impact though."

"What has Mom got to do with this?"

"Tom and I will be working in Waterton, and we plan to live together in Pincher Creek because it's a bigger town. I asked your mom for some direction on how to make this work for you."

"And?"

"I'm not comfortable with you staying in Banff alone. Eddy is okay with living here with you as a last resort but being tied down in one spot is not his style. He would only be doing it for us. Your mom isn't helping with the decision-making process."

"Does that surprise you? By not helping to make the decision, it leaves her clear by default of making the wrong choice. It's her go-to move when things get tough."

"Well, it's not helpful and not fair. I do not want to be the bad guy. I do not want to ruin your life by dragging you away from here if you don't want to go."

"You know what, how about I show up on Mom's doorstep with my suitcase?"

Steph pulls her head back and gives me scary eyes. "You want to move to Europe?"

"No, but I think it would be funny. Can you imagine the expression on Mom's face? She'd crap herself." I feel the temperature in the room cool down. Perfect.

"That would be an expensive joke. You'll be sixteen in August and whatever we decide, I want you to be happy. Really happy. I don't want you pretending to be okay with everything just to keep the peace."

"You know what?" I lift my hands in the air. "I want to work at the Frank Interpretive Centre for the summer with Afton. And then, who knows. Maybe you and Tom will decide there isn't room for me, and I'll stay here."

"That will not happen. There will always be room for you." She grabs my shoulders. "Tom knows that, and you know that. Right?"

I look at the mess on the floor. "Let's leave this for now. I'll go for a jog with you. And we'll run the crap out of our moods and maybe *happy* will find both of us."

"You don't jog."

"I can start." I take off for my room. "I'll be ready in ten minutes."

We take a right out of the back alley.

"Do you want to run along the river?" Steph pulls ahead of me.

"Sure."

There are few people out and about and the path is clear, so it's easy to just focus on not losing my lungs. Parts of the ice on the river have broken up and the water prisms in the sun. A small herd of elk paw through the snow for grass across by the picnic tables at the recreation grounds. A photographer has his gear set up, taking pictures of them.

"How far do you go?" I call out.

"Further."

Great. Why does helping someone out make my body hurt this much? At the train station, Steph turns and heads towards the Banff Park Lodge. I wore way too many clothes. Sweat drips down my face.

This is good for me. It's a distraction from all that sucks in my life. *I suck at convincing even myself.* The distance between Steph and me increases.

At Melissa's restaurant, she stops. Thank God. Steph does a few stretches in the doorway, and I look around to make sure no one is watching her attempt at aerobics or the fact I'm with her. Through the glass into the dining room, I see Barrett. I press my face against the window. Mika, Tom and Eddy are sitting with him.

I point to them and look at Steph.

"They're joining us for brunch," Steph says. "Maybe they'll be able to help us get happy."

We go inside and everyone sidles over on the benches to make room. I sit next to Barrett and Mika.

"Morning, gals," Eddy says.

"Water. I need water." I peel off my outer layers and Tom pours glasses of water for everyone.

"Training for a marathon?"

"Not anymore," I say. "There's not enough room in my life for jogging."

Everyone laughs and the chatter starts, and then the food comes.

Olivia and her family are at a table in the corner under a big screen TV. She's describing something to her mom, all animated with facial expressions and hand gestures. It makes me smile.

Barrett points his knife at the TV and presses against me. "There's our guy."

And there he is on the screen—a picture of Greg and the team. The ticker tape below says, *'Mount Logan Team to summit in September.'*

I clench my teeth. My heart stops and I blink fast.

"No talking," I whisper to Barrett.

"Got it. No talking."

The seconds it took to crash my world again went unnoticed by anyone but Barrett, and I hold it together, so I don't ruin anyone's fun.

Chapter 21

It has been two weeks since Greg left Banff. Some days still suck so badly. And they seem almost endless. And then there are days that I'm okay. I really am okay. It's weird how I actually know when it has been a good day and I wish for more of them.

This whole week I've been trying to figure out whether I should do this or not, but today is the day and I cannot ignore it. Greg was too important in my life.

I open my laptop and go to email.

Happy birthday, Greg. I miss you every day, but it hurts less than it did yesterday. I wish you a fantastic trip and many more summits to conquer in your life.

Ever always here.

Jillian of Banff

When I hit send, the little envelope spins and whisks off the screen. I close my laptop, kiss my fingers and press them on the cover. And just like that, the tears start. The hurt thumps in my heart all over again—like it was just yesterday.

But that's okay. It's a good kind of hurt. And I know I can handle it.

The End

Barbara (Wackerle) Baker is a Canadian author who writes realistic, fast paced wilderness adventure novels set in Banff National Park. Her books bring readers into the heart of her homeland, the mountains of Banff, where her characters must navigate their way through new surroundings as well as manage the turmoil life has in store for them.

Barbara grew up in Banff in the 60s and 70s when it was a quiet, nowhere place—not the iconic vacation destination it is today. Her childhood escapades exploring the wilderness has a huge impact on her writing. Her passions include writing, photography, exploring landscapes and time with her grandchildren.

Many of her short stories are published in magazines and anthologies. Carousel Pictures made a mini film of her essay, Life Support, which played in the Toronto International Film Festival (fall 2019).

You can contact her at bbaker.write@gmail.com and her author page at BWL Publishing https://www.bookswelove.com/baker-barba/

Other Barbara Baker books published by BWL Publishing

Summer of Lies
What About Me?

www.ingramcontent.com/pod-product-compliance
Lightning Source LLC
Chambersburg PA
CBHW070053120726
47909CB00002B/374

* 9 7 8 0 2 2 8 6 3 0 8 4 5 *